SHADES

Joseph Rubas

Parallel Universe Publications

First Published 2017 by Parallel Universe Publications
Copyright © 2017 Joseph Rubas
Cover design © 2017

Aokigahara originally published as "The Suicide Forest" in *The Horror Zine,* October 2013

Snowbound originally published by *Manor House* dark audio series, January 2016

The Ghostly Hitchhiker originally published in *The Storyteller,* July/Aug/Sept 2010

Just a Mask originally published in *HalloWEEn Tales,* October 2016

The Witching Hour originally appeared in *The Haunted Traveler,* May 2015

Confessional originally appeared in *The Literary Hatchet,* August 2015

The Lake House originally appeared in *Onyx Neon Shorts Presents: Horror Collection – 2015,* October 2015

The Traveling Show of 2016 originally appeared in *Beyond Science Fiction,* July 2015

Evildoer originally appeared in *Dark Dossier,* September 2014

A Perfect Life originally appeared on the *T. Gene Davis Speculative Fiction Blog,* August 2015

Fury originally appeared in *Schlock!,* April 2015

ISBN: 978-0-9935742-9-0
Parallel Universe Publications, 130 Union Road,
Oswaldtwistle, Lancashire, BB5 3DR, UK

CONTENTS

PASSING THE BUCK

Kayleigh Sherman was standing by the big fountain in the middle of the mall, rummaging in her purse for a piece of gum, when a young girl came timidly up to her. "Excuse me," the girl said, startling Kayleigh.

At a glance, she was fourteen or fifteen, mousey with pale blonde hair and creamy skin that looked almost translucent in the fall of sunshine cascading through the skylight overhead. She wore a rumpled black sweater and a pair of jeans; the knees were stiff and caked with mud. Her red Converse All Stars were also muddy.

"I need help getting a box into my car," she went on, nervously, her eyes darting left and right. "Can you help me?"

Kayleigh was surprised that the girl was old enough to drive. She started to say no, that she was waiting for someone (which was true), but something like sympathy rose in her chest. The girl looked, Kayleigh thought, like one of those hermits you see on TLC, the people who are kept home with crippling anxiety disorders, and only venture out when they absolutely have to. She could turn away from the girl, tell her to get lost, but she knew right now that she would feel like a bitch for the rest of the day.

"Sure," she said. She pulled her phone out of her purse, made sure that no one had texted her (they hadn't. Damn it. Where *are* you, Trish?), and then returned it. "Where's your car?"

"Out here," the girl said, gesturing with her head.

Kayleigh followed her past the food court, Spenser's, and Forever 21. It was noon on a Saturday afternoon, so the place was crowded with kids her own age and younger. At the south entrance, which opened onto a wide parking lot, the girl paused. "I hope no one took it."

Took it?

"Your car?"

The girl shook her head. "My box. I left it by the car."

"Oh," Kayleigh said.

The girl led her into the parking lot and down an aisle crammed with vehicles: trucks, sedans, crossovers, minivans, and even a moped.

"It's right up here."

They came to a light blue Camry parked apart from the other cars.

Kayleigh didn't see a box.

"Where...?"

Before she could finish, a man popped up from behind the car and pointed a gun at her.

"Don't fucking move," he hissed.

Numbness settled over her. The man hurried around the front end of the car, never taking Kayleigh out of his crosshairs. When he was close, he grabbed her by the back of her blouse and jammed the gun into the small of her back. "Be quiet or I'll kill you. Got it?"

Kayleigh's heart began to pound. The numbness was gone, replaced by terror.

"Do you understand?"

Kayleigh tried to speak, but her throat wouldn't work, so she simply nodded.

"Open the back door," the man told the girl, glancing anxiously toward the front of the mall. The girl obediently opened the door.

"Are you gonna let me go now?"

The man shoved Kayleigh into the back of the car and slapped a pair of handcuffs on her.

"You said you'd let me go if I helped you find someone else."

"Yes!" the man spat. He spun around and slammed the door. The girl jumped.

Kayleigh watched as the man placed his hand on the girl's shoulder and said something. She nodded. He kissed her on the cheek and came around to the driver side door. The girl looked after him. When he was behind the wheel, she looked at Kayleigh with haunted eyes.

"I'm sorry," she mouthed, and ran away.

That girl was the last person to see Kayleigh Sherman alive.

MIDNIGHT

10:48pm. "Are you ready?"

Jeffery Morgan read the text several times before starting to type his response and stopping. No. He *wasn't* ready. He wouldn't be ready even if he lived to be a thousand.

But he couldn't chicken out.

"Yeah," he typed and hit SEND.

Sighing, Jeff got up and grabbed his shoes from their spot by the closet door; he was already dressed in a pair of black sweatpants and a white T-shirt. Navigating by moonlight, he grabbed his black hoodie from the desk under the window and slipped it on.

He checked his phone, saw it was 10:55, and briefly considered texting Andrew back and telling him he couldn't make it. Something told him, though, that they would see through his excuse.

This is your chance, Morgan, Jeff thought. Outside, the old oak tree dominating the backyard swayed in the cold autumn wind. *Don't blow it.*

The thought of losing the only chance he'd had to make friends since coming to Westernport scared him shitless. He thought back to all the times he'd eaten lunch by himself that fall, and shuddered. When he and his family moved from Hagerstown in June, his father told him, "You'll make friends." Well, Jeff never made friends easily to begin with. On top of that, he was walking into a school where everyone knew everyone and had since elementary school. He was an outsider in Hagerstown, but that was okay, there were others. Here, he didn't have Jonny or Tim, didn't have the Magic: The Gathering gang, didn't have anyone. He was totally and utterly alone.

He was shocked then when Andrew Cooper sat with him at lunch last Monday. Tall and thin, with glasses, Andrew wasn't popular by jock or cheerleader standards, but he had a lot of friends and everyone seemed to like him. "I saw your deck," Andrew said, nodding to the deck of Magic cards sitting by Jeff's tray. During lunch he took them out and played against himself. Some of the other kids snickered as they passed by, and though he didn't have proof, he thought they were laughing at him.

"Yeah," Jeff had replied, "I used to play a lot."

"I used to be big into Magic," Andrew said, opening up his milk carton and taking a swig. "But that's, like, sixth grade stuff."

Jeff felt a flush of humiliation.

Sensing his faux paus, Andrew hastened to add, "I mean, compared to what I play now."

"What's that?" Jeff asked.

"Devilspawn."

Before the bell, Andrew managed to explain the basics of Devilspawn: Each player (typically between three and thirteen) played as either a demon or a light-bringer. Light-bringers were enemies of the demons. Sort of like Van Helsing to Dracula. The board was painted to resemble a fantasy world, with rivers, oceans, dense forests, and deserts. The goal (for the demons) was to bring hell on earth. For the light-bringers, it was to *prevent* hell on earth. Simple, Jeff thought, but Andrew and his "coven" upped the ante by playing a live action role play version in the woods north of town. They would meet in Andrew's basement on Monday evening, all thirteen of them (excluding Andrew), and make plans for that week's game. On Friday, they would steal out of their houses close to midnight and play the game, sometimes staying out until sunrise.

Andrew told him later, as they walked home from school, that he was planning a special game. "I've been reading a lot about Satanism," he said. "I found this book in the library that says you can summon him and use his power. I don't know if it's true or not, but I'm gonna try."

"Why?" Jeff asked. They were on his street now, a narrow, tranquil lane flanked by big houses and shady trees. A few other kids walked along the sidewalk on the other side of the road, lost in their cellphones.

"Because I'm sick of being a no one, that's why."

Jeff opened his mouth, but closed it again; he was afraid he'd say the wrong thing and offend Andrew.

"I want to be powerful," the older boy went on. "I want people to listen to what I say."

Jeff didn't know how to respond, so he said nothing.

"I can't do it without thirteen apostles, though."

Jeff looked at him.

"Robbie Horner moved away two weeks ago. I need someone else, and you seem pretty cool..."

Later, in his room, the lights off and his hands laced behind his head, Jeff pondered Andrew's invitation. He was elated to be a part of something, but he had the nagging feeling that Andrew was just using him. Regardless, by the time midnight rolled around, his mind was made up. He would join the coven.

They met that Wednesday night at Andrew's. Andrew introduced him around, but even now Jeff couldn't remember all the names. There was Stephen Hunter; Simon Jamison; Sean Johnson; and Kayla Winston.

He remembered *her*.

A tall girl with shoulder-length black hair and hazel eyes, Kayla Winston lived in McCool, the next town over. She was fifteen, a year older than Jeff, and wore black eye shadow and bright red lipstick. Sitting around the card table with the others that night, Jeff found himself repeatedly stealing glances at her, his eyes lingering on her smooth, graceful throat and the soft curve of her face. She caught him several times and smiled.

"Next Friday," Andrew said. "We'll do it Friday."

To Jeff's surprise, the others were as enthusiastic about raising the devil as Andrew. They talked of revenge and domination the way other kids talked about football or video games. Did they really think Andrew could summon the devil? Did they really think they could bring forth the prince of darkness and use his powers? That was crazy!

Still, Jeff found himself wondering. Here, alone, the idea was madness. But in Andrew's awesome presence, it seemed true. He *could* call on Satan; he *could* use his power.

"He's really smart," Kayla had said. "If anyone can do it it's him."

It was Saturday afternoon. Jeff was reading a Terry Pratchett novel in his room when his mother poked her head in. "There's a girl at the door looking for you."

She winked, and Jeff's cheeks blushed.

When he found Kayla Winston standing on the doorstep dressed in jeans and a black T-shirt, he was shocked but also pleased.

"Hi," she chirped.

"Uh...hi," Jeff responded, hating the stupid sound of his voice.

"You wanna hang out?"

"Sure."

Fifteen minutes later, they were walking south along the street. It was a mild day, and sunshine filtered through the treetops.

"I figured if you're going to be in our coven I should get to know you better. After all we're like brother and sister now."

"Yeah?"

"Yeah," she said. "Andrew says we're a family. Us against the world, you know?"

"I guess."

South of town, Kayla led him onto a path disappearing into the woods.

"So what are your parents like?" she asked. The trail ran straight and true for several yards before bending. Through the trees ahead, all yellow and red, he could see the Potomac.

"I don't know," he shrugged. "Cool, I guess."

"They don't hit you?"

"No."

She looked at him, genuinely surprised.

"Must be nice."

"Do your parents hit you?"

"Sometimes."

Eventually the path led to a tall, barren hill. Standing on it, Jeff had a sweeping view of the fiery autumn treetops stretching toward town. The only signs of mankind were a church steeple, a blue water tower, and the sewage treatment plant, the latter a big, boxy brown building.

"It's beautiful," she said.

Jeff swallowed. He wanted to tell her that she was beautiful, wanted to kiss her, but he was afraid. Afraid that she would say no, afraid that he would creep her out and they couldn't be friends anymore.

Instead, he muttered: "Yeah."

Presently, he shook his head and turned from the window.

"The old cemetery," Andrew had said on Monday. They were in the cafeteria, occupying most of a large table. "We can do it there."

Jeff felt strange being with such a large group. He was used to being by himself.

"It's out of the way," Stephen Hunter said. "Not many people go there."

"Some do," Simon Jamison pointed out. "There's a caretaker, right?"

Andrew flapped one hand. "He only goes out there to cut the grass. We'll be fine. Right, Jeff?"

Jeff, hearing his name, looked left and right. They were all watching him, their eyes boring into him. His face flushed and he licked his lips.

"Sure," he said.

It was settled. They would meet in the old cemetery off Ridge Road, overlooking the Potomac.

Now, at his bedroom door, Jeff listened, and when he didn't hear anything, he slipped out into the hall and pulled it softly shut behind him. The hall was pitch black, and he had to wait a moment for his eyes to adjust. When they did, he crept to the top of the stairs and stopped to listen again. His parents' door was closed, but even so he could hear his father's snoring. The snoring would hide any sounds he made, or so he hoped. His father could sleep through Judgement Day, but his mother would wake at the drop of the hat...if she heard anything out of the ordinary.

Swallowing, his heart racing, Jeff started down the stairs, being careful to avoid the third one down, since it creaked. Halfway, he paused and listened. Nothing.

At the bottom, he went to the front door and unlocked it. The sound of the tumblers was deafening in the silence, and he winced, certain that his parents would wake. For several stomach-churning minutes he listened, and when he heard nothing, he slipped out, shut the door behind him, and locked it.

The night was clear and cold. A biting wind swept up the street, stirring the trees and pushing dead leaves along the pavement. *Scritch-scritch-scritch.*

Taking a deep breath, he tumbled down the stairs and followed the flagstone path to the sidewalk. He glanced left and right, saw no one, and crossed the street.

From his house, Jeff followed Pine Street north through a neighborhood crammed with houses smaller and grimier than those on his street. At the intersection of Pine and Hill Avenue, he turned left and passed the elementary school (HOME OF THE BOBCATS!). Hill Ave meets Main Street just south of the Union Inn. Shuttered storefronts glinted in the light of the moon. To the south, a car turned onto Driscoll Street, its taillights glowing red, and for a second Jeff had a bone-chilling thought: What if it was his father out looking for him? He checked his phone. 11:14. He'd been gone almost fifteen minutes, *plenty* of time for his parents to wake up, discover his bed empty, and come looking for him. Flashing to the dreadful rite ahead, he thought that maybe being dragged home by his ear wasn't such a bad thing.

Shaking his head, he started north. A half mile from the town limits, the buildings lining the street fell away and were replaced by forest. At the clapboard sign reading WELCOME TO WESTERNPORT, MD'S NICEST TOWN!!! Main turns into Route 228, which winds twenty miles through the forest before reaching Kitzmiller. For the first ten miles it matches the Potomac bend-for-bend; Jeff walked along the gravel shoulder overlooking the river below, its inky surface dappled lunar white. The wind blew harder outside town, and Jeff shivered despite his hoodie.

Two miles past the edge of town, Jeff left the main highway in favor of a dirt road nearly hidden by foliage. Andrew had pointed it out on a topography map on Thursday night. "It's called Fried Meat Ridge Road. The cemetery's in a clearing at the very end of it."

Jeff couldn't remember if it was one mile or two.

The road ran fairly straight at first before bending to the right and then beginning to climb into the hills. Moonlight filtered through the trembling treetops, and the only sound he could hear was the forlorn hooting of an owl somewhere in the distance. Shivering, he licked his lips and walked as quickly as he could without breaking into a run. He tried not to imagine what might be hiding in the forest, watching, waiting to stumble out with its arms raised and its mouth open. He remembered a movie he saw once as a kid where a woman opened a door and this *thing* was lying on a bed, its skin sallow and its hair red. It giggled and said something about "coming back" presumably from the dead.

Stop it! Jesus, stop it!

After what seemed like an eternity, he came to the end of the forest. The road wound left and passed clear of the cemetery. From here, it looked sinister; its iron gate and slanted stones reminding him of something from a Lovecraft story. He could imagine some great entity living beneath the soil, waiting to strike.

Shut up!

Shaking his head, Jeff started across the lumpy field skirting the graveyard. At the gate, he paused and swept the graveyard with his gaze, hoping to see Andrew and the others.

He didn't.

What if it was a prank? What if they lured him out here just to laugh at him?

Pushing these thoughts aside, Jeff went into the cemetery.

"Hello?" he called, his voice refusing to echo.

"Over here!"

Jeff looked to his left. Someone was sitting on a tomb five feet high. As he drew closer, he saw it was Andrew.

"Great, now we can start," Andrew said, shoving off the tomb.

The others were arranged in a rough circle beyond the slab. They looked up and muttered their greetings.

"Glad you made it, preppie," Kayla Winston said with a wink.

Preppie? Did she think he was a *prep*?

While the others got to their feet, Andrew sparked a lighter and touched it to a pile of wood in the center of the circle; Jeff didn't notice it when he walked up.

"Tonight, we call forth the powers of Satan," Andrew said and backed away from the rising flames. Feeble orange light flickered across the night. "Jeff, stand next to Kayla. Steve, stand next to Mike. Hold hands."

Feeling slightly stupid (and *very* nervous), Jeff walked over to Kayla and stood next to her. Her hand crept into his and he felt a rush of warmth. That warmth dimmed when Luke Johnson took his other hand.

"I wonder if he can actually do it," she whispered.

Jeff looked at her. "You think maybe he can't?"

She shrugged. "I've never seen him do it, so I don't know."

"Yeah."

Andrew was standing apart from the group now, leafing through a large book. When he spoke, his voice rolled across the burial ground:

"This is *The Forbidden Book*. It was written by Le-Yu-Kang in 1905 and contains secret prayers to summon Lucifer. I will read from it and He will come. Never break the circle. If you break the circle he will be drawn back to hell. Do you understand?"

Everyone nodded or muttered that they did.

"Good."

Looking at the book, Andrew opened it and flipped through it. Jeff was surprised to find his chest tightening with anticipation. He stole a sidelong glance at Kayla, saw that her face was serene, and fought to push down his anxiety.

"Alright! Silence."

After a silent second, Andrew began to read. Jeff didn't recognize the language at first, it sounded like gibberish. Then he realized it was Latin.

> *"Dies irae, dies illa*
> *Solvet Saeclum in favilla*
> *Teste Satan cum sibylla.*
> *Quantos tremor est futurus*
> *Quando Vindex est venturus*

Cuncta stricte discussurus.
Dies irae, dies illa!"

"Satanas – venire!" everyone replied in unison.
Except Jeff.
"What's he saying?" he asked Kayla.
"Shhhhh," Luke admonished.
Andrew:

> *"Oriens splendor lucis aeternae*
> *Et Lucifer justitae: veni*
> *Et illumine sedentes in tenebris*
> *Et umbra mortis."*

"Satanas – venire!"
Something began to happen then. Jeff wasn't aware of it at first, but suddenly, all at once, he was: a strange, teeth-chattering *vibration*. The fire, burning low, flared up now, and seemed to turn blue. Jeff felt his hand going slack, but Kayla held tight.
"Satanas – venire! Satanas – venire! Satanas – venire!"

A roar filled the night. Looking up, Jeff saw dark clouds rolling across the stars. Lightning crackled within.
Dumb wonder filled him.
It was happening.
Andrew was actually doing it.
"*Satanas – venire!*"
The storm opened with a crash. Lightning flashed down, and someone screamed.
The world went white, and Jeff felt himself falling, his hands slipping away from both Kayla and Luke.
"Lord Satan!" Andrew yelled.
When Jeff opened his eyes, he saw Andrew on his knees, a bolt of lightning seeming to pour into him. The others also had lightening drilling their chests; they shook and jerked like men in the electric chair.
"Jesus!"
Kayla was on the ground next to him, supported on outstretched arms. She wore an expression of horror.
Another crash came, and the world shook. Jeff realized that the ground was parting. Panicking, he jumped to his feet.
The lightning winked out, and the others collapsed.
"Oh, my God..." Kayla started, but stopped.
Hands were beginning to come out of the ground, clawing through the grass and dirt. A fissure had appeared lengthwise before them, and

from it poured sulfurous smoke.

"Jeff!"

Jeff was so scared he couldn't move.

Things were beginning to climb out of the fissure. In the orange glow coming from the hole itself, Jeff could see that they weren't human.

"Jeff!"

Kayla was tugging on his arm.

The hands coming through the ground had become arms. In a few places, dead, rotten faces showed through the dirt, eye sockets squirming with maggots.

Jeff's paralysis broke. He turned from the horror and began to run.

*

Donald Graves, an accountant from Pittsburgh on his way to a convention in Charleston, tapped the steering wheel and sang along to Billy Joel's "The River of Dreams"; he knew most of the words, and compensated for what he didn't by humming.

It was 12:28 am by the green dash clock, and Donald was starting to think about finding a motel. He told his wife, Jean, that he was just going to drive through the night, something he had done many times before, but now, with the lines blurring on the road before him, he had to admit he wasn't a young man anymore. He would turn fifty in January, and he felt it.

Donald had been following Route 228 since crossing into Maryland at 10:30. Back there it was wide and well-lit, lined with restaurants, gas stations, and shopping malls. But here, just north of Westernport, it was narrow and dark, writhing through the woods like a snake in the throes of death. If he remembered correctly, there was a motel in Keyser. Maybe he would...

So quickly Donald could barely register, something jumped out into the road and slammed into the windshield, cracking it. Screaming, he instinctively jerked the wheel to the left and slammed into a ditch, his head bouncing off the wheel.

When he came to, white smoke curled from the crumpled front end of the Nissan. He moaned as a wave of agony crashed over him.

Jean's gonna kill me... he thought groggily. He touched his fingers to his scalp and they came away bloody.

Shit.

For a moment he sat where he was, letting his mind clear. When he was sure he was steady, he pulled his cell from his pocket.

Suddenly, the driver door jerked open, startling him.

When he saw the thing grinning at him, his blood ran cold and the phone dropped from his hand.

The thing, its white face partially obscured by matted black hair, reached for him with hooked fingers, the devilish red glow of its eyes shining hypnotically.

Before it caught hold of his shirt and dragged him out, he saw others behind it; a snarling dog-faced *horror* with ram's horns; a decomposing woman whose skull shone eerily in the moonlight; a midget with blue skin and jagged yellow teeth.

On the radio, Billy Joel searched for the desert of truth.

In real life, Donald Graves had found it.

And it was hell.

*

Jeff stumbled, went to his knees. His side burned and each breath was fire in his lungs.

Beside him, Kayla stopped. "Come on!"

Jeff tossed a glance over his shoulder. The woods were dark and empty. Here, far from the cemetery, the only sound was the wind in the trees.

"Jeff!"

"We're okay," Jeff panted. "They aren't following us."

Something moaned nearby, contradicting him. It sounded like it was off to the left.

"Jeff, come *on!*" Kayla pleaded.

Jeff got to his feet. Something moved between the trees; in a flash of moonlight, it looked dead.

"Let's go."

They walked quickly through the leaves, Kayla in front and Jeff behind. He occasionally looked behind to make sure they weren't being followed.

"Where are we going?" Jeff asked at one point. The trees pressed close against them, and the underbrush was starting to get impassably thick.

"I don't know," she breathed.

The land rose up, forming a hill. At the summit, Jeff could see the lights of town over the tops of the trees. At the bottom, on the other side of a narrow stream, a dirt road ran east-to-west. Jeff looked back. Faintly over the treetops, he could see the blue light.

"Come on," Kayla said, already starting down.

Sighing, Jeff followed.

At the water's edge, Kayla paused.

"How deep is it?" Jeff asked.

In the distance, a scream split the night, high and unearthly.

"Not deep enough," she said, and bounded across.

Jeff stayed close behind, wincing as the icy water engulfed his feet. On the far bank, he looked back. He thought he saw something in the trees.

"Quick," he said, pushing Kayla forward.

The road bordered the forest for several hundred yards before turning away from the stream. Trees loomed over them.

At the end of the road, the trees fell away. A building with a pitched roof sat in the middle of a clearing, a gravel parking lot to one side cast in the harsh orange glow of an arch sodium light.

A church.

Jeff's heart leapt. "It's a church," he said. "We'll be safe in there."

"Okay," Kayla said.

They started toward the building. Half way there, Jeff looked back, and saw with a start that over a dozen *things* were coming from the woods, moving at odd angles, their heads flopping bonelessly back and forth. As he watched, something appeared on the road. Jeff couldn't tell what it was, but it loped on all fours.

"Shit," he said.

Kayla screamed.

"Hurry!"

They ran, Kayla falling behind. Fifteen feet from the front door, Jeff stopped, grabbed her, and started dragging her. The things were closing in, twenty, twenty-five feet behind.

At the door, Jeff tried the handle but it was locked.

"Jeff!"

Jeff looked back. Three ghouls were so close he could see the emptiness of their eye sockets

Panicking, Jeff pulled back and kicked the door as hard as he could. It flew open with a crack and slammed against the wall. Inside, just as the first zombie reached them, Jeff threw the door shut. There was a bolt that hadn't been engaged. Jeff slammed it home and backed up a step. Kayla unthinkingly grabbed him.

The door shook as the things pounded against it. They couldn't come in, though, right? God, they *shouldn't* be able to. They were demons!

But what if they did?

"Here," Jeff said, going into the nave. "Help me with one of these pews."

Catching his drift, Kayla helped him drag one of the short back pews to the door. It was too long to fit lengthwise, so they pushed one end against the door. It wasn't perfect, but it would hold.

"What do we do?" she asked.

Jeff thought, his mind whirring. He didn't know. He was just as scared as she was.

"A phone," she said suddenly. "There has to be an office somewhere. And offices have phones."

Yeah. A phone. That made sense.

They went off in search of a phone.

Ray Tomlinson, Westernport's resident drunk, staggered off Maple Street and onto Main, his head throbbing and his stomach rolling. Grabbing an iron lamppost, he held on for dear life and fought back a wave of vomit.

When it passed, he chuckled to himself.

Ray had been drinking since he was thirteen, when he and a couple of his friends raided his old man's liquor cabinet. Thirty years. And in that time, he had only puked three times, the last being in 1991.

Vomit free he thought, and smiled. He pushed himself away from the lamppost and started across the street. He was almost to the other side when he heard something.

Turning woozily, he saw a group of people walking up the middle of the street. They passed under an arch of light falling from a lamp, and even in his present state, Ray knew something wasn't right with them. They moved jerkily, some of them dragging their feet along the pavement. They didn't speak or sing or shout like a team of drunks coming home from a bar; they hissed, moaned, and screamed.

As they drew closer, Ray's heart began to pound. Though he couldn't say why, he knew he was in danger.

"There's one!" one of them called, pointing. In the light, Ray could just make out its face: drawn, blue.

A noise went through the crowd, and they started coming faster. Ray turned to run, but something hit him like a freight train, slamming him to the pavement.

Just before the thing ripped out his throat, Ray saw its face: wolf-like, elongated, its teeth crooked and yellow.

When he screamed, it came out a bloody gurgle.

*

From Main Street, they spread out into Westernport. At the corner of Maple and Oak, they pulled a man from his car and ate his skin; his screams rose into the night, reaching a fever pitch before dying down as his vocal cords slipped from his gaping neck. Lights along the street flipped on; curtains drew back from upstairs windows.

They started toward the houses then, pounding on front doors and smashing through windows. In one house, a man appeared at the top of the stairs with a pistol and fired. Only then did he realize what he was facing. The bullets had no effect.

On Staples Drive, they dragged a screaming infant from its crib and feasted on it as its shrieking mother watched in horror. When her mind snapped and she sank into catatonia, one of them, a rapist in life, ripped her pink bathrobe off and took her, using the rotting penis of a body possessed.

On Bower Road, Sheriff Bill Wyatt jerked the wheel of his squad car and skidded across the pavement, the car doing a half circle before stopping. Next to him, his deputy, Roger Yancy, wore an expression of horror. The street was filled with *them*, some wandering aimlessly, others bending over fallen bodies.

"Jesus fuck," Wyatt said, unclasping his safety belt and grabbing the shotgun from its place between the seats.

He flung the door open and got out into the bitter night. Several of them saw him and started coming forward, their hands outstretched. "Skin!"

Wyatt pumped the shotgun and raised it to his shoulder. "Freeze!"

Yancy was crouching behind his door, his pistol in his hands.

The things continued advancing.

When the first calls came through, Wyatt didn't know what to think. People running amok in Westernport? Why? This wasn't Ferguson.

Then, when more calls came in from hysterical people reporting *monsters*, he knew something was seriously wrong. Monsters, mass hysteria, crooks *dressed* as monsters. Who knew?

Now, watching the creatures shambling down the street, Wyatt saw that they *were* monsters. Men with the heads of dogs; crawling horrors with upside down skulls; fangs; horns; skulls; all bathed in the throbbing red and blue lights from the cruiser's roof rack.

Shivering, saying a silent prayer to a God he hadn't spoken to in twenty years, Wyatt aimed at the closest monster, a rotting corpse in a tattered burial gown, and fired, the recoil of the shotgun nearly knocking him down; he wasn't steady.

The thing turned and fell. Wyatt pumped the shotgun again and swung it around, taking aim at a seven-foot-tall giant with red skin and horns (Satan himself?) Yancy was firing now too, his gun going *pop-pop-pop* like small scale fireworks.

Wyatt fired, but the monster took the buckshot like it was a warm summer wind. "Shit!" He pumped the shotgun again, sending the empty shell to the pavement, and aimed higher, hitting it in the head.

Nothing.

"Bill!" Yancy said, his voice full of fear.

"Hold steady!"

Giving up on the devil, Wyatt fired at another corpse. This one went down, but got right back up.

They were so close he could *smell* them. Sulfur. Rotten eggs.

Wyatt cocked the gun again, but it was empty; they would be on him before he could load it again.

"Run!"

He turned, but a black shape with large, ragged eyes rushed him. For a moment, he felt cold...then he felt himself changing. The world went gray, then black. The sound of Roger Yancy's screams as the things took him was muffled, distant.

His mind tingled.

I'm being possessed!

That's the last Bill Wyatt knew.

His body, now cold to the touch, joined the creatures feasting on Roger Yancy's insides.

*

At 2:30am, nearly two dozen creatures attacked the Westernport sewage treatment facility, killing a night watchman and several third shift technicians. One of the things, a hulking bat-like horror, laughingly pulled levers and pushed buttons, sending a tidal wave of waste spilling into the Potomac.

Up and down Main Street, they cavorted with satanic glee, smashing windows, starting fires, and killing anyone they could find. By 3:00, Westernport was silent, fires raging unchecked. In search of blood, many started south toward McCool. Some crossed the Potomac into West Virginia. At 3:25, they attacked a homeless camp by the railroad tracks.

At 3:48, a dozen, including many former Westernport residents, reached McCool, a collection of buildings around the foot of a bridge rather than an actual town. They raided houses, stopped cars, and marched into Keyser. Their first victim was a Potomac State College student on a late night walk. Following Front Street through the downtown business section, he heard strange laughter several times before something swooped in and grabbed him from the air. Talons dug into his flesh. He screamed, and the thing, cawing like the world's largest crow, lifted him higher and higher before dropping him. The last thing that went through his mind, other than the pavement, was: *Fuck!*

At 4:01, Brian Scott, night watchman at Potomac Valley Hospital, looked up from his magazine, a strange feeling suddenly coming over him. The emergency room was empty and tranquil at that hour, the florescent lighting harsh, cold.

Shaking his head, Brian went back to his magazine. An interview with Hilary Clinton. Fucking crook.

The automatic doors whooshed open then, and Brian looked up.

Five *things* stood before them. Their faces, Brian saw with a jerk, were varying shades of blue and gray. Their clothes hung from their emaciated bodies in tatters.

"Food!" one of them screamed, and they came toward him.

Heart knocking against his ribcage, Brian moved to stand up, but another, unseen creature grabbed him from behind, wrestling him to the ground.

When Brian Scott was dead, the ghouls split up, two going down separate corridors and one descending a flight of stairs to the morgue, where it found a stash of cold bodies and began to feast. In Room 2A, Elvira Johnson, an elderly widow lost in the grip of dementia, watched with dumb blankness as one of the monsters shuffled to her bedside.

She was too far gone to know what was happening, but not too far gone to scream.

Two miles away, Josh Simmons, fifteen, woke to the sound of something tapping at his window. The sound was frightening in the dark; what made it even more frightening was that Josh's room was on the second floor.

"Hey," he whispered to his roommate, Matt.

Matt snorted.

Josh tried to ignore the constant *tap-tap-tap,* but couldn't. Finally, he got up, went to the window, and opened the curtain.

Nothing.

Josh stuck his head out into the night and looked around. It was windy, so maybe...

A cloud of acrid smoke washed over him, and suddenly he was cold.

Possessed, he smiled. First, he beat Matt to death with his fists, then he went out into the hall and listened.

Group home, the boy's mind said, two boys in each room, two staff members downstairs.

Creeping as silently as he could, he went down the backstairs into the darkened kitchen. A light glowed in the living room. On the TV sirens wailed.

From a drawer, the boy selected a butcher knife and went back upstairs. He stabbed each of the remaining four residents, panting with pleasure. When he was done, he went downstairs and found a black man lounging on the couch.

"What are you doing?" the black man asked.

"Killing people."

The black man tried to fight, but he wound up just like all the others.

At 5:00 am, one of the creatures stumbled into the path of a semi screaming down US50 north of Burlington but south of Keyser. Hanging on for dear life, it made it all the way to Romney before letting go. There, it caught a stray cat and ate it.

Back in Keyser, things ran rampant through the streets much as they had done in Westernport. Within half an hour, they had reached New Creek in West Virginia, and Barton, Dawson, and Moscow in Maryland.

The night was theirs.

*

Jeff Morgan jerked awake just as the first light of dawn fell through the window. Kayla was next to him, her head lolling on his shoulder.

She was asleep.

For a moment Jeff listened to the silence of the morning. Was it really dawn?

The night had seemed to stretch forever. The things pounded on the door and appeared at the windows, including Andrew and the others, their faces pale and their eyes black. *"Come on,"* Andrew said at one point, smiling, *"the power of Satan!"*

They never came through the doors or windows, even though they easily could have. Jeff suspected they were afraid of the church.

Or the spirit of God.

"Wake up," he said, shaking Kayla.

"They here?"

They found a phone in a back office and called the police. They never showed, however.

"No," he said, "but I think it's over. Listen."

Kayla cocked her head and did.

"Come on."

They moved the pew and opened the door. The morning was cold and orange and fresh. The field fronting the church was empty. The woods beyond, still cast in shadows, could have hidden demons, but he doubted. They probably couldn't come out in the daylight.

An hour later, when the sun was fully risen, they left, Jeff in the lead.

"Where are we going?" Kayla asked.

Jeff didn't reply. He had an idea.

Back at the cemetery, the ground was still wide open, but no bodies were visible. No signs. Nothing.

The only thing they found was the book Andrew had read from: cracked brown leather.

Jeff picked it up.

"What are you doing?" Kayla asked.

"You'll see."

They walked back to the church. Birds chirped happily from treetops.

At the church, Jeff opened the door and threw the book inside.

It burst into flames.

"I think it was a doorway," he said to her then. "That's how they came out."

Kayla didn't reply; they simply watched the book burning on the floor of the church.

"Let's go," she said finally.

Hand-in-hand, they walked back into Westernport

AOKIGAHARA

Johnny Yun lit a cigarette and sucked deeply, relishing the harsh smoke in his lungs. Money was tight these days, and packs of Marlboros were far more expensive in Japan than America. A two-pack-a-day kinda guy, Johnny had to limit himself to two a week.

Sighing, Johnny got out of bed and sat for a long moment in the gloom. Outside, Tokyo sat huddled against the dirty gray sky, a futuristic metropolis misplaced in a 1940s noir film. Looking out over the wan city, Johnny, for the thousandth time, regretted moving to Japan. Back in California, he'd had a good job, a nice apartment, money, and a car. Here, he had dick. And, from what the few friends he had said, he spoke with an American accent, which was just the funniest thing going.

Why the hell did he come here? Did he *really* believe that he would prosper here?

Apparently so.

Johnny sighed again. No money, no food, the rent was due, and he had five dollars to his name.

Yen, he reminded himself, *five yen*.

He grinned bitterly. Yen. What a stupid word. Everything about Japan was stupid. The fashion, the culture, the anime, especially the anime.

Puffing on his smoke, Johnny looked at the bedside clock. 9:15. At ten he would call Hedrio. Last night he said he knew how they could make some money, and, usually, Hedrio's harebrained schemes paid off.

Johnny finished his cigarette, and stubbed it out in the ashtray on the nightstand. When he went to stand, he nearly fell back down, his legs weak and shaky.

You drink too much, he told himself, but he already knew, and he really didn't give a flying dick. What else was he supposed to do with his free time? Sniff vending-machine panties and read tentacle porn?

In the bathroom, Johnny looked at himself in the mirror, disliking what he saw. His flesh was wan and drawn. He'd lost weight since the Big Move.

"Too much rice," he said, and croaked laughter. He didn't eat much of the stuff, but the quip was in keeping with his sour mood.

Still chuckling, Johnny stripped out of his boxers and wife beater and climbed into the shower. Nothing felt as good as a hot shower in the morning.

Nearly a half hour later, Johnny got out, toweled off, and put his shirt and underwear back on. It was 9:42. Fuck it. He'd call Hedrio now.

Lighting another cigarette, Johnny sat on the bed and dialed Hedrio's number. Six rings later, Hedrio sleepily answered. In Japanese.

"English," Johnny said, "do you speak it, motherfucker?"

Hedrio laughed. Like Johnny, he was a transplanted American. Unlike Johnny, however, he liked Japan. Poor and down on his luck, but happy in the land of the Rising Sun.

"What's goin' on, my nigga?" Hedrio asked, his accent comically thick.

"Not much, derp. Just lookin' to make some coin."

"Oh. I get dressed and come. We going to Mount Fuji."

Johnny raised an eyebrow. "Why?"

"I'll tell you later," Hedrio said, and hung up.

Whatever, Johnny thought, and hung the phone back up. If Hedrio wanted to waste 90 miles worth of gas (and tolls!), that was on him, just as long as they made some coin.

Shaking his head, Johnny got up and got dressed; jeans, a white T, and a leather jacket. In the kitchen, he made some toast and drowned it with a cup of instant coffee. Another thing he hated about Japan was tea. The Japanese were so fucking gaga over their tea. Kinda like the British, but only more yellow.

Johnny shocked himself into laughing. Jesus, he sounded like a self-loathing Uncle Tom or something. If his grandmother could hear him now, she'd probably bust out some judo or something. *You are forgetting your roots!* she had once said, when he was a kid in L.A. *You are too American!*

Yeah, grandma, he thought now, standing in the kitchen of his tiny apartment, drinking coffee and looking at his Spartan living room, *because being Japanese in an all-black school is just tops! I get picked on enough without wearing your dumbass kimono to school.*

Now, however, Johnny stopped. *Had* he forgotten his roots? *Was* he a self-loathing Asian?

Nah, he finally decided, he was just honest. I calls 'em as I sees 'em, and Japan sucks ass.

Checking his watch, Johnny saw that he'd killed over twenty minutes. Shit. If Hedrio was anything, it was quick.

Hurriedly, Johnny drained the rest of his coffee and sat the glass in the sink. After a fat piss, he was on his way down the stairs. In the lobby, Jenna Wong was taking her garbage out. Another American expedite, Jenna was probably the hottest Asian chick Johnny had seen since the Big Move; tall and slim, tits small but perky, hair like liquid oil and eyes dark and furtive, she was on point. Ummm. Johnny'd smash that ass any time.

"Morning, Jenna," he said.

Jenna, at the double doors to the street, turned, startled, and smiled. "Hi, Johnny," she said. "How are you?"

"I'm good. Here, let me get that for you." Ducking around her, Johnny opened the door.

"Thank you," she said.

Johnny watched her ass wiggle as she walked to the curb.

Before Jenna had even finished putting her trash in the can, Hedrio pulled up, loud rap music thumping from the speakers in the trunk. Sleek and lime green, his ride looked like something out of the *Fast and Furious* movies.

"*Konnichiwa*, Jenna!" Hedrio cried out the window like a madman.

Jenna, trash now deposited, gave him a stiff and tentative wave, and turned, hurried scurrying back to the building.

"Bye, Johnny," she said as she passed him. He couldn't be sure, but he thought she was blushing. In Japanese, that meant *I wanna suck your brains out*.

Giggity.

"Come on!" Hedrio screamed, "we got stuff to *dooo!*"

Shoving his hands into his pockets, Johnny hurried over, cold rain beginning to fall from the sky. He opened the door, climbed in, and slammed it shut behind him. It smelled like weed.

"Good morning, nigga!" Hedrio cried, snatching Johnny's hand and trying some new nigger handshake. Hedrio was one-hundred-twenty pounds soaking wet, dressed in leather, and wore his red-dyed hair in short, pointy spikes. He reminded Johnny of that loser in *Malibu's Most Wanted*.

"Man, get the fuck off me," Johnny said, shoving Hedrio away.

"You ready to hit the road?" Hedrio asked, gunning the engine. "We hit the road!"

Before Johnny could reply, the car rocketed off, slicing through the rain like a bullet.

"Slow down!" Johnny cried, "you're gonna get us busted!"

Hedrio eased up on the gas. They were leaving Tokyo and entering the outlying suburbs before Johnny spoke again. "So, you mind telling me what the hell we're doing?"

Hedrio looked at Johnny, a goofy grin on his face. "We're going to *Aokigahara*."

"What?"

Hedrio nodded. *Aokigahara*, or, the Sea of Trees, if you were poetic, was a dense forest cast in perpetual shadow northwest of Fuji. The foliage was so thick that it was dark even at high noon, but that wasn't the worst thing about it. *Aokigahara* was also called "The Suicide Forest," because every suicidal motherfucker in Japan decided to trudge their asses out there and kill themselves rather than just stay home and do it. In fact, it was so bad that despite the government's almost daily sweeps of the forest, some bodies stayed out there for months, even years, hanging from twisted trees like stick figures in an Asian *Blair Witch Project*.

A lot of people said that the forest was popular with suicides because some guy wrote a book in which a couple of people offed themselves there, but *Aokigahara* had always been associated with death. Some said it was cursed, or haunted, or some damn thing. Johnny didn't know, nor did he care. He didn't believe in that sort of shit.

But the place was creepy nonetheless.

"The fuck are we going out there for?" he asked.

"Man," Hedrio said, "think about it. All these dead bodies, all with money in their pockets. I know a guy who went out there once and came home with two million *yen*."

Johnny sighed. It *was* a good idea. There were suicides out there every day. Old bodies, new bodies, it didn't matter. Still...fucking creepy.

And money wasn't even guaranteed. They might find a shit ton of bodies, but who was to say any of them would have any cash in their pockets? There was a high chance of finding some, yeah, but it wasn't a sure thing. This could all be a big waste of time.

Johnny said as much, but Hedrio merely laughed. "We'll find some money. I know we will."

Whatever.

The ride was long and dull. The rain picked up as they put Tokyo behind them, and became torrential as they passed through the countryside north of Fuji. Finally, sometime after one, they left the main highway and took a secondary road through increasingly forested highlands. At two, they arrived, pulling into a gravel lot surrounded by thick woods on three sides.

Hedrio killed the engine and laid back against the headrest. "You ready for money?"

"Always ready," Johnny said, "but where the hell do we start? There're...what...fifty miles of this shit?"

Hedrio shrugged. "We start over there," he said, indicating a worn dirt path that led into the forest, "and go in. Most of the dead people will be off the beaten track."

This was getting stupider by the minute. Whatever. "Come on, gook," Johnny said, getting out of the car. Hedrio followed.

"So, do we split up?" Johnny asked as they slowly walked up to the path. About fifteen feet in, it turned sharply out of sight. It *was* dark in there. They should have brought flashlights.

"Good idea," Hedrio said, "let's go."

Deep into the forest they went. After half a mile, Hedrio stopped. "I'll go off here," he said, pointing to a large, overgrown clearing, "you stay on the path."

"Alright," Johnny heaved, "whatever."

Hedrio went to do one of his nigger handshakes, but Johnny stopped him dead in his tracks. "Just go on. I'll see you later."

Nodding, Hedrio turned his back on Johnny and carefully climbed down the embankment to the clearing.

Johnny watched him for a long time before sighing and getting back underway. This was stupid.

For almost an hour, Johnny walked the path, looking for a good place to enter the bush and seeing none. He really didn't feel like trudging through weeds like Indiana Jones or something. He should have stayed home. He...

...hit something with his left foot and went down, landing heavily on his hands and knees, his heart leaping into his throat.

The fuck!

Must have been a stone jutting out of the ground.

Muttering under his breath, Johnny staggered back to his feet and whipped around, intent on throwing the damn rock into the woods. What he saw, however, froze him in place.

It wasn't a rock, it was a human skull, eyes wide and dark, bottom jaw missing.

"Jesus!" he said, disgust washing through him. He turned back the way he'd been going, and saw a body hanging from a tree up ahead, swaying back and forth in the nonexistent breeze.

It hadn't been there a minute ago. Of that Johnny was certain.

Heart racing, Johnny looked right and left, his neck suddenly tingling. They were everywhere. There must have been two, three dozen, all hanging from tree limbs, all swinging back and forth, all gray and rotting, their clothes torn and dirty.

Taking a deep breath, Johnny closed his eyes. There was no way this was happening. It had to be a hallucination.

1, 2, 3...

At five, he opened his eyes again.

The bodies were gone.

For a long moment, Johnny stood in the middle of the path, panting and looking about himself, left, right, front, back, as if he expected them to reappear, which, to be honest, he did.

Fuck this, he finally thought, and turned the way he had come. He'd go back to the car and wait for Hedrio. He could have his dead money.

Johnny made it fifty feet before he noticed that the forest had fallen unnervingly quiet. Up until then, there had been noise, crickets, a stream babbling in the distance, the soft rustle of the occasional breeze, but now...nothing, it was as silent as the surface of the moon.

Not only that...but the atmosphere had changed as well. It was more oppressive now, darker and heavier, crackling with unwholesomeness.

Johnny ran. He had to get the hell out of here.

He ran, and ran, and ran...

...but went nowhere. He passed the same tree, the same moss covered stone, the same overgrown sign (LIFE IS PRECIOUS: RECONSIDER YOUR ACTIONS!) four, five, six times.

Finally, getting a semblance of control over himself, Johnny stopped and sank down against the base of a tree. The light filtering through the treetops was getting weaker now; twilight seemed to seep up out of the ground, pooling, higher, higher, higher. A cold wind gusted suddenly through the forest, and in it were voices, thousands of voices babbling imperceptibly.

This was crazy. He was having some sort of breakdown or something. He was lost and he was slowly going mad, giving in to panic and paranoia. He had to get out of here, but he had to keep his wits about him.

Breathing slowly, Johnny closed his eyes and tried to get a rein on his galloping heart. What he needed to...

A twig snapped before him, startling him. His eyes flew open, and there, shambling through the thick underbrush on the other side of the path, were a dozen rag-clad phantoms, their faces in various states of decay and their arms outstretched like zombies from some old movie.

Johnny's heart burst against his ribcage, knocking the breath from his lungs. He tried to stand, but his knees had turned to water.

"Hedrio!" he screamed, his frozen vocal cords suddenly unlocked. He squeezed his eyes closed and counted quickly to ten, missing nine and adding an extra eight. When he opened them again, the ghouls were closer.

"Hedrio!"

He pushed himself forward, but, with whip-crack suddenness, something (a vine? a rope?) shot out of the tree's gnarled trunk and wound itself around his neck, dragging him roughly back and cutting off his air supply.

He tried to scream, but it came out as a futile gurgle. The ghouls shambled ever closer, reaching for him, their jaws working hungrily up and down.

The world began to dim.

Closer, closer, the smell of death thick on the air. The first ghoul in line, a tall, slender woman, grabbed Johnny's shirt, pulling herself closer...

...and opened her mouth.

Hedrio Takanowa looked up from the body before him. He thought he'd heard his name. In fact, he was *certain* he'd heard is name, as if shouted from a great distance. The forest was preternaturally quiet; you could hear an owl fart three miles away. For the last fifteen minutes (half hour? hour?) all he'd heard were the frogs croaking from a nearby swamp, *ribbit, ribbit, ribbit* becoming *doit doit doit.*

Shaking his head, Hedrio looked about himself like a man coming out of a deep, dark sleep. Something was wrong. He didn't feel quite right. His memory was fuzzy, and his thoughts were muddled.

Oh well. He returned his attention to the body at his feet; tangled in the tall grass, it had once been a businessman by the looks of it. Most of the flesh had rotted from his skull, but he was clad in a shirt, trousers, and a tie. Hedrio opened the wallet hitherto forgotten in his hand, and removed the bills. He was too excited to count them, but he knew he had a lot. He hoped that Johnny was having the same luck as him.

Hedrio slipped the bills into his pocket, planning to count them in the car, and his fingers brushed something cold and hard.

Huh.

He pulled it out, a rusted razor blade, and studied it for a mystified moment.

It wasn't his. In fact, he'd never seen it before in his life.

So how did it wind up in his pocket?

Doit, doit, doit, croaked the frogs.

SNOWBOUND

Philip Garner waited three minutes before turning the TV off. He would have done it sooner, but one of the Weather Channel's field correspondents was dancing and hooting on a Boston street corner because it was thundering as it snowed, and Phil couldn't bring himself to look away. When it switched back to the studio, however, he quickly lost interest. He knew what they were going to say: 6 to 18 inches over the next two days, then another possible 4 to 6 on Friday.

"This is one for the record books," Jim Cantore said. Phil didn't know about that, but he did know that the snow was already nearly halfway to the first story windows. If it kept on, they'd be buried, literally buried.

Phil wasn't claustrophobic, but the walls were beginning to close on him nevertheless. Of course, that could have been simple cabin fever. It had been nearly a week since he arrived at the bed and breakfast on Pine Ridge Road, nearly a week since the first storm rolled over central New Hampshire. The pantry was getting bare and the other guests were beginning to bicker. Mr. Johnson got more potatoes than I did; Mrs. Baker complains too much. On and on and on. Fred Mansfield, the owner of the place, tried to walk into town the day before yesterday, but got as far as the main highway (an impressive two miles downhill) before the wind became too much.

"You couldn't even see the asphalt," Fred said, the wonderment clear in his voice. "It looked just like the field out back."

That was troubling. If the highway department wasn't maintaining the roads...

The TV was saying more than a million people across New England were in the dark, with another million or so expected to join in the coming days. They had power now, but Phil was almost certain it wouldn't last, not with the snow and wind.

Presently, Phil laid back on the bed and stared up at the ceiling; shadows pooled in the corners, along with the dust and cobwebs Mrs. Mansfield claimed weren't there. How long until the roof collapsed?

The thought was sudden, almost as if transmitted from an external source. How long until the beams gave way and all that snow came crashing down?

Phil sighed. This was the worst hunt he'd ever been on.

Philip Garner was a businessman, and his business, nay, his *passion*, was the paranormal. In the twenty years since he started his own investigations into the unexplained, he had been on nearly two hundred expeditions all over the world, from Italy to Mexico City to Beijing. He'd also authored three books on the subject, two of which made the New York Times bestseller list. If things panned out here, he planned to write another, this one dedicated entirely to the Wiltshire Bed and Breakfast (*Most haunted inn in New England*).

The thing was he hadn't found anything. Nothing on the cameras. Nothing on the EVP machine. Not even one lousy cold spot.

The stories, though...they were the stuff of *legends*. Voices, footsteps, disembodied heads floating over you in the middle of the night, their eyes glazed and their lips dripping blood. It took him nearly three years to convince the owners, Fred and Martha Mansfield, to let him study the place. Three years of phone calls and emails. Three years of asking politely and outright begging.

"We'd look like kooks," Fred said, as if they didn't already. The sign out front pretty much marked them.

"You don't have to talk to me," Philip assured them. "I'll just do my investigating and that's it. No interviews. No quotes. Nothing."

Everything they told him was off the record, though he supposed he could slip it in as having been reported by someone else. And he figured he might. Fred and Martha had some juicy stuff, hands grabbing their ankles as they got out of bed at night and such. The readers loved that kind of junk, even if it *wasn't* true. Phil...well...Phil didn't mind exaggerating occasionally if it helped sales.

But as Fred and Martha got further into their story, Phil realized he wouldn't have to embellish. It was wild enough as it stood.

"I think it's a demon," Martha told him, "the way stuff just flies around. And the cat!"

Phil choked at the word "demon." He wasn't a religious man by any means, but he did believe that there were evil spirits existing outside the realm of the living. *Powerful* evil spirits. If a demon had found its way into the Wiltshire...oh boy.

"What about the cat?" Phil had asked.

Back in the eighties, Martha claimed, they had a cat named Smuckers. (With a name like Smuckers, it *has* to be good). One day, poor Smuckers went missing. Martha looked everywhere. Two days later, he came crawling out of the woods, his body smashed and his brain seeping out of his ears. She figured he got hit by a car and dragged himself home. "He was probably at it the whole two days," Fred confirmed.

Shortly after he came home, Smuckers died, and Fred buried him in the yard. Later that night, Martha heard something.

"It was eerie. Echoing through the house. It sounded like scratching."

Scratching. On the back door. When she opened it, Smuckers was there, one of his eyes hanging on a stalk of nerves.

"He meowed...and it was the strangest thing. His voice was really deep."

The first thing the cat did was try to attack her foot. Fred jumped in, squishing his head, but he still kept coming.

"Finally, I grabbed him by the scruff of his neck and took him outside and burned him in the fire pit."

"I think a demon got into him," Martha said, shuddering.

Phil doubted the story...though his doubts had their own doubts. Demonic possession happens, yes, but it's rare. Demonic possession of a dead thing...well, that was rarer still. Some in the field believed that a corpse was simply an empty vessel that a demon, if powerful enough, could inhabit. Phil knew people, people he trusted, who had all sorts of wild stories about demonic possession. He believed them, he had just never seen it himself.

If there *was* a demon, however, Phil would have known by now. As far as he was concerned, there was nothing to work with here. He would have packed up and gone home four days ago, but that's when the first storm blew through, cutting the Wiltshire off from the outside world.

Sighing, Phil sat back up and rolled his neck. It was three in the afternoon and the wind was beginning to pick back up, howling in the eaves like the voice of the damned. Dinner would be soon. He should probably...

Someone knocked on the door, startling Phil.

"Yeah?" he called out.

"It's me. Fred. We have a problem."

*

Edith Baker, ninety-one, lay in her bed, her mouth slack and her eyes open, staring sightlessly into the gloom. Phil grabbed her wrist to check for a pulse, and her skin was ice cold.

"She's dead."

Fred Mansfield's face went white. "Jesus."

She was clad in a thin silk nightgown, indicating to Phil that she never got up that morning. It wasn't uncommon for the old gal to sleep in, so no one worried when she didn't show promptly at dawn.

"What do you think did it?"

"I don't know," Phil said. "It could have been a heart attack. Stroke. Brain aneurism."

Mrs. Baker was Martha Mansfield's first grade teacher. They remained close throughout the years, and when Mr. Baker died in 1998, Martha insisted Mrs. Baker come and live with them. It was either that or a nursing home.

For being ninety-one, Mrs. Baker was in pretty good health. She was the one who kept the garden nice and pretty; she was the one who did the wash and cleaned the bathrooms every week. Fred and Martha begged her to stop, but the old woman would only say, "Buzz off, I'm earning my keep."

Now she was dead.

"What are we going to do?" Fred asked.

31

Phil shook his head. "I dunno. We can't call anyone."

The phone lines were down, and cell service was nonexistent on a good day, much less during a Snowpocalypse.

"We could put her in the cellar," Fred offered.

That would work. When the storm let up, one of them could walk into town and get help.

"Alright," Phil sighed. "You should probably tell your wife first."

Fred nodded. "Yeah."

While Fred went off to break the news to Martha, Phil covered Mrs. Baker with a sheet and drew a chair to her bedside. The door was open (Fred really should have closed it), and when Mr. Johnson walked by, he turned and gawked.

"Oh, my God, what happened?" he asked.

A tall, chubby man of fifty-some with short iron gray hair and glasses, Ben Johnson was an accountant from Boston. Every so often, he came out to the B&B for a few days to unwind. Had been since 1990, Fred told him. To say he was close to the Mansfields and Mrs. Baker would be a stretch, but he certainly knew them.

"I don't know," Phil said. "Fred found her. Heart attack, probably."

Ben shook his head. "Jesus. What are we gonna do with her?"

"Cellar."

Fred returned. Behind him, Marcus Warner strained for a look.

"Oh, shit," he said.

Tall and lean, Marcus used to be a football player...from what Phil heard. The New England Patriots drafted him back in 2005, but he didn't make the final cut. These days, he...Phil wasn't sure what he did, but he had to do something, right?

"Aw, man."

"You're putting her in the cellar?" Ben asked.

"Have to," Fred said. "What else we gonna do?"

Ben didn't reply.

"Marcus, you help me with her."

Marcus nodded. Fred grabbed her arms and Marcus caught her feet. The others stood aside as they carried her out of the room and down the stairs.

In the living room, Martha Mansfield sat stiffly on the sofa. Next to her, Wanda Sines did her level best to provide comfort. When Phil walked in, Martha looked up, unshed tears standing in her eyes.

"What do you think it was?" she asked.

"I don't know," Phil said. "Heart attack, probably. It looked like she went peacefully."

Martha drew a big, watery breath and said, "Thank God for small favors."

Wanda rubbed Martha's shoulder. "She's in a better place now."

At sixteen, Wanda Sines was the sort of girl men went to jail for: tall, olive skin, almond eyes, long, black hair. She was Martha's niece or third cousin or something like that. Phil wasn't clear.

"She's in a better place."

Yeah. The root cellar.

Phil almost smiled.

Instead, he went into the kitchen. The door to the cellar stood open, and Fred's voice rang distantly out. "Set her down, nice and easy."

Phil went down the stairs, avoiding the fifth one ("It's weak," Fred told him, "so be careful if you ever have to go down there.")

The cellar was twenty feet by twenty feet with a dirt floor and cold stone walls. A long bench in the corner that may have once been part of a workshop served as a makeshift resting place: The white wrapped woman lay stiff and jagged. Fred, Marcus, and Ben stood around, the former two huffing and puffing; apparently she was heavy.

"She should be fine in here," Fred said. "When this storm blows over I'll go into town."

"I could go now," Marcus said.

Fred shook his head. "It's too windy. You'll never make it."

"It's only four miles, right? I can do that easy."

Fred looked at him. "I don't think you can. Hell, I don't think anybody can."

"*I* can."

Fred looked at Phil.

"If he thinks he can make it," Phil said. Better that than leaving her down here, he thought but didn't add.

Fred sighed. "Alright."

Back upstairs, Phil sank into one of the kitchen chairs and watched as Ben started a pot of coffee. They were down to their last couple of rounds. They still had plenty of coco, though, so that evened out.

"This is a nightmare," Ben said.

"You can say that again," Phil replied. Through the window over the sink, whiteness prevailed.

Ben noticed too. "You think he can really make it?"

Phil opened his mouth to reply but stopped. He didn't know. Marcus was young and strong. If anyone could make it, it would be him.

"I hope so."

When the coffee was ready, Ben poured some into a mug and sat it on the table in front of Phil. He poured another two mugs and went into the living room. When he came back, he said, "Mrs. Mansfield's taking it better than I expected."

"That's good," Phil replied. He picked up his mug, blew on it, and took a sip. "The last thing we need is someone going into hysterics."

"Yeah," Ben said, sitting down. "I wouldn't blame her, I guess. Mrs. Baker was like a mother to her."

"I wouldn't either," Phil said, "but we have enough on our plate."

Just then, Fred and Marcus returned, Marcus dressed in a faded maroon snow suit and a black ski mask. He sat, and Fred started attaching his snowshoes to the bottom of his boots.

"That looks uncomfortable," Ben said, smiling weakly.

"It ain't too bad," Marcus replied. "Now, when you got all your gear on and you're playin' in the heat, that's bad."

Done, Marcus stood up and dragged himself through the living room. Fred, Phil, and Ben followed. At the door, Fred clapped Marcus's shoulder. "Be careful out there. If you don't think you can make it, come back."

"Alright."

"If you aren't back by..."

"I'll be back," Marcus said. "I promise you that."

He opened the door and a cold gust blew in.

Then he was gone.

*

"What time is it?" Fred asked.

Phil checked his watch. "Five."

Fred was standing at the sink, a second cup of coffee in his hand. Phil and Ben were at the table, working on their second as well.

"It's getting dark," Fred observed. "I hope he gets back soon."

"He'll be fine," Ben said. "Blacks were bred for hard work."

Fred and Phil both looked at him.

"It's true," he said, taking a long, loud sip.

They lapsed into silence. Fred watched out the window, his face hard and set. Phil finished off his coffee and leaned back in his chair. Ben, chastised, stared down into his cup like a gypsy divining tea leaves.

"Well," Fred started, "I suppose I better start dinn..."

A muffled crash cut him off. Phil jumped and Ben looked up.

"What was that?" Phil asked.

"I don't know, it sounded like it came from...shit."

"What?"

Fred shook his head. "I think the bench collapsed. The one Mrs. Baker's on."

It dawned on Phil. It *had* looked a little...aged. It wouldn't take much for it to go, especially factoring in the nigh supernatural heaviness of dead weight. An image of the old woman, wrapped in white, lying amidst splinters and broken boards flashed across Phil's mind.

"Fred?" Martha called out from the living room. "What was that?"

Fred licked his lips. "Nothing."

Martha didn't press the matter.

"We better go see the damage," Fred said.

Phil got up. Ben started to say something, but closed his mouth and

34

went back to looking into his coffee. Phil went over to the cellar door and opened it, a cold blast washing over him.

The light was on. He remembered turning it off.

"What's wrong?" Fred asked.

"I could have sworn..."

A shadow flickered across the wall followed by a shuffling footfall. Phil froze.

"What?" Fred worriedly asked.

The shadow grew smaller and denser as the source drew near. Between the ceiling and the banister, Phil caught a quick movement, and Mrs. Baker appeared.

"Jesus Christ!"

Her shoulders were stooped and her head hung; her arms dangled limply at her sides. When he spoke, she looked up, her head flopping bonelessly back, and terror washed over him.

Her eyes were red.

Demonic.

She smiled.

"Mrs. Baker?" Fred asked, taken aback.

The old woman took one jerky step forward and threw her arms up, as if to embrace them. Her face, Phil saw, half-obscured by darkness, was blue and drawn. Her teeth – dear God, her teeth – were long and jagged.

"Skin..." she drew, her voice low, unearthly.

Phil panicked and slammed the door, throwing himself against it.

"What?" Ben asked from the table.

"Mrs. Baker," Fred said, "she's alive."

Ben looked at Phil.

Phil shook his head. "That wasn't Mrs. Baker."

"What do you mean it wasn't Mrs. Baker?"

Martha and Wanda had appeared in the doorway. "What's wrong?" Martha asked.

"Mrs. Baker's alive," Fred said over his shoulder.

"That wasn't Mrs. Baker," Phil said. "Mrs. Baker is dead. I checked her pulse. Her skin was cold. There's no way she's alive. She's possessed. Just like Smuckers."

Martha cocked her head. "Smuckers? But that was just a story."

"What?"

"We made it up."

"You *lied*?"

"Embellished," Fred corrected. "We had to say *some-thing*."

Phil sagged against the door, dark realizations breaking over him. "You invited it in," he said, almost to himself.

"What?"

Demonic spirits existed outside of humanity, in the ether, in the darkness. However, there *were* ways to bring them into the world. Ouija boards. Séances. Claiming a demon you didn't have...creating a role, an empty role.

A role something could fill.

"You opened a door," Phil said. "You invited it in."

Fred's face darkened. "I've had enough of your New Age psychobabble. Get the hell out of my way."

Phil didn't budge. "Fred, listen to me..."

Fred pushed Phil aside.

"Fred!" Martha cried.

Fred opened the door, and Mrs. Baker was on him, her long, boney fingers digging into the sides of his face as she bit his neck.

Martha screamed; Ben jumped up from his chair.

Fred wailed as Mrs. Baker tore out his throat. He thrashed and pounded his fists against her head and back, but she continued unfazed. Phil was frozen. He couldn't move.

"Oh, my, God!" Wanda shrieked.

Giggling darkly, Mrs. Baker threw her head back in delight, her mouth and nightgown covered in blood.

"Yum, yum, Freddy!"

She let go of Fred, and he toppled back; his face was almost completely white.

For a moment, the ghoul stood where it was, licking the blood from its blue lips. Realizing there were others, she moved toward Martha, but Phil came to life; he grabbed her by the collar of her gown and yanked her back, almost unbalancing her. She was strong. She ripped free of his grasp and turned on him. "More meat!"

She fell on him, but he was quicker; he spun with her and shoved, sending her flying down the cellar stairs with a sickening crack. She was up in an instant, her neck twisted and broken.

Phil slammed the door shut and threw himself against it. Martha and Ben were kneeling over Fred, Martha sobbing. Fred's eyes were open but he struggled to breathe. His neck was ruined. Blood was everywhere. Jesus Christ, it looked like Busch Gardens in hell.

"Give me a chair!" Phil screamed.

Ben pushed a chair over and Phil caught it; just as he shoved the back under the doorknob, it turned.

Phil backed away.

The knob rattled and shook.

Shuddering, Phil wiped his hands on his pants. He *touched* it. Jesus Christ, he *touched* it.

"Fred!" Martha cried. Phil looked back at Fred (he wasn't going to make it, even if they *could* just call 911) and then at the door. The knob was rattling. The Edith Baker-thing was trying to get out.

"I can smell your pancreas!" the demon behind the door salivated. "I want it!"

Phil swooned.

This couldn't be happening.

It couldn't.

*

Ben and Phil lugged Fred into the living room and onto the sofa. His eyes were starting to glaze. He was dead or close.

Martha was sobbing, Wanda was crying. Ben was white. When Phil dragged him back into the kitchen, he looked around like he'd never seen the place before. He was in shock.

"I...I...don't..."

"Does Fred have a gun?"

Ben licked his lips and looked at Phil. "A gun?"

"Yes, a gun."

"I...I think so. Yeah. He's a hunter."

"Go get it," Phil said.

Ben nodded and rushed off.

Phil turned to the door. The knob was silent now. If Mrs. Baker was still there, she wasn't trying to escape. Yet.

Ben returned with a double-barrel shotgun and a box of shells. Phil took it, cracked the stock, and slipped two of the bright red cartridges into the breech. With that, he snapped it closed and cocked it.

"What's...what's happening?" Ben asked. "Mrs. Baker..."

"That wasn't Mrs. Baker."

Ben looked at him. "What *was* it?"

"Something else," Phil said.

Outside, the wind howled.

The power dimmed.

Ben looked up.

He started to speak, but in the living room, Martha wailed.

Fred was most likely gone.

"Listen to me," Phil said. "I want you to take Martha and Wanda upstairs. Your room, my room, whatever, just lock the door. Put a dresser in front of it. Make sure nothing can get through. Okay?"

Ben nodded. "O-Okay."

"Good."

*

The power went out at 7:21 PM EST on February 17, 2015. Phil was sitting in a kitchen chair facing the cellar door when it cut out, plunging the house into darkness. Outside, the wind moaned.

Phil's grip tightened on the gun. Fred Mansfield lay still in the living room. Phil didn't like having his back to the man, but he doubted he'd

37

rise.

For the most part, the house was quiet. Ben and the women were upstairs still and the doorknob hadn't moved in nearly a half hour.

"Let me out..."

The words, rasped and low, startled Phil.

"Let me out. I want to eat your skin."

It wasn't coming from behind the cellar door; it was coming from the middle of his own head.

"Let me out, Phil. Let...me...out..."

"No," Phil said.

The demon banged on the door, shaking it in its frame. "Let me out! Let me out! Let me out!"

He hoped Marcus got back soon.

"Marcus is dead," the demon said.

"Shut up."

"Dead nigger, dead nigger."

"Shut up!"

The back door blew open, slamming against the wall; a swirl of wind driven snow danced into the kitchen.

Just the wind, Phil told himself as he tried to calm his racing heart. He got up, closed it, and came back to the chair. He was just sitting down when a sharp, echoing knocking filled the house.

Marcus.

Phil got up and went to the door. *I hope to God he found help.*

He unlatched the door, and the wind ripped it out of his hands.

Phil's relief evaporated.

Marcus was hunched over, as if under a great weight. His black face was crusted with ice and flecks of snow, and his eyes were the color of blood.

"Told you I'd be back," he said.

Phil screamed and brought the gun up. Marcus moved to knock it away, but he was too slow. Phil fired. The Marcus-thing staggered back and went down. Phil slammed the door and latched it again.

When he turned, he nearly screamed: Fred, his shirt and gaping neck caked with blood, was standing behind him, his face slack and his eyes red. The cellar door slammed open, and Mrs. Baker appeared behind him.

"So hungry," Fred said, and took a shuddering step forward. "So... cold."

Phil raised the gun and fired. The shot took Fred in the face, knocking him aside. Mrs. Baker came flying forward. Thinking fast, Phil swung the gun like a club; the stock connected with her head. *Crack!*

Phil backed to the bottom of the stairs to the second floor. Mrs. Baker was getting to her feet, her head split and her brains falling out. Fred was already on his feet again; his head was obliterated.

38

Marcus pounded at the front door.

"Give us your skin," Mrs. Baker said. "Give us your... organs!"

Phil bolted up the stairs. At the top, he slipped two more shells into the shotgun. Fred and Mrs. Baker were at the bottom of the stairs now.

Phil aimed the gun, but before he could fire, Wanda Sines leapt from the shadows, knocking the gun away. "Skin!" she cried. Phil elbowed her in the face, knocking her against the wall.

Frantic now, he grabbed the shotgun and brought it around. The first shot took her in the stomach, leaving a giant red crater. The second decapitated her, and flung her down the stairs.

He tried to load the gun again, but the shell dropped from his trembling hands and rolled away.

Martha Mansfield and Ben Johnson appeared from the darkness.

"Shit!" Phil muttered. Ben came toward him, his arms outstretched, and Phil swung the gun, striking him in the temple and knocking him back. Martha hissed and threw herself forward. Phil ducked around her and swung the gun, hitting her in the back and driving her to her knees.

There was nowhere to go. He was trapped.

They were all in the hallway now. Marcus. Fred. Mrs. Baker. Wanda. Ben. Martha. Their eyes glowed crimson and their fingers clutched. Marcus chuckled and Martha growled.

God help me.

He tried to load the gun again, but they were on top of him; he threw it into the crowd and ducked into Mrs. Baker's room.

Inside, he slammed the door, locked it, and leaned his weight against it. He was breathing so hard he was lightheaded. He looked hysterically around for a weapon. Something. Anything.

The window.

They were at the door now, pounding, and he fought to keep his balance. It wouldn't hold for long.

God help me.

Moving quick, weasel-like, Phil went for the window.

The door crashed open behind him.

*

Hours later, Philip Garner settled into a snowbank overlooking State Route 10 and listened to the wind. He wasn't cold anymore. In fact, he was warm.

The terror, too, had gone, and right before he closed his eyes and went to sleep, he couldn't remember why he was so afraid in the first place.

After all, it was only snow.

DÉJÀ VU

In the early morning hours of December 8, 1980, Richard Morgan woke from a thin and fitful sleep, his heart pounding and his stomach churning. Sitting up, he snapped on the bedside light and took stock of the room around him, half sure that he would find some presence crouching in a corner, waiting to strike. Instead, he saw nothing more than his furniture: an armchair by the heavily curtained window; a massive oaken dresser topped with a mirror; an end table by the open door. Beyond, the hallway lay in shadows.

For a long time, Richard sat where he was, attempting to process the strange feeling in his stomach. Foreboding, he thought, but that wasn't exactly right, was it? Richard was typically good at identifying and articulating his own emotions (as a writer it was his job to be expressive), but tonight he couldn't quite name what he was feeling.

I'm just nervous, he thought, *that's all.*

And why wouldn't he be? After all, he was going home tomorrow for the first time in nearly twenty years.

Shaking his head, Richard sank down and pulled the covers up to his shoulders, leaving the light on.

In the morning, he was leaving for Ohio, heading for Highland, a place he hadn't been to since Eisenhower was president. When he left it was a postcard perfect small town. Now? What would he find? His friends, and everyone he knew, would definitely be older. Mr. Johnson, who ran the soda shop on Main Street, was closing in on sixty in 1961. Surely he'd be long gone, his position taken by someone else, if by anyone at all. Denny Parker, with whom Richard once fished and played, would be nearing his fifties. The town itself...God himself only knew how it had changed.

Sighing, Richard closed his eyes and attempted to sleep, but couldn't; his mind raced aimlessly, and he couldn't shut it down no matter what he did.

December 8.

December 8.

December 8.

Something about the date seemed oddly familiar.

By five in the morning, Richard was caught in the firm grip of déjà vu, an emotion that he knew all too well. A temporary aberration of the mind that leads one to believe they are experiencing something that they've experienced in the past but haven't, déjà vu strikes most people rarely. Richard, however, developed a roaring case at least once a month. There was nothing wrong with him neurologically, thus he sometimes wondered if he hadn't lived this life already.

Finally, at close to six, he got up, showered, and dressed. In the gloom-washed kitchen, he made a pot of coffee and put a bagel in the toaster.

Breakfast in hand, he retreated to the breakfast nook and ate while looking out onto the sloping backyard. In the distance, the Royal River passed sluggishly by, its course choked with ice.

New York City, he thought for no apparent reasons. *December 8, 1980.*

Suddenly, something seemed familiar; déjà vu swept him with the force of a tsunami. *Something's going to happen there today. Something bad.*

He didn't know how he knew this, but he did; he knew it as well as he knew his own name.

Shaking his head, Richard got up, washed his dishes, and went outside.

There the air was bitter. Crows cawed and wheeled overhead. He went to the mailbox at the end of the driveway, opened it, and found a bulky object waiting for him. The return address was New York City.

Richard's heart leapt, but then he realized what it was.

Back inside, Richard sat at the breakfast nook and ripped the package open just as the first warm rays of the morning sun fell through the window.

The book was a hardcover, its dust jacket smooth and glossy. The cover art depicted a silvery rocket blasting out of earth's atmosphere and toward a distant planet. THE STORIES OF RICHARD MORGAN the legend read.

Feeling the same thrill that he always felt when one of his books arrived, Richard reverently opened the cover and looked at the table of contents, remembering where he was, what he was thinking, and what was happening in the world when he wrote the tales. The earliest was penned in the summer of 1959 and appeared in the December issue of *The Magazine of Fantasy and Science Fiction,* the premier sci-fi publication. The latest was written that past May and was exclusive to the collection.

Richard had always been fascinated with science. Something about the logic, the possibility, the *technology* enchanted him, made him long to be a part of it. His last novel, 1979's *Benton* was about a scientist in the year 2053, and Richard had so much fun putting himself in the professor's shoes that he was seriously considering a sequel.

Absently scanning the TOC, a title jumped out at him.

Déjà vu.

He remembered writing it, of course, but couldn't remember the particulars. It was written in 1960, after all.

Given his most recent brush with the strange emotion, Richard flipped to that page and scanned the first paragraph.

The actor was a longshot, but he won the election, defeating the one-term farmer from Georgia...

Something eerie seemed to pass close by.

Actor?

One-term farmer from Georgia?

That was an elementary summation of the most recent presidential election. Ronald Reagan, an actor, beat Jimmy Carter, a peanut farmer from Georgia, leaving Carter with a single term to his name.

Richard read on. The story was about a missile defense system called *Star Wars*, and how it successfully defended the United States from a Soviet strike. It accurately predicted a number of things. Vietnam (though in this case the "long and unpopular war" was a flare-up in Korea that ended with a North Korean victory); the moon landing (in the early hours of August 10, 1970...); and the gas shortage of the early seventies.

Richard closed the book, his heart thudding in his chest. He didn't remember actually writing this story at all.

How did he get so many things right?

He didn't know.

And for some reason, that scared him.

*

Richard Morgan left Rochester, New York, at half past nine that morning. He drove southwest, the radio firmly planted on a pop station from Syracuse. The book sat in the passenger seat. Every once in a while, Richard would glance over at it, as though it were a sleeping snake coiled in temporary repose.

At several points along the way, Richard found himself singing along to songs on the radio that he'd never heard before. He knew them, obviously, but he couldn't *remember* hearing them.

You've been working too hard. Six months on a single novel? No wonder you're losing it. All work and no play makes Jack a dull boy.

Richard thought of the manuscript locked in his desk, finished but crisscrossed in red ink. He didn't have a title for it yet, but it was set in the year 2015 and followed several government agents as they tried to stop a terrorist network from taking over the Middle East. *Songs to ISIS* was a contender, in honor of the goddess, but something about it didn't sit quite well with him. He started it earlier in the year and pushed most of it out in a single weekend. After that...

For most of the afternoon, Richard followed I-90 along the shore of Lake Erie. He was in Ohio and heading southwest when he realized something: he didn't know where he was going.

Though Richard vividly remembered the town in which he grew up, he couldn't for the life of him remember how to get there, or, for that matter, just exactly where it was.

Crazy, he thought. *This is crazy. Twilight Zone. Population: Richard Morgan.*

South of Ravenna, he pulled off the side of the road and consulted the atlas he kept in the glovebox.

He couldn't find Highland.

He searched several times, both the map itself and the handy index in the back that listed the name of every town. He went over the "H" section five times, sure that he was overlooking it and that this time it would pop out.

It never did.

Richard's head spun.

Did they change the name? It was possible. He scoured the Alleghany section of the state, certain that the town was surrounded by mountains (though he honestly couldn't remember *what* surrounded the town), but nothing jogged his memory. The place where he was born, where he spent the first twenty-five years of his life...was a black hole in his memory.

It was beginning to get dark now. Defeated, Richard turned around and started for Rochester, something like panic building in his stomach. He thought back to his hometown, and discovered that his memories weren't so vivid after all. He remembered Main Street and the park and the soda shop, the theater and the river, but he couldn't recall what they looked like. He remembered old Mr. Johnson, but his face was a shadow. Even Denny Parker was nothing more than a hollow silhouette.

It was nearly midnight before he passed the town limits. A news bulletin broke in on the radio, and before the announcer even spoke, he knew.

John Lennon, the lead singer of The Beatles, was dead.

"...New York police say John Lennon was shot three times near his home on Manhattan's Upper West Side. He was rushed to Roosevelt Hospital, was dead on arrival..."

Richard's blood turned to ice-water.

At home, Richard sat in his study, feeling like a balloon with no air. At one point, he got up, went to a shelf, and selected a copy of *The Catcher in the Rye*. He sat back down and flipped through it, savoring the yellowed pages.

The man who killed Lennon had this book with him. Not this exact book, but a copy. Richard knew it, but he didn't know how.

After nearly an hour of sitting as if in a daze, Richard got up and went to bed. There, he struggled to sleep, thoughts swirling through his head.

Highland isn't real; I made it up.

How did I know John Lennon would die today?

How did I predict Reagan, Carter, and Vietnam?

Shortly after two, Richard dropped into sleep...

...but snapped awake again, his mind suddenly clear.

He *remembered* now.

Remembered building the machine in the distant, untenable future.

Remembered stowing it in a cave, June 1, 1958.

Remembered taking the pill...the pill that would wipe from memory the past, now his future, remembered inventing a new past.

He remembered his name: Richard Benton.

From the year 2053.

THE GHOSTLY HITCHHIKER

"Hey," Kenny said over the rim of his glass, his brown mongoloid eyes sparkling in the last weak orange of the day, "I know what we can do tonight."

I finished off my soda with a sigh and sat the can back down onto the scarred kitchen table. Behind Kenny, who sat hunched childishly in his flimsy chair, gloom was quickly gathering in pools of dark shadow. The small window above the crowded sink, framed with the swaying multicolored leaves of autumn, showed the sky to be a poetic mixture of pink and bloodless orange.

"What?" I asked Kenny, who grinned like an idiot peering through a woman's bedroom window. His gaunt face and his messy black hair further lent him an insane air. He was probably thinking of promiscuous coeds or of toilet-papering the Dean's house.

"We take a ride," he said, "and look for that ghost on 45."

Though Kenny and I were of vastly different intelligence levels and of wholly different backgrounds, we both held a strong love of the occult and the macabre in common. When our classes at the university were finished for the day, we usually set out to "explore" one haunted venue or another.

We had recently visited a cave south of town reputed to be haunted by vampires, a legend dating back to the mid-1880s. We found nothing even remotely supernatural.

The ghost to whom Kenny was referring was the White Lady, said to haunt a lonely stretch of wooded Route 45 after dark. She had supposedly died in a car accident on a rainy night back in the seventies, and was still trying to make her way home. Some of the old farts in town even claimed to have given her a lift; upon reaching her obviously abandoned former dwelling, she was always gone. I had told Kenny that that was nothing but a local rehash of an old urban legend that went back a lot further than the seventies, but he refused to believe me.

"We won't see anything," I predicted.

"Sure we will," he retorted confidently, "she'll be out tonight."

I shrugged one shoulder. "I'm telling you, Kenny; she's not real."

"Whatever, dude; Bill Gates ain't real, either."

"Okay," I grunted. Despite knowing that the search would be in vain, I would happily go. It didn't seem right sitting around and reading or watching movies on a Halloween night; that one night above all called for occultic action, even if said action was lackluster and pointless. Riding the road was better than sitting in front of the TV.

We waited a bit longer before we piled into my Isuzu Trooper. The "ghost" was not on a definite time schedule, but it seemed inappropriate to start our rounds until true night had descended. We caught the beginning of *Night of the Living Dead*, and left at 5 'till eight, too eager to stall further. I shut the movie off just as a pack of cannibal corpses smashed into a black-and-white farmhouse, and we hurried side-by-side down the flagstone walk which led to the sloping street. Laughing children in sheets and cheap masks ran crisply up and down the leaf-strewn sidewalks with their subdued parents trudging behind.

Kenny slid into the passenger side and I climbed behind the wheel. For a moment or two we sat as a gaggle of pubescent girls too adult for costumes yet too childish to resist free candy, squeezed between the Trooper and the rusted hunk of an Impala which occasionally suffered our Costello-sized shut-in of a landlady. Kenny lit a cigarette, and I fished my own pack from my breast pocket.

"You finished with that damn book yet?" Kenny asked to break the silence. Never a reader before we had met and having decided that our one driving interest bonded more than our many other differences repelled, Kenny now found pleasure in reading some of the newer horror works.

I was currently rereading *The Stand: The Complete and Uncut Edition*, which Kenny yearned to tackle despite its massive length of over a thousand pages.

"I'm on 855; maybe the day after tomorrow."

"Okay, just hurry the hell up; you read like an old woman."

"Me?" I asked. "Okay, whatever, Two-Week."

"Shut up," Kenny replied. I called him that because it took him that long to finish *Carrie* by Stephen King, which weighed in at the astonishing length of 150 pages. "I have other things to do with my time; I can't sit around all day like a bookworm."

Without further reply I started the Trooper, filling the dim smoky cab with the sounds of *The Monster Mash*, which I had heard played several times on 98.3 that day. I glanced at Kenny's sharp face, bathed a ghastly orange in the spill of one of the many lamps lining the sloping street, and he smiled. "Turn around and get us going, man. I got the money for gas, don't worry."

"No you don't," I said sharply. I paid for our nocturnal rambles.

Once creeping out of town, Kenny and I lapsed into silence. As the radio played one spooky song after another, and as the hour grew steadily later, we cruised the same silent stretch of wooded road between Fredericksburg and Bowling Green, meeting nothing but the occasional glare of headlights carrying happy and sated trick-or-treaters home.

At 10:30 the last Halloween song faded from the radio and we once again reached the dim outskirts of Fredericksburg.

"Just one more," Kenny pleaded, "then we'll stop."

I turned around in a brightly-lit Fasmart parking lot, and once again roared into the silent black of the wilderness. We passed the same tired decaying roadside barns, the same shutdown mom and pop stores, and the same forlornly lit homes that we had all night; I wanted to at least take another road, but God knows that Kenny would have thrown a hissy fit.

Hard Luck Woman by Kiss came on the radio and I turned it up; Kenny's face squinted as if he had just sucked a lemon. He liked rap.

"Why do you listen to eighty-year-old music?" he asked. "You're such a nerd."

"This isn't eighty-years-old; this is the good stuff, unlike..."

My head being turned toward Kenny, I was in position to see a white blur as the Trooper sped by empty country. A cold jolt of panic impaled my heart and cast it rudely into the pit of my stomach. I trailed off and Kenny, inferring that something was amiss from my no doubt pale and slackening face, spun around in his seat. Slowing, I craned my neck around to look through the back window: in the outer edge of evil red taillight glare a tall figure in white stood high and erect on the shoulder of the road.

No, this is impossible; the White Lady isn't even real!

"Stop!" Kenny cried. "There she is!"

I hit the gas.

"Go back!" Kenny wailed, kneeling in his seat and peering into the darkness behind us like a child bidding a grudging goodbye to Disneyland.

"Nah," I breathed, "screw you."

"Go back! What are you, a bitch?"

My icy hands were trembling on the leather wheel, and I could barely hear the music above the roar of my pounding heart.

"Go back!"

I slowed and we halted with a jerk. Kenny was looking at me as if I were a stern parent who had taken something from him. "C'mon, man, what're you doin'?"

I licked my dry lips; I was out of cigarettes.

"Go back and pick her up; you can't just drive away after all we've been through." Kenny's face was pleading, his eyes shining with a familiar fire that I had only before seen in the mirror.

"We've been waitin' for this kinda thing for a minute, man. Now here it is, the real deal; you just gonna dip, really?"

Slowly calming from the initial shock, I took several more deep breaths and steadied myself. No, I wasn't going to "dip", I had wanted and waited too long to experience something extraordinary for myself, like a man who has read longingly of Hawaii and decides that the time has come to visit it in person. I had spent many anxious and fruitless hours in old decaying houses and ancient legend-haunted cemeteries awaiting the appearance of one alleged supernatural being or another. I had spent years yearning for something from a gothic novel to happen to me, and here I was, finally; fleeing was simply not an option.

"Okay, you're right," I said levelly and, with an unconscious shudder of both dread and exhilaration, spun the wheel and aimed the nose of the Trooper back down the empty highway.

"Alright," Kenny drawled excitedly, rubbing his hands crisply together, "let's go. Wonder what ghost butt feels like?"

"Probably like thin air," I guessed slowly, caught off guard by his bizarre question, "maybe warm air, but air nonetheless."

"I'll climb in back and lay my hand on the seat..."

"No you won't," I snapped, "you stay where you are and keep your mouth shut."

"Alright," Kenny grudgingly conceded, "don't poop yourself, pops."

In the headlights the ghost was still there, her thumb thrust casually into the air.

I pulled to the side, crunching gravel under the tires. The girl was about our age, with long straight raven's hair and a thin, pale face. My heartbeat quickened as I watched her glide liquidly around the front of the car and toward the door behind Kenny. She climbed silently in, bringing with her the sweet smell of flowers; my stomach turned upon speculating their nature.

"Where you going?" I stammered as I fought against my persistent eyes, which longed to study the ghost as a scientist might study a new species of beetle.

"825 Monmon Drive in Bowling Green," she said hollowly, her voice sending a shiver down my spine. My resolve almost crumbled then, but I kept a tight rein on my emotions. And had I not it wouldn't have mattered; she was already sitting within, stonily and dreadfully quiet like a grotesque statue escaped from Satan's personal collection.

I once again spun the Trooper around and shot off into the night, the back of my head tingling as if expecting a blow.

"So, you haunt the highways often?" Kenny asked through a stupid grin, sending an electric jolt of fearful shock into the depths of my soul. I backhanded his scrawny chest as hard as circumstances allowed, which wasn't hard enough by far.

"What?" he asked innocently.

"Sorry about my friend," I smiled, looking into the rearview mirror, "he's an alcoholic." The only thing that I could see in that tiny strip of glass was grainy darkness. Were ghosts like vampires when it came to reflections? Had she already gone?

A tiny judgmental sounding hmm alerted me to the fact that the White Lady was still in our presence, invisible or not.

"I'm weir' for beer," Kenny said with a smile, "and I say let's toast in honor of our new friend, the..."

"Shut up or I'll kill you," I hissed; I halfway meant it.

Kenny smiled back mockingly, as if daring me to lunge for his throat, which I would have loved to do.

The ride thereafter was a frightful misery. The girl in the backseat spoke not a word, but was tomb silent. I was the whole way aware of her thick, darkly imposing aura; the hairs on the back of my neck and arms stood rigid, as if in preparation for escape should the old legends of ghosts being harmless have been horribly mistaken, and my skin crawled as if covered in graveyard maggots. My breath came in short hot gasps; sweat coated my feverish forehead; and my heartbeat hammered dangerously. For the first time in my life I felt the cold hands of claustrophobia caressing my soul. I drove a bit over the speed limit.

When we found the unlighted section of Monmon Drive on which the ghost said she lived, I at once saw that the house she pointed us to was in the same state as a neglected toy left out in the elements by a careless toddler. It was a small, dark two story box covered in a film of grime; what white paint was left was peeling off in strips, revealing dull gray beneath like a bad memory not quite forgotten.

I drove up the bumpy gravel driveway wondering if the ghost had vanished from the backseat yet. Would her seatbelt still be fastened as if she were still there? would something of hers be accidently left behind, say a shoe? would the sickly smell of flowers linger after she had gone?

While looking at the old deserted house with a mixture of dread and parched wonder, the cloying stench of flowers enveloped me like a funeral shroud. I felt something firm and slightly slimy press against my cheek, and shuddered. I forced myself to turn, and saw the ghost pecking Kenny's cheek, corpse green in the dash glow.

"Happy Halloween, guys," she chirped and climbed out of the Trooper. She bounded across the shaggy front yard and up the warped wooden stairs just as a porch light came on. The girl was met at the flimsy screen door by a tall stern-faced woman in a pink bath robe.

"Son of a..." Kenny drawled slowly, his shocked mouth agape.

Both women disappeared into a lighted front room, the mother giving us a stiff and tentative wave.

"There's your White Lady," I chuckled, cleansing relief and burning shame at my own gullibility washing over me, "and past her curfew, too."

"Shut up," Kenny mumbled.

JUST A MASK

"Go on," Jake Warner said, his tone mocking, "don't be a chicken."

Tommy Wilford shot him a dirty look. "I'm not a chicken," he said.

"Yeah?" Jake's eyes were narrow. He looked like a shark moving in on its prey. "Prove it."

They were standing on a cracked sidewalk running past big, expensive homes. Younger children streamed past them, giggling and making monster noises. Across the street, an identical sidewalk ran past identical homes.

Except for one.

Smaller than the rest (two floors instead of three), it was pretty in the sun, its roof red and its porch shady and inviting. But now, in the night, it looked haunted, so big and dark. Plastic gravestones dotted the front lawn, and cheap ghosts and demons hung in the trees, rustling softly in the wind. From the porch, bright white light flashed dizzyingly. It was like opening and closing your eyes really fast; light, dark, light, dark.

Tommy didn't know who owned the house, but every year they went all out for Halloween. Music. Lights. Decorations.

And every year, he was scared.

Not this time, he thought, trying to be brave, *I'm almost thirteen; only babies get scared on Halloween.*

Thirteen or not, Tommy was still afraid. It wasn't the decorations (those were lame), it was the light machine. It disoriented him. Anything (or anyone) could come rushing at him, and he wouldn't see them until it was too late. And running? Forget about it. He'd probably trip and wind up dead meat.

But that was stupid. It was only a house. So what if it was spooky? And so what if his heartbeat sped up every time he passed it? It was a nice house in a nice neighborhood. There weren't any monsters inside, because monsters didn't exist. If he knocked on the door, some guy would come out and give him candy. That was all.

A cold gust of wind swept down the street, kicking leaves along the pavement.

It's just a house, he told himself, *stop being a baby.*

"You're not scared, are you?" Jake asked.

"No!" Tommy said.

Jake smiled. He was Tommy's best friend, short and skinny, small for twelve. He could run fast and everybody liked him.

He was the opposite of Tommy.

Tommy didn't make friends very easily. He was shy, awkward, and a little pudgy. His mom said it was just baby fat, but he overheard her talking to his doctor on the phone once, and she sounded worried.

He gained ten pounds since school started. I don't know. He doesn't eat very much.

No one at school made fun of him, but that didn't matter. He felt like an outsider, like he didn't belong. Jake, on the other hand, was everybody's friend. All the popular kids hung out with him, and he always had a date to dances. Sometimes Tommy envied him. But mostly, he was just thankful for him.

He *wasn't* thankful that he was such a jerk, though.

"It's okay if you're scared," Jake said. "We can go somewhere else. I hear the kindergarten kids are having a party."

"I'm not scared," Tommy said again. He was determined. He was going to go up to that house, knock on the door, and carry away as much candy as he could.

"Are you *sure*?"

Tommy started crossing the street.

"Hey, wait up!" Jake called.

At the other side of the street, Jake caught up with Tommy. "What do you think he has in there?"

Tommy stopped to think. Images of Skittles, Reese's Pieces, and Carmelo's danced through his head.

You're too old for trick-or-treating, Tommy's mom said before they left that evening. Maybe that was true. He felt stupid in his costume (the Grim Reaper, only he left the mask and plastic scythe at home) and his face flushed whenever adults passed by and looked at him weird, but that didn't mean he was too old for free candy.

"I don't know," Tommy finally said. "But it better be good."

By now they were standing at the end of the little stone path that led up to the porch. The lights flashed hypnotically and, from a radio hidden out of sight, spooky sounds played: Wind, rattling chains, and high, scary screams.

Tommy gulped. "Maybe they'll have brownies or something," he said. Even the thought of brownies couldn't distract him from his fear.

"Maybe," Jake said, and Tommy was surprised that he too sounded scared. "Or candy apples."

"Yum," Tommy said, even though candy apples were the last thing on his mind. "Let's go."

Tommy started up the path. Jake stayed close behind. On either side, tombstones and plastic skeletons loomed out of the darkness; Tommy caught only quick glimpses of them in the light.

Halfway up, something grabbed his foot, and he screamed.

Jake screamed too.

"What?" Jake asked, panting.

Tommy was afraid to look down, but he forced himself to.

His pant leg was caught on one of the stones lining the path.

That was all.

He laughed at himself. "It's nothing. Come on."

At the bottom of the stairs, Tommy stopped. Next to the door was a table with a big bowl of candy on it. Next to it was a chair, and in the chair, some sort of monster, its face green and its eyes red. Its chest was all puffy, like it was stuffed with something.

It's a dummy, Tommy thought, just a dummy.

"Get the candy and let's go," Jake said. He was whispering.

"Okay. Okay."

Tommy went up the stairs slowly. The world around him pulsed with light. Light, dark, light, dark, light dark. He was just in reach of the candy. He stretched his arm out...

...and the dummy came alive, jumping forward with a loud roar. Tommy screamed and stepped back. The porch was gone and he was falling down the steps, his arms flapping.

When he hit the ground, all the air in his lungs was knocked out of him. Jake was screaming and crying. Tommy tried to get up, but he couldn't; he could only lay and wait for the monster to get him.

Suddenly, the lights and music went off, and the porch light came on, soft and yellow against Tommy's tightly closed eyes.

"Oh, no," the monster said, its voice muffled. Jake let out a sharp yell, and Tommy closed his eyes even tighter.

"I'm so sorr..."

"Please don't eat us!" Jake yelled. He was so scared he sounded like a girl. "We'll do anything you want! We'll be your minions!"

"What?" the monster asked. "No, I'm not going to eat you!"

Tommy opened one eye. "You aren't?"

The monster, standing over him now, only laughed. "No! Why would I do that?"

"So..." Jake started, "you're *not* a zombie?"

The monster laughed again. "Of course not! It's just a mask."

Tommy sat up. Boy, did he feel stupid. What was he thinking? Only babies got carried away and thought monsters were going to eat them.

I guess we're babies.

"It's just a mask," the monster repeated. "Look." He pulled it off...

...and Tommy froze.

The man's face...it wasn't a face at all; it was a gray, grinning skull.

"See? It's just a mask."

MEETING RAY BRADBURY

"I've finally finished it," Paul LeMond said proudly, his hands flying unconsciously to his hips.

Next to him, Bill Hadder made a small noise of agreement, though, in truth, *he* was the one who finally finished. All LeMond did was point and tell him what to do.

"I can't believe it," LeMond was saying, his voice dreamy and faraway. "I simply can't. I've built a time machine!"

The time machine was a simple metal box roughly six feet tall by six feet across. On its front was an airlock door and a porthole built to withstand the rigors of time and space.

Hadder nodded. "Yup. She's a beaut, doc. You gonna test her out?"

LeMond tittered. "Of *course* I am!"

He stepped forward and laid his hand on the machine's shiny metal exterior like a boy touching his first breast. A small grin played across his gaunt face.

"Should we do it right here?" Hadder asked.

"I don't see why not."

They were in Doc LeMond's detached garage: benches laden with tubes, vials, jars, and auto parts lined the dirty walls. Through a window, bright summer sunshine filtered through the pepper trees clustered along the outer wall. Hadder imagined the doctor would want to load the machine into the truck and take it to a remote spot before trying it out...though he didn't know why. Who cared, anyway? Less work for him.

"Such a fine piece of equipment," LeMond was marveling, running his hands all over the time machine. "Beautiful."

"Where you gonna take it?" Hadder asked.

LeMond's hands froze. "I've given that quite a bit of thought, actually." He turned, furrowed his brow, and continued. "I considered taking it to meet Einstein, to the birth of Christ, to the day the apple fell on Newton's head. But in the end I decided on something a little more...personal, I suppose. I want to take it to meet Ray Bradbury as a child."

"Who?" Hadder asked.

"Bradbury," LeMond replied. "He was a science fiction writer. When I was a child I fell in love with his work. In fact, Bradbury is the one who introduced me to science. His...homespun origins fascinate me. He grew up in a small town like I did."

Hadder knew the story. In six years of working for Doc Paul LeMond, he must have heard it a hundred times. Poor. Living in a shack in the hills of West Virginia. Falling in love with science and technology. Blah-

blah-blah.

LeMond had that faraway look on his face again. "Might as well do it," he said.

*

LeMond climbed into the capsule and closed the door behind him.

The inside of the machine was cramped: A single seat sat amongst a mountain of buttons, levers, screens, and blinking lights.

For a long moment LeMond simply admired the beauty of his design, then he sat in the seat and buckled in.

Bradbury, he thought, his heart skipping a beat. He remembered long summer afternoons under the tree in his backyard on Russell Road, a glass of lemonade close at hand and a Bradbury paperback in his lap. He remembered the *feeling* he experienced on reading the master's works, the sense of wonder, astonishment, familiarity. He remembered taking endless trips to distant planets on shiny rocket ships, the cold October world forgotten around him. He remembered visiting far off places, realms of fantasy and boyhood.

I'm going to meet Ray Bradbury.

He relished the thought.

He had the chance to meet the master once in L.A. back in the eighties; he was signing copies of *The Stories of Ray Bradbury* at a science fiction bookstore in Culver City. If it hadn't been for the damn traffic making him late...

LeMond shook his head.

It didn't matter now.

At a keyboard, LeMond typed: Waukegan, Illinois; July 18, 1933, and Bradbury's address at the time. When he hit ENTER, the machine began to shake.

This is it, he thought.

The shaking increased, followed by a loud wail as if of steam.

Here we go.

The world went white.

*

For a long time, LeMond sat unmoving in the capsule, his hands still clutching his harness. Colors danced and whirled before his eyes; bells rang in his ears.

When the side effects began to subside, LeMond unclicked the belt.

Did it work?

God, *did it work?*

LeMond opened the door, wincing at the sunlight falling into the capsule.

My God, he thought, *it* did *work.*

LeMond was standing in a spacious backyard abutting a row of ramshackle houses along a dirt street. A Model T lumbered down the road, a cloud of dust rising in its wake.

I'm here. 1933.

The sky was dazzling blue. The wind smelled of flowers and honeysuckle.

"Wow," LeMond muttered, spinning around, "I..."

It was then that he saw it: two small bare feet poking out from under the machine.

At first he didn't realize what he was looking at, but when he did, his heart leapt into his throat. A child. His machine had landed on a child.

A terrible thought struck him then.

What if...?

Behind him, a screen door creaked open. "Ray!" a woman called. "Raymond Bradbury! Dinner!"

5051 BARTLEY SQUARE

(*From* Ghosts of the British Isles, *by Chester Compton, 1937*)

In a rather dumpy section of ancient London, where tall monuments loom over narrow lanes and the sun is rarely beheld, there sits in the shadow of a defunct meatpacking plant Bartley Square, a row of tall, slender townhomes enshrouded in perpetual darkness. There are four separate domiciles in one, each adhering to the same rough diameter and layout: 5050, 5051, and 5052. The flanking two have no notable qualities, it's the middle one that we are concerned with, for here is centered the most bizarre case of the supernatural that I, in my long and illustrious career, have ever encountered.

The homes at Bartley were originally one, built in 1790 by Lord Mulberry, an astute and God-fearing gentleman who had commanded a rather large force at Yorktown. Construction began in the sweltering summer, and ran through 1791, many of the laborers being African slaves secretly imported from a planter cousin of Lord Mulberry's in Virginia. Several of them were said to have died and been entombed in the foundation for fear of detection, but these savory bits should be taken with more than a grain of salt, as stories of fallen workmen bricked up have been making the English rounds since the 1680s, when it was discovered that a foreman was sealed up in Jamaica Lane after an unfortunate accident. Today, there is no motivation to tear up Bartley Square and see, so a healthy dose of skepticism should be employed.

Either way, the home was finished in September of the aforementioned year, and Lord Mulberry moved in with his young daughter on the twenty-fifth. Little seems to have distinguished 50 Bartley, as it was then known, from its surroundings. At the time that part of the city was fashionable, and between 1788 and 1828 many opulent homes were risen. Lords and poets and wealthy landowners mingled in the sun-washed thoroughfare, and life flowed languidly on as it does in such places. In 1801, the highly regarded Pastor Buckles took over the local church in Stoker Street, and for many years his weekly service was attended by masses of the regal and sophisticated. Lord Byron lived for a time not far from Bartley before leaving for the Continent, and his place was briefly taken by a group of bohemians who anonymously published *Reflections in August,* a compilation of poems still highly regarded in English and American academic circles.

Lord Mulberry grew old and died, as the natural course of time dictated, and the home passed to his daughter and her army captain husband, who had moved to the north. In May, 1819, they took possession of the house at Bartley, which had been kept for a year by a young Negro couple brought from Massachusetts in 1815 to look after the ailing Lord. The husband, who had frequent business in Manchester, was often gone for long periods of time, leaving his wife in the sole company of their maid, a warm Greek woman. He was home only several times during 1821, the last in March, when a mysterious fire broke out in the lower portion of the home.

The next morning, cresting dawn shewed the extent of the blaze, which had burned with freakish intensity most of the night; Bartley was a blackened shell of its former self, quite literally. The only survivor was the maid, who jumped from the attic window to the cold cobblestones below and broke her arm. She was understandably incoherent as she was led away by concerned neighbors, babbling on and on about black things that reached out from the flames.

For several long years, Bartley sat in decrepit abandonment. During this time odd noises, thumps and whispering voices, were reported by neighbors. One man, who had grown tired of Bartley acting as an inn for the homeless (so he thought it was), rushed into the charred skeleton one midnight to confront whoever needed confronting, and found the place entirely deserted.

By the late 1830s, the region had begun to stagnate, and many of the wealthy residents left, leasing their homes out to the lower class sorts that poured in like ants to a fleshy carcass. In 1835, a shrewd investor named Roger Watson purchased the hallow framework of Bartley, and in 1838 finished massive renovations, dividing the gross area and opening it as three homes in one. While it wasn't an architectural delight, the new Bartley Square was clean, moderately pleasing, and reasonably priced. In 1840, it was rented by an elderly widow named Freely from Newcastle who took up residence in December.

With her were two companions that she had neglected to mention, one a Persian cat, which I'm sure Watson wouldn't have objected to, and the other her adult son, Jonathan, who had been diagnosed as a teenager with insanity. He had been in several institutions over the years, but his mother found the conditions appalling, and decided to care for him herself. Locking him in the attic and feeding him through a hole in the heavy door seemed perfectly humane to her, and that's what she had done at her previous lodgings.

She was cast out because of her son's tendency to scream and beat his head against the walls at night. She fully didn't expect to be long at Bartley Square before she was evicted again, and that appears to have been a reasonable assumption. But it so happened that Jonathan only had several nights to disturb the peace before he choked to death on a bit of gruel, alone in the attic.

As you might expect from a grieving mother, she quickly fled from painful memories of her son and, it has been rumored, a police investigation. Watson, who had managed to keep the whole dreadful affair under wraps, almost immediately found a young, recently married couple to lease 5051. They left after a week, complaining of odd sounds coming from the attic. An old Frenchman then moved in, and left several months later, saying that on several occasions he had heard the most ghastly thumps, grunts and groans in the night.

The last to inhabit the house was a young third-class family who escaped in the night twenty-eight days after moving in. Enraged, Watson is said to have followed them to a relative's home and dragged the tale from the reluctant father: Not only had inexplicable voices and footsteps been heard in the attic, but the daughter, seven or eight, had been choked awake by "a monster" one night in her upper bedroom. Their mad flight came only after a week of nightmares on the part of the children (who had taken to sleeping with their parents), and an assault on the father by something in that same upstairs room, which he had taken to prove to his children that no "ghosts lived there."

Watson knew then that something was wrong with Bartley, and immediately, before talk could spread, sold the townhouse to an American investor. By this time, most of South London was abuzz with the "haunting," and several passersby claimed to have seen a ghostly face peer from the attic window at night.

Soon, Bartley was entirely deserted, and the perplexed American hired an impoverished elderly couple to act as live-in caretakers. Within a week the old woman died in the upper bedroom whilst folding sheets. Her husband told an inquiry that he was at the breakfast table when he heard a short scream and a great thump. Upon entering the room, he found his beloved lying on the floor, her face bloodless and twisted in primal terror.

Deep in mourning and suddenly afraid, the old man appealed to his master to assign him to other duties, but was told to hold down Bartley or leave. The American *did*, however, send his young niece to keep the old man company and to supplement his meager janitorial powers.

She lasted not even a month. On a Tuesday, her fifth on the job, the old man was preparing dinner when a horrid wail issued from upstairs.

He found her huddled in a corner, her face white and her eyes staining grotesquely. She pointed to a spot next to the man and babbled hysterically about "it."

With her insanity and eventual death, an ember flared, and suddenly the entire city was talking about the wretched place "down south." One of those who happened to overhear such babble was Lord Westover, a notorious dandy and rake who, on a damp night in November, stepped into a pub not too far north of Bartley after inspecting an orphanage he regularly donated to. He was taking a drink when two men began loudly arguing at the end of the bar.

Lord Westover stepped between them, and laughed unabashedly when it was revealed that the two were arguing over whether the room down the road was haunted by a routine ghost or a demon.

"Poppycock!" Westover exclaimed, "nothing of that sort exists!"

But the two men united in the face of the unbeliever, one of them stepping so far as to question Lord Westover's intelligence.

"Me a dullard?" the Lord cried, "show me this room then, and let me prove to you there are no ghosts!"

The two men led Westover to Bartley's doorstep. The old caretaker was hysterical, and threatened to shoot Westover if he came *near* "that Devil room." Somehow, though, he was mollified, and reluctantly allowed Westover to remain.

The two pub-rats bid their powerful friend a good-bye, assuring him they'd be back in the morning.

"Now!" Westover said boisterously after they left, "where is this room?"

The old man took him to it, and left only after giving a bemused Westover his pistol and making him promise that he'd ring the bedside call-bell "at the first sign of trouble."

The old man left Westover to his devices, and settled down in his room with the Holy Bible, praying strenuously that the Lord protect and keep Westover.

But God seems to have taken offense to Lord Westover's disbelief in Him, for not an hour later, as the poor old man battled for sleep, a bell began eerily echoing throughout the house.

As the old man struggled to his feet, the ominous tinkling was drowned by a thunderous report.

When he reached Westover's room, the Lord was dead, one hand wrapped around the velvet pull-cord and the other the smoking pistol.

The old man fled into the night, and refused to ever return, telling a reporter that he'd rather die in a poorhouse than live in a spook house.

The death of Lord Westover caused a sensation, and for the first time England the public in general became aware of the supposed malignancy at Bartley Square. The public, fascinated by phantastic accounts in the evening papers and by "true" tales in the *Penny Dreadfuls*, turned a collective eye to the shadowy patch of London horror, and Bartley became a sideshow attraction.

The American sold the house in 1848 to a noted spiritualist and alleged sadist named William J. Hanover, who lived there for three days before finally establishing a watch in the accursed room with several friends. One of them was found next morning wandering the streets gibbering, his eyes glassy and far away. A group of policemen grudgingly went to Bartley, and discovered a scene of appalling terror. Hanover sat in a darkened corner of the room, the top of his head dissolved and a pistol clutched loosely in his hand. His two remaining acquaintances were laid out on the wooden floor, one dead of fright and the other savaged as if by wild dogs.

Even the sturdiest of men in run-down industrial town taverns quaked at the mention of Bartley Square after the Hanover incident. The Hanover estate realized that selling it would be madness, so the "Spook House" sat empty, decaying and festering like an open sore on the face of lovely Britain.

By 1918, as the Great War came to an unsatisfying close, the building had deteriorated considerably, the windows cracking from frigid winters and holes widening in the sodden roof. A sign had been placed on the door of 5050 declaring the entire structure a hazard, and warning people away, though no one would dare enter it.

The final, and perhaps most grizzly, chapter in our saga was begun by two young, unnamed sailors on shore leave. They had just returned from the European meat-grinder, and had been making the rounds, visiting every pub and whorehouse from the East End to the West. In one tavern, they ran into an old enemy from France, and a fight broke out when they mocked his imaginary cowardice.

Upon being ejected into the street, the three continued their brawl. A bobby broke them up, and watched them part, the sailors to the south, the solider to the north.

It wasn't long before our two subjects became drunkenly lost in the maze-like streets, and were forced to seek refuge in one of the many abandoned buildings along the walk. Taking no precaution, as drunkards often do, they threw open the first rusted gate they came to and strode boldly into the middle number of a row-house.

They settled down in the front parlor, but the pervading dampness quickly drove them up the narrow staircase. Taking to the first room on their left, each man fell quickly asleep, but were almost as swiftly started awake by a horrid mewling, as though from a cat in pain. Before either one could clear his mind, they heard the heart-freezing sound of heavy footsteps descending the stairs to the attic. The younger of the two, a mere lad of nineteen or twenty, jumped up and readied himself for escape. The other, however, sat paralyzed with fear.

Creak.

Creak.

Creak.

The footfalls suddenly faded, and not a moment later, the threshold was filled with a hulking, translucent shadow that seemed to move in an aura of frigid air.

It then "seeped" into the room, flowing deliberately toward the senior. The junior was able to break the shackles of terror that bound him, and escaped into the street, unaware of what was being done to his wailing companion.

He was found several hours later hiding in an alleyway and trembling like a dog before the boot of a cruel master. He spilled his incoherent story to the officer who discovered him, but was mistaken for a madman and locked in the local stationhouse. Not an hour later, however, a frantic man burst through the door to report a ghastly scene outside Bartley Square. He led the officer to Bartley's front gate, upon which was skewered a savaged human body that had fallen (or rather had been thrown) from a smashed upstairs window. Its stomach was laid open and its entrails dangled from the gaping hole, swinging in the early morning breeze.

In the years since, Bartley has been boarded up and abandoned. A sign hangs upon the door warning people away, and a bobby is compelled to pass the doorstep every hour. I haven't had the chance to investigate the house for myself, but a colleague of mine has, and while he escaped with his sanity and his life, he reported being set upon by a ghostly force that attempted to strangle him. He was half-asleep at the time, so it's possible that he was beset by a nightmare or some form of apnea, but, given the history of the house, this is unlikely.

What haunts Bartley, and where did it come from? Surely, if the testimony of the Greek maid is to be believed, then something odd had taken residence there as early as 1821. Some, however, discount her and blame the ghost of the mentally ill Jonathan. As I have not poked around for myself, I will reserve final judgment; I will say, however, that the nature of this "ghost" leads me to believe that it is something more, something infinitely worse...

THE WITCHING HOUR

Alexandru Anton watched nervously out the window as the car navigated the winding road to the village of Zela, high in the steep forests of Transylvania. Since leaving Bucharest early that morning, Alexandru had been reading the dossier provided by the Securitate, and with each page his disquiet grew. Now, the lush green hills and hunkered country cottages seemed sinister, a façade masking menace and magic. The weather didn't help. In the city, it was warm and sunny, but the farther into the wild they got, the darker the sky became, so that now, at one in the afternoon, it verged on twilight.

"How much farther?" Alexandru asked.

The driver, a large, broad shouldered peasant in black, grunted. "Ten kilometers."

Ten kilometers. They were close. Alexandru swallowed.

Despite the reassurances of his handlers, Alexandru had the distinct feeling that they would know him when he arrived, that the witches would watch him through drawn curtains as he pulled up, aware of who he was and for whom he worked. That was ludicrous, of course, for witches possessed no actual powers, but, even so, he couldn't convince himself otherwise.

"Proceed with extreme caution," the dossier said. "Consider them dangerous."

From what he'd read, he agreed wholeheartedly; reports of missing persons, harassment, and murder. Was it all true? Could it possibly be?

It all began five months before, when a loyal member of the Party wrote a letter to the regional committee complaining of "Witchcraft and Devil worship." "They meet in the woods at night," he charged, "and practice black magic. My own daughter was approached to join them but wisely declined. Now we fear for our lives."

The committee replied, asking for more details, and his next letter was full of them. "I don't know who precisely is involved, but the night before last, I left my house about midnight and went into the woods south of the town. Shortly, I came to a clearing where a fire roared. In the shadows, I saw roughly a dozen people dancing about. They were chanting. I couldn't discern the language, though I thought it was Latin. The next day, I found a dead dog lying on my doorstep. Its throat had been cut and its eyes were removed. I took it to be a warning."

Later in the day, he returned to the clearing and found bones from multiple animals, along with "other signs of witchery." Not too long thereafter, another Party member wrote to the committee, claiming that an old woman by the name of Dalca had placed a spell on him, and now his son was sick and his car no longer started. "She's a terrible old woman with no teeth and a puckered face, a prime candidate for Lucifer worship."

Several days later authorities were informed that both men had mysteriously died and been buried in the local cemetery. No other explanation was given.

"Religion is the enemy," the director of the Securitate said, and that was the Communist Party line through and through. "It distracts man from his social obligations and diverts his loyalty from the state. Witchcraft is especially heinous."

Now, here he was, on his way to see for himself whether witches really met at midnight. And if they did, he was to report back to headquarters. After that...

"We are close," the driver said.

The road rounded a harrowing hairpin curve and there, in the distance, Zela rose on its hill, a tight cluster of ancient European buildings along a narrow cobblestone street. In the flat lands leading up to it, lone cottages rotted in the twilight. An old wooden bridge carried the road across a lazily stagnant river; from there, the road began to rise. On the right, an old woman in a headscarf forked hay into a wooden carriage. She stopped to watch as they passed.

His official story was that he was a college student from Targoviste touring the countryside. If pressed further, he was to profess a love for the novel *Dracula*, which was partially set in Transylvania. That would, the Securitate hoped, allay suspicions, as *Dracula* was banned by the Communist Party. If his favorite novel is one that is banned, they reasoned, people will trust him not to be a government agent.

But people, even peasants, aren't so easily fooled. Not always. What was one small lie from a government that told many big lies? And would they accept him as a college student? Though he was young and fresh by agency standards, he was still close to thirty. It was true that he had a boyish face, but could he pass as twenty-two?

Presently, the car entered the shadow of Zela. On either side, brick and wood structures loomed, blocking out the remaining light of day. A few people moved sluggishly along the sidewalks, bags of groceries in their arms. Their clothes were old and threadbare, their faces hard and weather-beaten. A few Romanian flags hung over open doorways, the red, yellow, and blue bars just as faded as the people who flew them. At least one of them lacked the coat of arms of the Romanian People's Republic. A sign of disloyalty.

The car came to a stop in front of the town inn, a quaint two floor building with a pitched roof, its crisp white face crisscrossed with wooden beams, reminding him of buildings he'd seen on a trip to East Germany. A wooden sign hung above the door: INN.

"Two days," Alexdanru said as he got out.

The driver nodded. "Two days."

He would return in two days. If, by then, he'd found nothing, the government would send another man.

Alexandru was afraid that if he didn't find anything he'd be demoted.

Outside, the day was damp and chilly. Alexandru took his bags from the back, and the car pulled quickly away.

He was alone.

Sighing, Alexandru went into the inn. Its lobby was dim and warm. An archway to the left led into a type of sitting room. A fire burned in the stone hearth. Chairs sat empty around it.

Ahead, a desk flanked the foot of the stairs, which turned before disappearing. Alexandru sat his bags down, rang the bell on the tabletop, and waited several minutes before a short, plump man in a white shirt came in through a doorway leading who knew where.

"Good afternoon," he said with a smile. His face was red and warm. Alexandru thought he resembled Nikita Khrushchev, late leader of the Soviet Union, except Khrushchev had never been particularly plump.

"Good afternoon," Alexandru said with a nod, "I'd like a room, please."

The man smiled. "Of course. For the night?"

"Two nights, actually."

The man beamed. "Wonderful. Are you alone?"

"Yes," Alexandru said.

The man pulled out a big logbook and wrote down the details. "Would you like dinner? We eat at six."

"Are there any cafés around?"

The man nodded. "Yes. Directly across the street is one. The food there is good."

"I'll probably eat there."

The man noted that in his book. "Let me show you the way."

The man (who introduced himself as Adam) led Alexandru up the stairs. There were six rooms along the hall, and two of them were already taken. Alexandru's was small and Spartan, boasting only a bed, a nightstand, a desk, and a single forlorn chair.

"It's perfect," Alexandru said.

*

The café was busy when Alexandru ordered his dinner; though he sat in a far off corner, he could feel himself being watched. The waitress, a pretty woman, brought him his food with a smile and left him alone. He thought he saw something in her eyes, suspicion maybe, but she was gone before he could study it.

People in the countryside were naturally suspicious of outsiders, he knew that, but he couldn't help feel that the suspicion here was different, more profound. Several times as he ate, he looked over to find people openly staring at him.

Shortly before he finished, a man slid into the chair across from him, startling him.

"Good evening, sir."

The man was in his sixties, thin with a thick gray mustache. His eyes were sparkling blue and his lipless smile revealed rows of yellow, rotted teeth.

"Good evening," Alexandru replied. Though he could feel the eyes of everyone on him, he resisted the urge to look.

"My name is Florin."

"I am Alexandru."

"It is nice to meet you, Alexandru."

They shook.

"Are you on vacation?"

"Yes. I am touring the countryside."

Florin nodded. "I was a traveler as a young man. When the Soviets liberated us from the Nazis, I traveled with them to Berlin."

"I've never been," Alexandru lied.

"It's a beautiful city. How are you liking our town?"

Alexandru swallowed. "To be honest, I feel like a zoo animal."

Florin laughed. "Do not take offence to it. We rarely see anyone from the outside. We have no television, no radio. The world is a stranger to us."

"What is a stranger but a friend you haven't met?"

Florin laughed again. "That is true. What do you do for work?"

"I am a student," Alexandru said.

"So you are a Party member?"

"Yes."

Florin nodded. "Good. It is good to know you are a friend. I apologize for interrupting your meal. Have a good night."

"You too."

Later on, back in his room, Alexandru went over the encounter in his mind. Had he handled it correctly? Florin would most certainly spread the information he had given him, thus the entire town (or most of it) would know that he was a student and a member of the Communist Party. Would that tip them off that he was a government agent? Many people were members of the Party, including many people who didn't particularly like the Party; being a member was the only way to advance in life.

Presently, it was close to eight 'o'clock. At eleven, he would leave the inn and set out for the clearing. The dossier indicated that it was on the other side of the bridge into town, nearly a kilometer into the wilds.

Now, the wait.

*

At eleven sharp, Alexandru left the inn and began walking toward the edge of town. The streets were empty save for a few men staggering home from the tavern. They didn't seem to take any special notice of him as they passed.

Past the lights of Zela, darkness crashed down around him like black sea water. The sky was still overcast, so neither moon nor stars lit the way.

At the bridge, Alexandru paused for a moment to get his bearings. The clearing was to the east, which, after a quick calculation, was to his left. The papers said it was rather large, and so shouldn't be too difficult to find.

The brief stop lasted roughly ten minutes, and by the time he was ready to get back underway, the sound of voices in the night stopped him cold. Someone was behind him, walking the same route he had. For a beat, he was paralyzed. How would he explain being here, at this hour?

Just as quickly as it set in, the paralysis broke, and training kicked in; moving quickly yet quietly, he ducked off the road and into a cluster of reeds at the water's edge, startling a frog into flight.

The voices drew nearer. Footfalls came on the bridge. *Clunk-clunk-clunk.*

"...night."

"I know. I know. I hate it too. But we must in order to keep His blessings."

Women.

Alexandru listened closer.

"How is she taking it?"

The second woman sighed. "As well as can be expected. It is *her* child being killed tomorrow. She knew this day might come, and she's willing, but she isn't happy."

Child? Killed?

"I wish there was some other way."

"So do I, but He demands a sacrifice. It's for the good of the village."

God in heaven! They were going to sacrifice somebody!

The women were on the road now. They steered left, and shortly disappeared into the woods.

For a long moment, Alexandru remained where he was, digesting what he had just heard. A child was going to be killed tomorrow tonight. A sacrifice to the delusion of Satan! Righteous anger flooded him. Leave it to religion. It didn't matter who was in charge or who was worshipped, they were all the same, kneel at the altar of fantasy and render unto the killer-god your children or theirs. Wasn't that the central tenet of all faiths? Death? God smites this group, Allah smites that. God commands blood. The vampire in the sky needs nurture.

These beasts...their sacrifice was literal. No crusades or fatwas here, just simple, pagan murder.

More voices approached.

Resisting the urge to strangle whoever else was coming along, Alexandru huddled down and waited.

He recognized Florin's voice.

"...of him. You can't trust Communists. They have a lot of funny ideas."

"No," a man said, "you can't."

Florin sighed. "If Martin was one of ours, I'd have him killed tonight."

"Do it anyway," the other man said. "How can he stop you?"

Florin was quiet for a moment. "We're not to harm him. He doesn't want it."

It was the other man's turn to be silent. "If he *is* a spy, we have His protection. What's the worst that could happen?"

Florin grunted. "I wonder."

They crossed the bridge (*clunk-clunk-clunk*) and disappeared into the woods.

So, the innkeeper wasn't in on it. That was good. When he got back later, he'd have to talk to him.

Alexandru remained in the reeds for a while longer; several more people crossed over the bridge. When his watch read midnight, he decided it was safe to move on; they would all be at the black mass.

The woods were alive with the croaking of frogs and the chirruping of crickets. He found a well-worn pathway, and followed it through the thicket; around him, trees and snarls of undergrowth loomed and sought like undead hands.

After several hundred yards, Alexandru began to notice a flickering light through the branches ahead. Closer, the sound of low, monotonous chanting rose into the night; it had the quality of a thousand bees buzzing in a hive.

When he reached the edge of the clearing, Alexandru crouched down, making himself as small as possible. A massive fire burned in what he took to be the center of the clearing, its light dancing across the shaggy ground; even as far back as he was, Alexandru could still feel the heat against his face.

The figures amassed around the blaze weren't dancing, rather, they were standing, their hands, or so it seemed, linked to form a circular chain of Satanism. The chanting continued apace. It *did* sound curiously like Latin. The buzz was maddening. His eardrums thrummed with it, and his brain ached. A wave of nausea crashed over him, and he fought back the urge to puke.

As he watched, the chain broke, and the worshippers all took several steps back in unison. In time with each other, they raised their arms, and the flames themselves appeared to mimic the gesture. When their arms dropped, the fire dropped, devolving into a mere bed of embers. When they raised their arms yet again, the fire roared back to life, only this time it wasn't red or orange or yellow, it was purple, trimmed with green.

Alexandru's breath caught. The revelers began dancing at this point, and the fire kept time. The buzzing intensified, like tape wound too quickly through a spool, and an icepick of pain cleaved Alexandru's brain. Clapping his hands over his ears, he fled, staggering back down the path. When he was out of earshot, the agony in his head disappeared, and his eardrums no longer vibrated, though his ear canals itched.

Free from that damn oppressive buzz, he became aware of a strange, body-wide pins-and-needles sensation. It was slight, but pronounced.

He had to get back to the inn.

He met no one on the way.

Inside, he shut the door and locked it behind him. He pulled the curtain away from the window flanking it and peered out; nothing moved. He wasn't followed.

At the door to Martin's private quarters, Alexandru knocked loudly and waited, glancing occasionally over his shoulder, each time half-expecting Florin to be there.

Finally, the door creaked open and Martin appeared, dressed in a bathrobe and a pair of slippers. His eyes were puffy with sleep and his voice was thick. "Mr. Anton? Is everything alright?"

"I need to talk to you," Alexandru said.

Martin looked puzzled. "I'd be happy to talk to you, but can't it wait?"

"No."

"Alright," the innkeeper sighed, stepping out of the way. "Come on."

*

"I know what's going on in this town," Alexandru said, concluding his tale. "Or some of it."

Across the kitchen table, Martin Seczk was pale. He hadn't touched his coffee, and when he moved his hand, he nearly knocked it over.

"I heard Florin say you're not one of them. I can trust you."

Martin nodded woodenly. "I suppose. I don't know much. I'm an outsider here."

"Tell me what you do know."

The old innkeeper shifted uncomfortably in his chair. "It started when the Communists took over. There were...shortages of everything. People didn't have enough to eat. They were dying. When Gheorghiu-Dej sent his men to collectivize everything, they were...so brutal. People reached their limits. They said "If God won't protect us, the Devil will.""

"Florin started it. Didn't he?"

Martin nodded. "He was the mayor long ago. People looked up to him, they respected him. When he said that the Devil would do for us what God wouldn't, people listened."

"So he was doing it long before anyone else."

Martin nodded. "Behind closed doors. When he saw his chance, he spread it. You have to understand *why* they're doing this. When the Germans invaded us, they took everything. Our food. Our clothes. When the Russians beat them back, they came right through Zela. Our buildings were burned, our friends and neighbors were dead. The years right after were hard for us, but when the Communists took over, it got worse, and they were desperate. They were tired of seeing their children sick and hungry. They lost their faith in God. They started...doing what they do now, and things got better. The Dark Prince watches over his own."

"You think the Devil is actually rewarding them?"

"Yes," Martin said, "I do."

Alexandru sighed.

"They can still be saved, though. If I can just get them..."

"That's why you haven't said anything? You think you can save them?"

Martin only nodded.

"Well, you aren't doing a very good job of it. A child's going to be killed tomorrow. If you won't stop it, the State will."

Alexandru stood, and Martin did likewise. "Do what you must," Martin said, and Alexandru detected a hint of weariness. "God's Will will prevail."

In his room, Alexandru locked the door and wedged a chair against it. Still dressed, he sat down on the bed and thought about what he'd seen...the strange purple fire and the buzzing, the damned buzzing.

When he slept, his dreams were dark and devilish. Florin, clad in a black robe, chased him through the empty streets of Zela, a spear fashioned out of bone held high above his head. When he reached the clearing, dead bodies began coming out of the ground, their faces rotted and their clothes hanging in tatters.

Alexandru woke with a start long past dawn. Pale morning light fell through the window.

Downstairs, he knocked on the door, and Martin appeared, as if he had been expecting him.

"Do you have a telephone?"

"Yes."

In the parlor, Alexandru dialed his driver's number. He answered on the third ring.

"Come get me. I've seen enough."

"I'll be there in half an hour."

Back in his room, Alexandru gathered up his things, and then carried them down the stairs. He was surprised to find the car waiting for him; the driver must have driven like a madman.

Back downstairs, he paid Martin for both days, and then carried his bags out. The driver helped him put them into the trunk.

"Are you okay?" he asked as they pulled away. Several people in the street watched them depart, their mouths and eyes wide as though they'd never seen a car before.

"I'm fine."

Thirty kilometers away, they stopped at a police station in the town of Kalza. When Alexandru flashed his Securitate ID card, the desk sergeant went from gruff and suspicious to warm and servile.

Alexandru's fingers trembled as he dialed the number. When his commanding officer answered the phone, Alexandru said, "We have a problem."

"What problem?"

Alexandru quickly ran through what he had seen and heard.

"Damn it. Okay. I'll contact the base of Medvala. Proceed there. I want this town razed."

*

The village of Zela huddled darkly against the sky. Alexandru Anton turned to the man behind the wheel of the armored transport and said, "The orders are to kill everyone."

The driver nodded.

Behind them, several other armored vehicles plodded along, each one featuring a wicked machine gun turret on top. If they couldn't gather everyone up nicely, they had orders to open fire with the machine guns. "Satan will recognize his own."

The bridge was coming up. Beyond it, Zela.

"I want this..." Alexandru started, but stopped. All of a sudden, the buzzing was in his head, stronger than it had been the previous night. The driver heard it too, for his face contorted in something like discomfort.

"What the hell is that?"

"It's..."

The driver burst into flames.

"Jesus Christ!"

The fire seemed to come from within, starting at his center and spreading forth, creeping along the ridges and contours of his body. Within moments, he was fully engulfed.

Alexandru felt no heat.

Wailing, the driver jerked the wheel. The transport left the road and splashed into the river. Cold water gushed into the footwell. Screaming, Alexandru forced open the door and half-fell into the water. Behind him, the other vehicles were also in distress. He saw flames in the cabs of each.

Slack-jawed and wide-eyed, Alexandru watched as the last truck in the convoy exploded. The one directly in front slammed into the one in front of *it*, and the flaming driver smashed through the windshield.

Screams of agony rose into the day. Troops began piling out of the transport directly behind Alexandru's, and each one in turn erupted in flames. Smoke. Screams. The odor of burning flesh. Heat.

Alexandru turned toward the town, and there, on the bank, was Florin.

He was holding a pistol.

Alexandru screamed and threw his hands up.

The first bullet ripped through his outstretched palm and tore through his right eye, exiting out the back of his head.

The second struck him in the nose.

But he was already dead.

*

"We have to leave," Florin said.

The townspeople were gathered in front of the inn. Below, smoke and fire billowed into the sky.

"But we're protected," someone said.

"How far?" Florin asked. "How far will He go for us? How much of a burden will He allow?"

No one spoke.

"They'll send more. And more. And He will not expend his powers etern..."

Florin burst into flames.

POTTER'S FIELD

Sam Potter, a big, roughly-hewn man with close cropped brown hair and a neck as thick as a package of hotdogs, backed the black Chevy van into the garage and got out, the warm summer night redolent of flowers, foliage, and motor oil.

It was shortly past midnight on Sunday morning; outside, the street was dark and quiet. The houses slept in shadows, and the only sound was the fragrant wind in the trees along the sidewalk.

With a single-minded determination that could only be called robotic, Sam went into the house and retrieved the long, lumpy burden from the bathroom. A woman's limp, naked corpse, wrapped in black trashbags.

Relishing the hot, coppery smell of her blood (which was so fresh it was still tacky), Sam carried her into the garage and heaved her into the back of the van; she made a dead, hollow "thump" when she landed.

"Your chariot, madam," Sam said with a crooked smile, and closed the doors.

In the van, Sam adjusted his rearview mirror and found a radio program hosted by an aging shock rocker with a woman's name: Krokus was singing "Screaming in the Night," a long, windswept ballad that fit the mood perfectly.

Set and ready to go, Sam pulled out of the garage and down the brief driveway to the street; he pressed a button clipped to his visor, and the garage door descended creakily.

The streets were all empty and forlorn at that hour; traffic lights cycled red, yellow, and green for motorists that weren't there; storefronts snuggled deep against the darkness; and icy stars twinkled in the void, showboats without an audience.

On the short drive to the lot, he thought of the woman in the back. Sherry, her name was. She was tall, roughly his height or slightly more (5'8, 5'9) and "thick" as the niggers said. Her eyes were a faded, cynical shade of blue and her hair was a dull, carroty mess, nappy, curly, like one of those troll dolls kids used to buy. She had a tattoo of a dolphin on her left leg and wore a toe ring. Her kisses were sloppy and hot and her breath tasted like cigarettes and Vodka.

Sam remembered the warm, soft feeling of her throat under his hands, pulsing, pulsing, pulsing. When he squeezed, her eyes went wide and her rank, ragged womanhood tightened around him.

Krokus gave way to ELO, and Sam's pants seemed a tad more snug than they should have been. With one hand, he reached down and rubbed himself. The memory drove him wild; need and desire rose once more in him, and something like fear with it.

He tried to control it. God, how he tried. But it was getting away from him lately. He felt like he was losing his grip. And the worst part was *he liked it*. All the years of denial, of sitting home on his hands and biting his lip...looking back now, they were hell. He was a shark. Once he tasted blood, he *needed* blood.

Fifteen years he denied himself the joys and the pleasures of sex, true, honest, totally fulfilling sex. After Karen Longwood, he stopped. He was fifteen then, tall, lanky, and pimple-studded, his hormones raging and his thoughts always, yet lazily, returning to deathsex. He didn't mean to kill her. When he came upon her walking home through the streetlights on that bitter November evening, her skirt hanging well above her warm, fleshy thighs, he only meant to fuck her. But his hands got away from him, like in that movie. He didn't know she was dead until he was done and her hazel eyes stared beyond the veil.

It scared him. It exhilarated him. He knew he could do it again and again, but shouldn't. They'd catch him and put him in prison.

So for a decade and a half, he told himself no. But then, last March, it became too much and he relented. He took a woman home from a bar and choked her to death with her own panties. It was okay, though, he had a plan even before he killed her; his father had owned a parcel of land off of Route 3, just outside Warsaw; vast, dense, and heavily forested, chopped nearly in half by a narrow, rushing river.

That's where he put all six of them.

Now, with a seventh in tow, Sam Potter turned off of Route 3 and onto the rutted dirt road which wound through the property. His father had been talking of building a house on it for years, and sometimes came out and surveyed locations, parking on the road and walking back and forth like a hound on a convict's trail, but he was too old and poor to do anything with it now.

Sam followed the road for a half mile before pulling into a wide, dusty turn-around. He killed the engine, cutting Brian Johnson off mid-growl, and checked the time; 12:58 the green dashboard clock said. From here, he could still see the road through a screen of trees. He'd wait ten minutes.

He turned the key and put the radio back on. Led Zeppelin was in the middle of "Whole Lotta Love."

At the end of the ten minutes, just before Sam climbed out, a pair of headlights passed by on the highway, doing maybe thirty. Slower than normal, but not slow enough to scare him. The Virginia State Police barracks was three miles north (what irony, he thought), and gray police cruisers were a common sight on the road after dark. But unless they were shinning a spotlight directly at him (and squinting *real* hard), they couldn't see him from the road.

Sam gave it another ten, smoking a cigarette and trying his best not to remember Sherry's sweet, grunting moans as he strangled her. He was real cautious. He had to be. But if he let himself go, if he took another so

73

soon, he'd be done.

When he was satisfied that he was really and truly alone, he killed the engine and got out; the night was alive with cricket and frog songs.

Sam stubbed out his cigarette and went around the back of the van. Somewhere, an owl hooted, and above, a full, pregnant moon appeared as if by magic, bathing the woodlands with its pale, cemetery glow.

Nice night for a dig, Sam reflected. He opened the doors, the rusted hinges shrieking ghoulishly, and paused.

He thought he heard something, something under the canopy of noise, something quick and furtive, something intelligent.

He listened, his heart suddenly dancing a jig. It sounded like movement. Most likely a deer or a fox, yes, but what if it wasn't? What if it was a cop? Maybe they were on to him. The disappearances were big news; women disappearing up and down the Northern Neck, from King George to Tappahannock, all from seedy dive bars, all white and haggard. He never took one from Warsaw, though. You don't shit where you eat. But maybe that's what gave him away.

Calm down, he told himself; he had started to breathe heavy. No panicking.

Instead, he listened.

The wind in the treetops. The croak of bullfrogs down by the pond. The sweet cricket symphony from everywhere and nowhere. The babbling of the river. Nothing more. Raccoon. Deer. Possum. Whatever it was, it wasn't a cop.

Sam swallowed hard and forced a smile. He was safe. They wouldn't catch him. They had no idea.

Momentarily mollified, Sam reached into the van to retrieve his latest lay.

Behind him, something moved.

Sam jumped.

The human mind is hardwired to detect patterns where no patterns exist, and the mind, by its very nature, tends to cast these patterns in the darkest, most ominous light possible. Sam knew that, but in the nanoseconds between the noise and his turning to face it (a time in which his also whipped out the pawnshop .38 he bought from the Fauquier County gunshow three years before), Sam *knew* that that noise was a scraping footstep.

And he was right.

For in the silvery spill of moonlight, a figure stood dark against the shadows, face hidden and obscure.

A part of Sam, deep, deep down, believed that he was being paranoid, thus even though he "knew" the sound was a footstep, he didn't expect to find anyone standing behind him. When he did, an electric bolt flashed through his soul, a bolt of surprise, of shock.

And of fear.

The figure, scarcely more than six feet away, stood stock still, like a statue.

Sam, shocked speechless, fired from the hip. Once. Twice. Three times.

The figure took the rounds without so much as a flinch, much like you'd expect a ghost would.

Instead of falling back, the figure stepped forward, and a rogue moonbeam fell across its face.

Sam's blood ran cold.

The figure before him was a study in terror. Its face was a sickly blue-gray, and its eyes were missing from its sockets. In their place, maggots squirmed and writhed as if in horror of their lot. Its flesh was torn and rotting, ripped to shreds around the mouth and nose, the latter of which had partially decayed, providing a glimpse into its deep, black nasal cavity.

The creature, Sam saw, was nude but for a pair of long white socks which nearly reached its ruined, seeping vagina.

Yolanda Skinner was wearing socks like that the night he killed her.

The creature smiled as if in acknowledgement of his revelation, its crooked, yellow teeth showing through.

Sam couldn't move. The weight of the horror was too great.

The Yolanda-thing took another shuddery step forward, her/its hands raising as if for a long, cold embrace. Her fingers. Jesus Christ, her fingers were cracked and caked with dirt.

Sam came suddenly alive. He raised the gun and shot the thing in the head. The previous three shots, all to the chest, had had no effect. This one, however, succeeded in putting the creature down. She fell back, tottered, seemed about to save herself, but then went heavily down, thudding to the dirt.

To Sam's left, the bushes moved.

He spun around, his heart in his throat. Another creature was coming out of the woodwork. Its face flesh had long since rotted away, revealing the grinning, dirty visage of a barren skull, its gaping eyes two long, black chambers of madness. Its torso had also begun to rot in earnest; broken and splintered ribs jutted through its long, thin burial shroud. Brenda Meeks, the first of his adult consorts. Had to be. He beat her chest in before he strangled her.

Sam screamed and brought the gun up. The Brenda-creature's head was touching the barrel when he fired; the shot shattered her skull, sending a shower of hard, yellow fragments raining into the night.

The Yolanda-thing had regained her footing. Others, some dark forms, some fully revealed in the moonlight, were advancing from the forest. Here. There. Everywhere. Their movements jerky and unsteady.

A sound like crinkling plastic woke Sam from his dark paralysis. Before he could register what it was, two long, cold arms wrapped themselves hatefully around his shoulders.

From behind.

Sherry.

Sam screamed. The other creatures were closing in, their heads cocked and their empty eyes wide and hungry.

Strong, possessed of the strength of the dead, Sherry dragged him into the van, kicking and screaming.

Revenge, the creatures found, is a dish best served not cold but warm. 98.6 degrees warm.

THE WARLOCK

Fifteen minutes. Fifteen minutes since the old man hobbled out the front door, looked nervously around, and stumbled off into the woods, crunching dead leaves underfoot.

Fifteen minutes...or maybe longer. Charlie Parker wasn't sure. Sitting against the fallen tree, waiting for the old man to get far enough away that he and the others could do what they needed to and then get away, he fell into a doze. The day was hot and humid, and the August sun was directly on them. When he dragged himself out of it, he thought that the light looked slightly different, like an hour had passed instead of a couple of minutes.

"Wake up," Charlie whispered, hitting Scott Fallow's shoulder. The skinny red-head started awake, looking around and muttering.

"It's time."

Eyes clearing, Scott shook Matt Barlow awake and passed on the message.

Charlie raised his head over the dead tree. The cabin sat in its grove, coddled in the bosom of rampant vegetation. Its façade was sunken and dark, its roof pitched and threadbare, its windows dirty.

"Alright," Charlie said, glancing at Scott. The latter's face was a mask of worry. "Come on."

Charlie scrambled over the log and started toward the house, the layer of leaves blanketing the forest floor rustling crisply. When he looked back, Scott was watching him from over the tree. Sighing, Charlie stopped. "Come on, you fuckin pussy."

Scott glanced down at Matt, shrugged, and scrambled over the tree. Matt followed, bringing the red gas can with him.

Charlie reached the front of the cabin and crouched down below one of the windows. The door was to his right. Matt and Scott were soon there, Matt handing him the gas can.

Starting where they sat, they worked their way around the entire house, splashing gas on the ancient wooden walls. When they reached the front again, Charlie produced a lighter from his jacket pocket.

"Maybe we shouldn't," Scott whispered.

Matt nodded. "Yeah, this is big."

"Fuck you," Charlie said.

With that, Charlie opened the front door, splashed some gas on the floor, and threw the can inside. He lit the fuel, stepped back as the fire *whumped* into life, and slammed the door. He then held the lighter against the wall. Flames shot up and raced across the cabin's front. The wood was old and dry. In minutes, it was consumed.

"Come on!" Charlie said, and started back the way they had come.

Matt and Scott followed. At the tree, Charlie paused and looked back to admire his handiwork. The cabin was engulfed, and the trees crowding it on either side were alight as well.

In one of the windows, Charlie thought he saw movement, a quick flash, as if someone were watching, and then moved away.

His heart sputtered.

Impossible.

The old man was in the woods, and he lived alone. He was out doing whatever hermit witches do. Praising Satan. Killing babies.

The window exploded, and a long stalk of flame shot out, curling up and over the roof.

"Let's go," Charlie repeated.

*

Dan Mars, Sheriff of Holyfield Florida, followed the rutted dirt track through the dense forest south of town and slowed when he came to the smoldering ruins of the cabin. A fire engine sat off to one side, spraying a stream of pressurized water at the wreckage from a cannon mounted to its roof. Firefighters, in full regalia, were moving aimlessly back and forth, or so it seemed. Beyond the fire engine, the chief of the department stood against the front end of a red and white Range Rover, talking into a handheld radio. When he saw the police car, he lifted a hand.

Pulling off to one side of the road, Dan killed the engine and got out. The day pressed against him like a wet blanket. The smell of gasoline hung heavy on the air.

As he passed close to the house, the heat rose, becoming dryer. He watched the blackened rubble as he went by.

"Thank God someone saw it," Chief Curtis Jones was saying. He was a tall man, black and thin with a tiny mustache crawling across his thin upper lip. "The entire forest woulda gone up."

Central Florida was currently in the middle of a rare summer drought. Typically, storms moved through the area every day during June, July, and August, dumping afternoon rain, but since the beginning of August, nary a drop had fallen. If the fire had gone unchecked, there's no telling what could have happened.

"Who caught it?" Dan asked.

"Hiker," Curtis said, clipping the radio to his belt.

"Now what was a hiker doing out this way?" Dan asked. The dense underbrush west of US1 wasn't the kind of place someone would normally hike. There were few trails, and the route wasn't very scenic, with thick walls of vegetation pressing close.

"Who knows?" Curtis began walking toward the house, and Dan followed, his hands on his belt. The hiker, a college-aged kid with short black hair, was sitting up against a fallen tree. When he saw Dan, he looked nervous and stood up.

"I'm Sheriff Mars," Dan said. "What's going on here?"

Dan could see that his attempt at sounding friendly hadn't swayed the kid to his side.

Shaking his head, the kid said, "I was walking along the trail back there," – he gestured vaguely beyond the house – "when I saw the smoke."

The trail he was referring to started in town, went out to a swampy marsh, and wound out into the brush before emptying onto US1, just before the bridge across the Chokeeoko River.

Dan wrote the kid's statement down and let him go with a smile. When he was gone, he looked at the pile of burned wood that had once been Keynard Mays's hidey-hole. "What do you think, Curt?" he asked.

"You smell the gas?"

Dan nodded. "Hard not to."

"Someone did it on purpose."

Dan sighed. He knew the moment he stepped out of the car that someone did it on purpose. Still, Hollyfield was a quiet town. The worst crime he'd ever dealt with was a break-in at Conner's True Value. Things like murder, rape, and arson were so far removed from Hollyfield as to be nonexistent.

He tried to imagine someone coming out here and lighting the fire, but couldn't.

As if reading his mind, Curtis said, "A lot of people in town didn't really care for Key."

That was true to an extent. Keynard Mays had been living in the cabin since anyone could remember. A gnarled, twisted old man with a hunch back and jagged features, he ventured into town only two or three times a month to buy groceries. Some said he was a criminal hiding from the law, others that he was some sort of witch. The kids in town scared each other with stories of how Keynard Mays would grab you if he saw you on his land and drag you back to his cabin to do only God knows what. The adults...well...bigotry runs strong in the south. If it isn't against blacks, like it once was, it's against people who are different or "weird." After all, it has to be against *somebody*.

Even so, there was a line between not caring for someone and burning their house down.

"Have you found a body?" Dan asked.

Curtis shook his head. "Not yet. We haven't really combed the place over, though, so it's anyone's game."

An hour later, they found the body.

*

Danny Parker cried out as his Charlie snatched the remote. "I was

79

watching that!"

"Too bad," Charlie said, settling down on the couch and changing the channel. The movie Danny had been watching, *The Thing from Outer Space*, became MTV2; Lil' Wayne was sneering at the camera while half-naked women danced in the background.

"This is stupid!" Danny protested.

"*You're* stupid," Charlie countered.

Sighing, Tommy got up and stormed away. Mom was in the kitchen, clipping coupons at the table.

"Mom, Charlie..."

"I don't wanna hear it," Mom said.

"But Mom..."

Mom looked at him. "I can't take this right now. Just leave me alone."

Danny sighed. "Fine."

He went out the back door. The afternoon was hot, the sun weakening as it approached the horizon.

Their backyard, open to all the other backyards on the block, was bordered by a narrow alleyway. Danny went through the gate and started south. Kids played in the distance, their happy squeals salting the evening air.

No one cared! Charlie got to do whatever he wanted and Mom let him. "I can't deal with your brother," she said. "He's on my last nerve." He'd been on her last nerve for three years. She said he was a juvenile delinquent and that he needed to go "somewhere." But that's all she ever did, talk! Danny was sick of Charlie. He was sick of the Indian burns, the titty twisters. He was sick of it all!

At the end of the alley, he turned left onto Palm Drive. Tiny stucco houses marched into infinity on either side. At the second house on the left, he knocked on the door.

A few minutes later, Josh and Megan Barlow were following him east. Both tall, gangly, and pushing thirteen, Josh and Megan bore an uncanny resemblance to their older brother, Matt; black hair, dark eyes, bronze complexion.

"Where are we going?" Josh asked.

"I don't know," Danny replied sullenly, "and I don't care."

"Are you okay, Danny?" Megan asked, worry in her voice.

"No, I'm not," Danny said. He told them about Charlie, and how sick he was of him and of their mom letting him do whatever he wanted. They both sympathized. Matt was kind of the same, though not as bad.

Ten minutes later, they were on Hollyfield's main drag, a four block section of shops and restaurants lined with wavering palm trees. At the corner of Main and Ponce, they turned left, and wound up at the town park. It was empty.

"Let's just...hang out," Danny said. "For a little while."

He didn't want to go home.

*

Larry Caulfeld III listened as Sheriff Dan Mars recounted the fire and the discovery of the body, his chest growing tighter with every word.

When Dan was done, Larry sank back in his chair and sighed. "That's my second client gone in a week."

Mrs. Bush, an elven old lady who lived across town, died of a heart attack on Monday. She simply keeled over at the dinner table. Thank God Mrs. Waylon was with her, otherwise she would have laid there for weeks.

It was scary how quickly death could come.

"I just figured you should know," Dan said. "We don't have any next of kin. Maybe you...?"

Larry shook his head. "Key didn't have anyone. Not that he ever told me about."

It was Dan's turn to nod. "We don't know what caused the fire yet, but we're looking into it."

"You do that."

When the sheriff was gone, Larry opened the bottle he kept in the bottom drawer and poured himself a glass.

Keynard Mays was dead.

Larry couldn't say he was happy about it, but he certainly wasn't upset, either. In the twenty-six years since he'd taken over the practice from his father, Larry had met with Kenyard Mays maybe a half dozen times, and each time Larry came away with the distinct (but inexplicable) feeling of *corruption*. Shaking his hand had been like fondling a live eel, cold, wet, and repulsive, and the smell he gave off, like sulfur, reminded Larry of things he'd heard about the Devil. Worse than all of that, however, were his *eyes*. Yellow. They were yellow through and through. When they fell upon you, your stomach withered and your soul rebelled. Whenever Keynard Mays walked into a room, the atmosphere clouded with tension, and when he rasped laughter, your blood turned to ice water.

Larry was well aware of what people in town whispered about his client. They called him a witch, a warlock, a Devil worshipper. While Larry didn't believe in things like magic or the Devil, he couldn't confidently say that the old man himself didn't believe in them, and even pursue them.

In all their years of association, Larry had been out to the Mays cabin only once. It was dirty, shadow-soaked, and stank. The only adornments were strange and terrifying images carved onto the walls. Monsters. Charts. Pentagrams. When Larry asked the old man, slyly, what he believed in as far as religion went, he simply winked and said, "I believe in me."

Presently, Larry drained the glass and shuddered.

81

At midnight, Dan Mars stood over the body of Keynard Mays and tried not to lose his dinner. The man was black and shriveled. In places the char wasn't complete, giving one a view of the red, pulpy flesh beneath. Fluid had drained and pooled on the metal gurney, and Dan couldn't stop himself from wondering *what* exactly it was. Spinal fluid, maybe?

They found the body in the middle of the wreckage, facedown and clutching a book bound in cracked leather. The book, which sat on the passenger seat of Dan's car, was the most intriguing find of the day; though it went through a massive fire, it wasn't burned. The pages, yellowed and brittle, weren't even so much as charred. When Dan picked it up, it was warm and slimy in his hands, like skin, and seemed to *hum* slight and low, like a power line. The first thing he saw when he opened it was a drawing of a demon, complete with fangs and ram's horns, and tight, tiny writing on the facing page. He remembered what everyone said about Keynard Mays and shuddered. He hadn't told the lawyer about the book. He didn't know why. It wasn't evidence, and should have been turned over, but a strange compulsion filled him.

He wanted to read it.

To read it and *know*.

Know what was inside.

Now, as the Holly County Medical Examiner, a petite Cuban woman named Flores explained the body and what she'd found, Dan's thoughts turned back to that book.

"...understand?..."

Dan nodded, though he didn't.

In his bed, washed in the light of the moon pouring through his bedroom window, Charlie Parker thrashed and moaned, a thin sheen of sweat covering his face. He clawed at his sheets, muttered a single word ("no") and started panting as though he were running. When he sat bolt upright at three in the morning, a scream lodged in his throat, he was certain someone was in the room with him, watching from the shadows. Shaking, he switched on the bedside lamp.

Nothing.

He was alone.

For a long time, he sat in his bed, hugging the blankets. He tried to remember the nightmare and couldn't, but the terror still lingered.

When he was sure he would be okay, he got up, went downstairs, and got a Coke from the fridge. He was just shutting the door when he heard it.

A whisper from the darkness.

Charlie's blood froze.

"W-Who's there?" he asked, his heart beginning to pound.

No one replied.

*

Danny Parker woke early on the first day of school. He showered, dressed, and poured himself a bowl of Coco Puffs, which he ate in the kitchen. Danny liked school. Not as much as he liked summer vacation, but he liked it enough. His favorite classes were history and English. He did okay in everything else, but those were the two he really looked forward to.

At 7:50, with his brother and mother still asleep, Danny left by the back door and started off along the alleyway. At the end, as always, Josh and Megan Barlow were waiting for him, their bookbags slung over their backs. Josh was wearing a black T-shirt with jeans, Megan a white tank-top and light blue caprices. Danny felt his heart flutter when he saw her.

"You guys ready?" he asked.

Josh shrugged.

"*I'm* ready," Megan said. "I was up early."

"Me too," Danny said.

"You guys are nerds."

The school was three blocks north, near the cemetery, a long, low two-story building dating from the nineteen seventies. Crowds of kids stood around the front door talking, while big yellow buses ambled along the horseshoe drive, emptying their loads before lumbering off.

Halfway to the entrance, a strange feeling overcame Danny. He glanced over his shoulder, and froze.

An old man stood on the street corner, leaning heavily on a knotted wood cane. His hair was white and wild, his shoulders stooped, and his eyes burning red.

He was looking directly at Danny.

Danny's eyes widened.

The old man raised his cane and pointed it at Danny. When he spoke, his lips barely moving, Danny heard his voice as though he were right next to him. "You're going to die, little boy. You're all going to die."

"Danny? Are you okay?"

It was Megan.

Danny nodded. "I'm fine."

He looked back at the corner, but the old man was gone.

*

Dan Mars spent the morning at his desk, drinking coffee and glancing at the book on his desk. He'd read some of it already, but every time he

83

touched it, an uncontrollable shudder passed through him. Last night, before going to bed, he locked it in the bottom drawer of the desk in his study; he knew it was crazy, but when the book was around, he had the creeping sensation of being watched. The sense of *power* he'd felt last night remained. When he laid his hand on its cover, he could feel...*something*.

Or perhaps it was only his own nerves. Presently, Dan drew the book near and opened it. Most of the writing was in Latin, though a good portion of it was in Old English. "Tho'"s and "Thy'"s abounded. The text was interspersed with drawings of monsters and demons. What he could actually *read* wasn't much better: Spells for death, spells for drought, spells to make your enemies sick.

He that owns this Booke will have its Power; He whose NAME is in the Booke will command its force. The Booke shalt not be corrupted lest He who owns it lose its favor.

In the back, Dan found a handy little index of past owners, their names scribbled in faded ink. The last one in line was Keynard Mays.

*

Charlie Parker put his chin in his hand and tried to listen to the teacher, but it was no use: He slipped into unconsciousness, only snapping himself awake before the final plunge. But during third period, he couldn't save himself. He fell asleep at his desk...and never woke up.

*

All day Danny kept seeing the old man. First outside, standing on the grass during math, and then in the mirrors every time he went into the bathroom. By lunch, he was scared. He wanted to tell Josh and Megan, but decided not to. What if they thought he was crazy?

Then again, maybe he was.

"I don't like Mr. James," Megan was saying. She took a long sip from her milk carton, leaving a thin line of milk on her upper lip. "He's boring."

"*School* is boring," Josh said, resting his face in his hands. "Why do we even have to come here?"

When lunch was over, Danny went to history class. As the teacher introduced the subject of American History, Danny's gaze drifted out the window, and there, under a leafy oak, stood the old man.

He was smiling.

And his teeth were sharp.

When school let out for the day, Danny waited for Josh and Megan outside. He scanned the yard and the streets, but he didn't see the old man.

Danny was just getting ready to go back inside when his mother's car pulled up. "Get in!" she cried.

Looking around, Danny went to it.

"What's wrong?"

"It's your brother!"

Charlie Parker was dead.

*

Dan Mars stood in the long, locker-flanked hall as they wheeled Charlie Parker away. A few teen girls stood further down the corridor, looking and talking. When the teacher emerged from the classroom, a tall, thin woman with frizzy red hair, her face a mask of pale shock, Dan's stomach sank. He could already tell she wouldn't be able to give him much.

"He just...died," she said, her voice thick. "He fell asleep. I went to wake him up. And he screamed and fell. That's it."

There were no outward signs of trauma. No wounds. No burns. Nothing. It wasn't exactly unheard of for an otherwise healthy teenaged boy to simply *die*, but it was rare. He'd have to check the kid's medical records, see if there were any clues.

Dan Mars was starting to hate his job.

*

Mom spent the rest of the afternoon in bed, sobbing. Danny tried to comfort her, but she was inconsolable, and after a while, he retreated to his room. Unable to stand the overwhelming charnel house atmosphere, he left an hour later, and walked slowly along the alleyway, his hands shoved deep into his pockets.

Charlie was dead.

He tried to wrap his head around the concept but couldn't. He knew what death was, of course, but to think that his own brother was dead, never to return...

At Josh and Megan's, Danny knocked.

"Josh isn't here," Megan said, coming out the door. "What's up?"

"I just need to talk."

"Okay."

They unconsciously made their way to the park. After settling down in the shade of a leafy tree near a stream, Danny told her about Charlie; her mouth formed a perfect O of shock.

"I'm so sorry, Danny," she said, hugging him. Danny's heart fluttered again. The warmth and smell of her intoxicated him; he could have held her forever.

He briefly considered telling her about the old man, but didn't.

You're going to die, little boy; you're all going to die.

He did say that, didn't he? Now Charlie was dead...

"Are you okay?" Megan asked.

Danny nodded.

He wasn't.

*

Megan Barlow finished painting her toenails at ten, let them dry for fifteen minutes, and got ready for bed. In the next room, Matt yelled, startling her. Last night, some time before three, she woke from a deep sleep to hear her brother screaming. She was worried about him. Today he looked terrible and didn't speak to anyone.

Fifteen minutes later, Megan was in bed, with the light off, and right before she dropped off to the sleep, she thought she heard someone whispering her name.

*

Danny Parker woke at five from a nightmare he couldn't remember. He was sweating, shaking, and somehow *certain* that he wasn't alone.

When he turned on the bedside lamp, scattering the shadows, he saw nothing.

The feeling remained, however, and for a long time he stayed where he was, his arms wrapped around the blanket.

Finally, after nearly an hour, he got up and went to the bathroom. When he came back, he thought he saw a quick, blurry movement outside his bedroom window.

Something strange was going on.

*

The morning started off bad. First, Scott Fallow, sixteen, was found dead in his bed, his eyes glazed and his face twisted in fright. Standing in the boy's bedroom, the golden early morning sunshine bathing his shoulders, Dan Mars remembered the Parker boy from the day before. He and Fallow were friends. Now they were both dead.

Coincidence?

Dan didn't think so. There had to be something in common here. A bad batch of drugs, maybe. It happened from time to time. That these two were friends and were now dead meant something.

There was a third boy Charlie Parker hung around with a lot. What was his name? Barton? Barlow?

Barlow. Matt Barlow.

Dan decided to go and talk to Barlow at school.

Before he could, however, a call came across the wire. Break-in at Messers and James Funeral Home. A body was stolen.

Keynard Mays's body.

Dan drove through the sun washed streets of Hollyfield, a knot of dread forming in his stomach. In less than forty-eight hours, Hollyfield went from sleepy little town to madhouse.

Ever since Keynard Mays's house burned down.

Thinking back to the spellbook, Dan shook his head. Coincidence.

At the funeral home, Dan listened as John Messer recounted coming in that morning and finding Keynard Mays missing.

"I don't understand it," he said. "The security system was engaged. I had to turn it off before I came in. There's no way someone could have gotten in here."

Oh, there were ways.

"You have a surveillance system in place, correct?"

Messer nodded. "Yeah. The whole place."

"Have you watched the tape?"

Messer shook his head. "No. I called you as soon as I realized what happened."

Dan nodded. "Alright. Let's watch the tape then."

Fifteen minutes later, they were sitting in front of a TV screen in a little closet off the main hall. Messer rewound the tape to midnight, when he left, and let it play.

The mortuary was before them; Keynard Mays's body was on the embalming table, a crisp white sheet covering his head.

"I did the best I could," Messer said, "but there wasn't much left to embalm."

On the screen, nothing happened.

"Can you fast forward it?" Dan asked.

Messer nodded, hit a button, and the scene fast-forwarded, When the time code in the upper right hand read 3:00 AM, the sheet covering Mays started to twitch.

"Hit play!"

The scene slowed down.

Under the sheet, Mays moved, twitched. His arm fell off the gurney and hung suspended over the floor.

Then it moved.

"What the hell?" Messer breathed, leaning closer.

Suddenly, Mays sat up, and Messer fell back. The sheet slid away, and the corpse of Keynard Mays, in all its charred, blackened glory, was revealed.

Kicking the sheet aside, Mays got hesitantly to his feet and swayed for a moment, in danger of falling over. Steady, he shuffled off camera.

For a long moment neither one of them spoke. When Dan finally opened his mouth, he said, "Either he's still here, or he left when you weren't looking."

"That's impossible," Messer said. "He-He wasn't alive. I swear to you, Sheriff. He was *dead*."

Dan nodded. "I know he was."

After searching the funeral home top to bottom, Dan said, "Just...keep quiet about this, okay? We'll figure something out."

Messer nodded dumbly.

It was noon. On the drive across town to the high school, Dan replayed the tape endlessly in his head. Keynard Mays was dead, yet he got up and walked away. It was impossible, but tape didn't lie.

Then again...

Either it was a prank or an elaborate ploy. How easy would it be to have someone dress up as a charred corpse and walk away for the sake of the camera? Not hard at all. The only question was *why*? Why would someone do that? The only thing that made sense to him was a prank, but, then, a lot of things criminals did didn't make sense to him. If he didn't have this Barlow thing breathing down his neck, he would have spent more time at the funeral home. But as it stood, talking to Matt Barlow was more important than hunting a dead body; Barlow might be in danger.

Five minutes later, Dan slid the cruiser into one of the slots facing the school. Inside, the halls rang with the murmur of kids laughing and talking in the cafeteria. In the front office, he asked to see the principal.

"Sheriff," Howard Krebs said minutes later, emerging from his office.

Dan nodded and followed Krebs into his office.

"To what do I owe the pleasure?" Krebs asked, sitting.

Dan dropped into his own chair and said, "Matt Barlow."

Krebs's face puckered. "God, what's he done now?"

Dan told him his suspicions, and Krebs concurred. "Those boys are bad apples," he said. "Barlow's in math. I'll call to the room."

Ten minutes later, Barlow, dressed in a long black T-shirt and baggy jeans, entered the room, his eyes furtive. When he saw Dan, a look of fear crossed his face.

"Hi, Matt," Dan said with a smile. "I'd like to ask you a few questions."

Matt looked at his principal, nodded, and muttered, "Okay."

Barlow sat in the chair next to Dan.

"I assume you know about Charlie," Dan started.

Barlow nodded. "Yeah," he said, his voice low.

"Well, this morning we found Scott Fallow dead."

Barlow's eyes widened. "Scott?"

Dan nodded. "We don't know what happened. His dad found him in his bed and called us. Looks like he died sometime in the night."

The realization that his two best friends were dead seemed to stagger

Barlow; he shook his head from side-to-side, slowly, amazedly.

"What I need to know," Dan said, "is did you guys do anything together recently? Drugs? Alcohol? Hell, did you go swimming in the same creek? I'm worried something might happen to you next. If it's drugs, don't worry about me busting you. I just wanna keep you safe."

Barlow broke down in tears then, hiding his hands in his face. He sobbed something that Dan didn't quite hear.

"What was that?"

"We burned down old man Mays's house," he cried. "We thought it was empty. It was a prank."

Dan sat back in his chair.

It *was* connected.

*

Danny Parker spent most of *his* morning looking over his shoulder, sure that the old man would be right behind him, his eyes glowing and his mouth twisted in a terrible grin.

He never was.

After school, he walked home alone, his hands shoved into his pockets. He was at the end of his street when he realized that he didn't want to go home. The sense of grief was palatable, oppressive; his mother would be in bed, with the curtains closed, crying into a Kleenex.

Instead, he went to the park, where he sat under the tree near the stream. In the distance, beyond a wooden fence, Juniper Road passed by, heading east to Daytona Beach, DeLand, and Flagler. He was just starting to fall asleep when a voice startled him awake.

It was Megan.

"Hi," she smiled.

"Hi," Danny said, sitting up straight.

Megan sat down, and for a long, silent moment, they both stared into the distance.

"How's your mom?" she asked finally.

Danny shrugged. "Sad."

"Yeah," Megan said. "How are *you*?"

Danny nodded. "I'm okay."

They lapsed back into silence. Finally, Danny said, "How are you?"

Megan looked at him, her dark eyes worried, and he felt a clench in his stomach. He wanted to put his arm around her.

"I think I'm going crazy," she said.

"Why?"

"All day, I've been seeing an old man watching me. First on my way to school, then outside, then...what?"

Danny's face had dropped. He told her about his experiences the day before. A look of relief came across her face. "So I'm not the only one."

"No," Danny said.

"Who is he?" she asked.

"I don't know," Danny replied. "But...never mind."

"What?"

Danny took a deep breath. "I was thinking, maybe it's the old guy who got burned up the other day."

"Old man Mays?" she asked.

"Yeah. Everyone says he's a witch..."

"But witches aren't real."

"How do you know?"

She didn't reply.

"I only saw him one time," Danny said, "when I was little, but I think it was him I saw yesterday."

"But he's *dead*, even if he *was* a witch."

"Then he came back."

Megan looked scared.

*

Dan Mars lived in a modest ranch house on Palmetto Drive, a long, shaded street lined with comfortable old houses and well-manicured front lawns. As evening drew on, Dan sat in the den, leafing through the spellbook and replaying the events of the day in his mind. First the Fallow boy, dead in his bed, a twisted look of terror on his face, (what happened to you, Scott?), then the break-in (or break-*out*) at the funeral home, Keynard Mays getting up and slouching off toward God only knew where.

After leaving the high school, he went back to the funeral home and grilled Messer some more. Being a good judge of character, Dan was pretty sure he was telling the truth. He had *nothing* to do with it.

But if not him, then who? And, more importantly, *why*? A black market existed for dead bodies, of course, but not ones that have been burned to a goddamn *crisp*. If people want dead bodies, they'll want them fresh and unmarked, for organs or, God helps us, sex. What purpose could a lump of charcoal have?

Dan finished off his third beer of the night and sat it on the end table with the other empties.

What if, for the sake of argument, Keynard Mays *was* a witch? What if he really *did* just get up and walk away? Forget the how. Chalk *that* up to "magic." Magic was the *how*, but what was the *why*?

Revenge.

The word came him from the ether, freezing his blood. Two of the boys who killed him were already dead. The third...

...the third was in the town jail, on a lonely hall behind a heavy metal door. If he were to scream, no one would hear him.

Suddenly uneasy, Dan got up, pulled his uniform back on, and drove to the police station. The night was warm and damp. Inside, Deputy Rich Martinez looked up from his computer and grinned. "Hey, Dan, what're you doing here?"

"I'm checking up on Matt Barlow."

Martinez stood. "He's fine. I just went back there fifteen minutes ago."

The door to the cellblock shrieked as Dan opened it; a short hall terminated at a brick wall with a small, barred slit through which the harsh orange light from the parking lot cascaded in. Two cells flanked the hall on either side. In the last one on the right, Matt Barlow was a shadowy lump on the cot.

"Barlow?" Dan asked, clanging the bars.

Barlow didn't move.

Dan looked at Martinez, shook his head, and opened the door with a key. Inside, he shook Barlow.

Barlow rolled over.

His eyes were glazed.

His throat was torn open.

"Jesus Christ!" Martinez exclaimed.

*

Danny Parker made himself a microwave dinner, and ate in front of the TV, watching but not really seeing what was on the screen. When he was done, he put his fork in the sink, turned the TV off, and went upstairs.

At his mother's room, he paused.

"Mom? Are you okay?"

No reply. The room was a pit of darkness.

"Mom?"

He switched on the light...

...and screamed. On the bed, his mother was mutilated, her stomach laid open and entrails heaped on the mattress next to her. Her eyes were open and glazed, staring into nothing, and her mouth hung slack, blood oozing forth.

Danny turned to flee, to run and put as much distance between himself and the terrible sight as possible, but was stopped by something.

The old man.

He stood in the hall, at the top of the stairs, his eyes burning fire. This close, Danny could see that he was translucent, like a ghost.

"Revenge is upon you, boy," the old man said.

Behind Danny, the hall closet slammed open, startling him. He spun around. A terrible mass of blackened flesh came shambling toward him, its arms outstretched. Its legs shook as it came closer. Its eyes, like the old man's, were red, glowing with the infernal light of hell.

Danny screamed.

*

Megan Barlow sat cross-legged on her bed, trying but failing to lose herself in her homework. Matt was in jail, Mom and Dad were fighting.

Even as bad as that was, she couldn't get her mind off the old man. *You'll die for what happened to me,* he said, shaking his cane, *you and* all *the children will die.*

Danny thought he was a witch, and that maybe he put a curse on the town. He was probably right. Danny was smart. He knew a lot.

Finally, she gave up on her homework and climbed between the sheets. She didn't think she'd be able to sleep, not with all that was happening, but within moments she was out. When she woke again, it was past midnight, and the house was silent. She turned over, toward the window, and there, in her room, *right in front of her,* was the old man, his face twisted and ugly and his eyes glowing red.

"You'll pay, missy, you'll pay dearly..."

She tried to move, to scream, but she was frozen.

Then her closet door opened and a terrible black *thing* emerged.

Megan's eyes filled with tears of terror.

When the thing reached her, it stopped, ran its hand up her leg, and yanked down her pants.

Megan didn't scream.

Couldn't scream.

Not even when the thing's fingers penetrated her.

*

Dan Mars drove aimlessly through the town, letting his wheels wander as far and wide as his mind.

On Palm Drive, Dan slowed and idly scanned the houses on either side of the street. Nearing the end, a little boy appeared in the street, his eyes wide with fright. Dan hit the brakes and got out.

"Please help me!" he screamed.

"What's happening?"

"Follow me! Hurry!"

The boy led him into the Barlow house. He was just here earlier.

The boy led him up a flight of stairs. In the master bedroom, his parents were dead, lying haphazardly across the bed, drenched in blood.

"My sister..."

The boy showed him what door it was.

Dan went in.

For an eternal moment, Dan Mars's mind couldn't register the scene before him. Keynard Mays, as transparent as a piece of glass, stood by

92

the window, smiling. On the bed, a terrible, deformed, charred *something* was on top of Megan Barlow, thrusting itself deep into her. When the little girl's eyes fell on his, shining with unshed tears, reality snapped back.

Keynard Mays looked up, his smile widening. The thing, the body to the spirit grinning at him, continued molesting Megan Barlow.

The gun was in Dan's hand before he realized it. The first shot took the creature in the head, knocking him off of Megan Barlow. The second drilled it in the throat; flecks of char splattered the wall behind it. The spirit of Keynard Mays laughed. *"It's not that easy, Sheriff."*

The thing came at him again, its eyes glistening with the moist terribleness of life. Dan shot it three more times, the last bullet decapitating it.

All the fight seemed to go out of it then.

Laughing still, the spirit of Keynard Mays vanished.

Megan Barlow was crying now. Dan went to her. She was nude from the waist down, her genitals red, raw, and bleeding, and her lip was split.

"It's okay," Dan assured her, "it's okay."

But it wasn't.

And, as far as Dan was concerned, it never would be again.

*

After taking the Barlow kids to the hospital, Dan Mars went to see Larry Caulfeld. The lawyer listened as Dan babbled out his tale, his eyes widening and mouth slackening. When Dan was done, Larry said, "If you're right, and I'm not saying you are, we have to stop this."

"How?" Dan asked.

"I don't know," Larry replied. Then: "Do you have that spellbook?"

Dan nodded. "Yeah. Why?"

Larry sighed. "It's a guess, but something tells me that that spellbook is where he gets his power."

Dan's mind flashed back to the passages about owning and caring for the book, and it suddenly made sense. If they destroyed the book, it would rob him of his powers.

Fifteen minutes later they stood in the middle of St. Anne's Church in the heart of town. The pews were all empty at this hour, and the church was awash in the flickering light of a thousand candles.

At the font containing the holy water, Dan Mars took a handful and splashed it on the book. Amazingly, it began to sizzle.

"Jesus," Larry muttered.

Dan splashed another handful onto it. The leather began to shrink and shrivel, even to blister in spots.

"It's working," he said.

It wasn't working.

In her room at Halifax Hospital in Daytona Beach, Megan Barlow woke from a deep, black, dreamless sleep.

Only it wasn't Megan.

It was Keynard Mays, born again.

The book was gone, he knew in an instant, but there were other ways, other means.

In the darkness, Megan giggled.

CONFESSIONAL

The old priest crossed himself and entered the confessional booth. It was late, approaching midnight, and the cathedral was nearly empty, the pews occupied by only a few nocturnal worshippers. The lights were out, the candles were lit, and, inside the confessional, it was dark.

Saying a quick prayer to the Virgin, the priest sat, slid the divider back, revealing the screen, and asked, "What did you do now?"

The voice that replied was low, mocking. "Hi, Father Thomas. Aren't you supposed to call me 'child' or something?"

Father Thomas didn't reply.

"And what makes you think I've done something wrong?"

"The newspapers," Father Thomas said tightly.

Beyond the screen, his face hidden, the killer laughed. "Ah, the newspapers. It's always the newspapers. Which one do you read?"

Sighing, Father Thomas said, "The *Chronical*."

The killer snickered. "How about that crime photo they had? I was kind of shocked they published it. No class, that's what I say. I mean, kids could see that shit."

"Please don't curse in the confessional booth."

"Goddamn it, I'm sorry, Father. I have a dirty mouth."

Indeed. His hands weren't clean, either. If the first murder the police knew about was, in fact, his first, the San Francisco Slasher had been active for two years; his first victim was a college student named Mary Parkins they dragged out of the bay on January 8, 1970. His next, a grandmother named Dotty Mason, was found in a wooded area north of the city, her panties wound so tightly around her throat that she was nearly decapitated. Father Thomas knew all of their names, their faces; at night, instead of sleeping, he gazed into their eyes, praying for them and their families.

For him, the nightmare began in October 1971; the killer came to him.

"I just have to get it off of my chest," he said, "it's too good *not* to share."

Father Thomas was bound by his oath to never reveal the sins that he heard in confession, no matter how disgusting they may be.

Even if the penitent was a mass murderer.

His inability to go to the police conflicted with his yen for vengeance, a sin. At times, he almost broke his oath and went to the authorities. But he was weak. He was a God fearing man. His entire life had been dedicated to the Lord, all sixty-three years of it, thus the thought of going against the Lord flew in the face of everything he had ever known.

"You whackin off in there, Father?" the killer asked.

Father Thomas swallowed.

"I'm not here to talk about what happened last night," the killer went on. "I wanna talk about *tonight*."

Tonight? Oh, God. He killed another.

As if divining the priest's thoughts, the killer chuckled. "Her name was Rebecca. Pretty redhead. Twenty-two, twenty-three. Nurse at the hospital. Good person. Loved animals, wanted a family, said her prayers. I finger-fucked her with a switchblade."

Father Thomas's stomach turned.

"Cut her clit off, threw it in a pan with some olive oil, onions. She didn't like it. Guess it wasn't cooked right. My fault. I'm not much of a chef."

Father Thomas prayed for this Rebecca, that her agony in her final moments pale in comparison to the Glory of Heaven.

"She had a daughter. Two-years-old."

If a man's heart can actually stop without killing him, Father Thomas's stopped in that confessional booth.

"I've never fucked a toddler before. Tightest pussy *ever*."

Father Thomas fell back, his head clunking softly off the wall behind him.

The killer laughed as if fondly reminiscing with an old friend. "Good times, Father. Look, I gotta get going. I can squeeze one more in before sun-up. Happy trails."

The confessional door opened, and the killer walked happily away, his footfalls echoing.

Father Thomas wept.

*

Father Thomas couldn't sleep that night. He couldn't even sit still. So, at nearly three in the morning, he threw on his coat and hat and went for a long walk through the dark, predawn streets of San Francisco. Around him, the city was quiet, stores closed and homes buttoned up against the night. Inside his own heart, however, chaos reigned. What could he do? Something. He had to do something. He couldn't just let this beast continue on his way. Especially not after tonight.

He had to tell the police.

But he couldn't.

He was duty-bound to silence.

Surely the Lord wouldn't mind him talking to the police if it meant a murderer was taken off the streets?

But all were children of God. And all children of God were to be afforded the same standing in God's eyes.

Dawn found Father Thomas halfway across the city in a depressed industrial neighborhood by the ocean; the waves lapped gently on the shore, and the damp, cold air had begun to warm.

On the final corner before he turned around, Father Thomas came across a 24-hour pawn shop.

He went inside.

*

Night fell over San Francisco, a city under siege. A pretty twenty-three-year-old nurse and her two-year-old daughter were found dead in their apartment near Ashbury. A thirty-year veteran of the force puked on his shoes when he saw what the Slasher had done to them. Young patrolmen slept uneasily for years afterward, and men with children and families hugged their kids just a little tighter that night.

At midnight, Father Thomas, wearing a pair of brown trousers and a blue checkered shirt buttoned to the throat went into the confessional, sat down, and slid the divider back.

"Good evening, Father," the killer said, his voice light and gay. "No Roman collar tonight?"

"No," Father Thomas said.

"Why's that?"

"I don't deserve to wear it."

The killer chuckled. "No one does. We're all sinners, Father. We all fall short of grace. I think it's funny how people put priests and deacons and pastors and whatever up on a pedestal like they're above it all, true consorts of God. Please. You're just as bad as I am."

Father Thomas nodded. "I know," he said, his voice barely above a whisper. Tears stood unshed in his eyes.

"So how did you like my double header last night?"

"I never heard of another," Father Thomas said. "Just the woman and her daughter."

"That's who I was talkin about, though I did get another one after I left here last night. Old lady on Russian Hill. I beat her over the head until her brains started seeping out of her ears..."

Father Thomas stood. "I'm going to be sick," he said. "Excuse me."

He stepped out of the confessional, but instead of heading for the bathroom, he walked over to the other booth and threw the door open, startling the man inside, a chubby cherub with black, natty hair and sensuous lips.

"What are you doing?" the man asked, his smug tone suddenly gone.

Father Thomas pulled out the .38 he'd bought from the pawn shop that morning and aimed it squarely at the Slasher's head. "God forgive me," he said, and pulled the trigger.

*

The body of twenty-one-year-old David Mauer was found three hours later, slumped in the confessional booth of Saint Anthony's on Coates Street, a neat, expertly placed bullet hole in his forehead. The murder was never solved; neither was the disappearance of Father Matthew Thomas. Police suspected Thomas was kidnapped by whoever killed Mauer, and possibly murdered later; he probably saw it happen. Wrong place, wrong time.

Others thought that maybe *he* was the murderer. But that was ludicrous. The poor man was dead, shoved into a shallow grave somewhere in Death Valley, or out in Napa's wine country.

Certainly, that was the case.

THE THING IN THE WOODS

Moonlight cascaded through the treetops, bathing the forest floor in bright, slivery light. The girl, naked save for socks, stopped and leaned heavily against the trunk of a gnarled tree, her breaths coming in quick, painful gasps. Behind her, voices rose in the night, muffled by distance. They were closing in.

Panting, she pushed herself away from the tree and bounded on. Tree branches slapped and scratched her body, lashing across her breasts and buttocks with uncommon fury, as if they, too, were against her.

Ahead, the land gently rose. Near the summit, she stepped into the cold, metal jaws of a monster, and her ankle snapped. Screaming, she fell back.

The voices were louder, more excited.

Desperate now, she struggled to a sitting position, hot tendrils of pain snaking up from her ruined foot. Bear trap. In the thin lunar light, she saw bone and blood and tendon. Faintness came over her.

"There she is!" someone cried.

She tried to stand but couldn't.

Then they had her.

There were six of them, their faces hidden by hoods and their bodies lost in the folds of their robes. The girl screamed, tried to fight, but it was useless; something cracked her in the back of the head, and darkness swallowed her.

When she woke next, she was back in the cave, the rough stone walls bathed in the flickering light of a thousand unseen candles. On those walls paintings, drawings, demons and naked women, monstrous maws and screaming faces. She struggled, but her hands were tied above her head.

From the shadows, they appeared, forming a rough semicircle around her. Their chanting was low and buzzing. She tossed her head left, right, and left again. In one direction, night and normalcy reigned. In the other, the deep, inky blackness of a fireless hell. And in that hell, giant red eyes appeared.

She screamed.

*

They met at the trailhead on US12 early on a hot August afternoon. Tim Warner, his pack on his back, stood facing west, while his son, Derrick, leaned against a post in the ground, playing on his phone.

"You should really leave that thing in the car," Tim advised, scanning the blacktop. In either direction, the highway curved out of sight, steep, rocky hills rising over it.

"It's fine," Derrick said absentmindedly, his fingers blazing across the keyboard.

"Whatever," Tim said with a sigh. Derrick already didn't want to be here. Pushing the boy would only make things worse. If he fell into a creek and his phone got ruined, hey, that was on him. He was seventeen, old enough to accept some responsibility. God knew, Karen wouldn't teach him any.

He's failing all but one of his classes, she told him over the phone a week before.

It's because you let him stay up all night playing that goddamn X-Box.

Karen was permissive with Derrick to a point of insanity. Of course, Tim knew the reason why. She didn't want to be a mother. She wanted to have her fun, her friends, and her freedom. How many times in the past year had she left him alone for the weekend to go gallivant here and there? How many evenings did he spend engrossed in that game, his homework undone and unremembered, while she went to movies, plays, restaurants?

Too many.

If he had his way, Derrick would live with him, where he had at least a fighting chance. Family court, however, always sided with the mother...

The sound of an engine in the distance brought Tim out of his reprieve. Looking east, he saw the gleaming front end of the Conners' station wagon appear from the summer haze, a pile of luggage lashed to its roof.

"There they are," Tim said. Derrick grunted.

The car pulled in behind Tim's Jeep, and David Conner got out from behind the wheel. He was wearing a beige fishing vest and a fishing hat. When he saw Tim, he threw his hands up. "Timmmah!" he said.

"'Bout time you got here," Tim said, going to meet him. "We were about to head in without you."

They shook. Dave's grasp, even after nearly ten years, was as strong as iron.

"You know girls," he said, glancing back at the station wagon. "Takes 'em forever to get ready."

Dave's wife Megan was getting out of the car then. Tall, blonde, and fair-skinned, she reminded Tim of a china doll. Two days in the sun, and she'd be toast.

"Come *on*, Jenny," Megan was saying. The back door flew open, and Jenny Conner climbed out. Short, petite, and fair like her mother, she wore her dirty blonde hair in a side ponytail which hung just above her slender right shoulder. Clad in a pair of jeans and an old white tank top which left *far* too much room around her arms, she looked ready for the weekend, if not especially willing.

Tim stared at her for a few minutes. The last time he saw Jenny

Conner, she was two-years-old. Where had the time gone?

Seeming to sense what he was thinking, Dave said, "Is that your boy?"

Derrick was still leaning against the post, but his phone was forgotten; he was watching them.

"That's him," Tim said.

"Wow," Dave marveled. "Where's the time gone, huh?"

"That's exactly what I was thinking."

Megan and Jenny were coming to them now. Megan was smiling. Jenny was sullen.

"Hi, Tim," Megan said, offering her hand. Tim took it.

"You haven't changed a bit."

She blushed. "It takes a lot of effort to keep from getting *old*." She spat the last word out as though it was particularly distasteful.

"Well, you guys better get your stuff together," Tim said. "Daylight's wasting."

*

Derrick Warner watched as the Conners gathered their gear off the top of their station wagon and shrugged into their packs.

He paid special attention to Jenny.

The last time he saw her she was a baby, shambling around the Conners' living room, now she was a full blown woman. Her soft, dark hair streaked with blonde; her pale, creamy skin; her clear green eyes; her lips; the soft curve of her chin. God, she was *beautiful*. Several times she glanced at him, and looked away, smiling. Did she think he looked goofy? He made a conscious effort to keep his eyes off of her, but they always drifted back. Her neck was graceful, gazelle-like; her budding breasts under her shirt were small but, he imagined, pert; and her hips were beginning to curve into womanhood. He tried to swallow, but couldn't.

When everyone was ready, they came over to the trailhead; in addition to his pack, Mr. Conner wore a hunting rifle slung over his back.

"Alright," Dad said. "Everyone keep close together and *stay on the trail*. The campsite's two miles in. The terrain is hilly and rocky, so it won't be a cakewalk. But if you stay on the trail and be careful, you'll be fine."

Jenny groaned and threw her head back. Her mother, next to him, pushed it forward. Even petulant, she was beautiful.

"Let's roll," Mr. Conner said.

Dad went in first. Mr. Conner was next, then Mrs. Conner. Jenny followed her mom, and Derrick brought up the rear. "This is stupid," Jenny said, more to herself than anyone else.

Heart thudding, Derrick licked his lips and said, "I know. Why

101

couldn't we vacation in the city?"

"Because my dad's a big kid and he wants to play in the woods."

Derrick laughed.

From the highway, the trail turned right and wound into the hills. Around them, tall trees pressed close, their bows blocking most of the sunlight. As they walked, Derrick watched Jenny; her butt wiggled under her jeans, hypnotizing him.

What should he say to her? He had to say *something*.

"I hope we find a lake so we can swim."

"There'll probably be piranhas in it," she said.

"Or sharks."

"Or serial killers."

"Or Kanye West."

"'Hold up, lake, I'mma let you finish."

They laughed, her giggle the sound of music.

"I read an article about a lake that's so salty it kills anything that goes into it," she said. "It turns animals into statues."

"What?" he asked, disbelieving.

"It's true," she said, half-turning.

"That's crazy."

"I know. That's probably what the lakes out here are like. If you go in you get butt rot and die."

Mrs. Conner heard. "Jenny!" she said, shocked. "That's a *terrible* thing to say."

"But it's true, Mom," Jenny defended. "It's like those parasites in the Amazon. They swim up your pee-hole..."

"That's enough, Jenny," Mr. Conner said from the head of the pack. "Unless you want my hand to swim across your ass."

Jenny fell silent.

"I thought that was funny," Derrick said lowly.

She turned to him and smiled. So radiant. "I know. *They* don't appreciate my humor."

"I do."

She smiled again. "You're sweet."

She turned back around.

She said I was sweet!

Was that good or bad?

*

"She's smart," Tim Warner said. The trees had fallen away from the trail, and the hot August sun washed over them. To the east, tall pines huddled close together beyond a brown, wavering field. In the west, a rocky blue mountain thrust up into the sky.

"*Too* smart," David said.

Megan and the kids had fallen behind some. Dave and Tim were alone.

"She makes me feel like a moron sometimes," Dave went on. "Hell, half the time I don't even know what she's talking about."

Tim remembered Dave telling him how Jenny made the honor roll and whatever else. But he had no idea the little girl was as smart as she was.

"They moved her up a grade, didn't they?" Tim asked.

"A grade and a half," Dave said with evident pride. "She keeps it up she'll be in college by the time she's sixteen."

"Huh."

Tim couldn't properly name the emotion that went through him. Jealousy? Derrick was seventeen, and he was nowhere *near* college ready. Little Jenny Conner, on the other hand, Miss twelve-going-on-twenty-five...

Tim shook his head. He was being stupid. Derrick was normal...more or less. Jenny was advanced. So what? In the army, Tim was a better shot than Dave, but, at the end of the day, what difference did it make?

If it wasn't for Karen...

"Being as grown-up as she is," Tim said, "you're gonna have to worry about boys a lot sooner."

Dave chuckled. "Already there, pal."

He didn't tell Tim about the time, last summer, he caught her touching herself. God, he wished *he* didn't know about that. It was normal at that age. He knew that. When he was that age he was doing it three times a week. And girls...well...even though he was raised to think of girls as frigid, for lack of a better term...girls were really no different.

"So what's this campsite look like?" Dave asked, turning the conversation in another direction.

"It's a level clearing on the shore of a lake," Tim said. "Nice place."

Tim had been here before, when he and Karen were still married. He knew the trails like the back of his hand...mainly because after they spent two days fighting, Karen stormed off and got lost, and he had to find her. The best way to familiarize oneself with something, Tim learned, was to jump right in.

"How much farther?"

"About a mile, maybe less."

The path disappeared over a rise, and they stopped to wait for the others.

"Tomorrow we'll set off early, hike a couple miles, and then come back. I wish we had longer. There're some pretty great views in the higher hills."

Dave sighed. "Yeah. Too bad. But, hey, we're both in So-Cal now, so we can do this more often."

They could.

The trees fell away in the east, and a sparkling blue lake appeared, its surface dappled by the light of the sun.

"Thank God," Derrick said.

"Looks like your prayers were answered," Jenny said.

"I could just jump right in now."

"You'd get all of your gear wet."

"Who cares?"

"Your pack, your sleeping bag, your tent..."

"Oh well."

She looked back at him. "You could always sleep in *my* tent."

Derrick's heart sputtered. Seeing the look on his face, Jenny giggled.

What did *that* mean? Was she being nice? Was she trying to be...suggestive? God, he hoped she was being suggestive.

"No sleeping bag?" he asked, his voice shaky.

"Yeah," she said after a moment, "you can sleep in my sleeping bag."

Derrick's penis twitched. He liked the thought of that.

Farther up, a little pathway led from the main trail down to the lakeshore, passing through a stand of trees before emptying out on the soft dirt.

"Pick a place for your tent," Dad said, clapping him on the back. "Try to not go *too* far away."

Derrick unshouldered his pack and took a swig of water from his canteen. "Over there, I guess."

"Over there" was a patch of flat earth next to a rising tree. Dad went over, checked it out, and came back. "Alright. Looks like as good a place as any."

While Dad and Mr. Conner pitched their tents, Derrick set his own up, and was done in half the time. Looking around, he saw Mrs. Conner sitting on a log by a makeshift fire pit someone built before them. Jenny was on the other side of the pit, sitting among the ruins of her own tent and carefully reading the instructions, her lips moving and her eyes flicking from line to line. Derrick walked over.

"Do you need help?" he asked.

Jenny looked up. "If you want."

She got to her feet, so close to him he could slip his tongue into her mouth if only she'd let him. "I can't figure it out."

"I got this," he said, and set about righting her wrongs. In five minutes, her tent stood proud and ready for service.

"Kudos," she said. "There's just one problem."

He looked down at her, his heart seizing. "What?"

"The flap is facing away from the camp."

She was right. The back of it was facing the firepit.

"I'm sorry," he blushed. "I-I'll fix it..."

She put her hand on his. "Don't worry about it."

He looked at her.

"It's okay," she assured him.

He took her hand in his and threaded his fingers through hers, his heart slamming so hard he could hear it in his head. Her eyes shone.

"Jenny!" Mrs. Conner called, startling him. "Jenny! Wanna swim?"

"Later," she told him.

*

Amu-Ne, once known as Ben Cramer, stood high on a rocky bluff overlooking the sparkling blue lake. On its north shore, five people buzzed busily about, setting up camp.

They were staying the night.

Amu-Ne raised the binoculars to his eyes and studied the campers. Two men. A woman. A boy. And a girl. From what he could see, the girl was roughly thirteen or fourteen. She was most likely a virgin.

His heart raced. It would work this time. The Great God of the Forest would accept this one, would fill her with His seed.

"Are they staying?" Mau-Na-Noc asked from behind him.

"Yes," he replied, lowering the binoculars.

"The girl?"

"We take her tonight."

*

Derrick drew a sharp, heavy breath when Jenny appeared on the shore. Her bikini bottoms clung lovingly to her form, and her top held her young breasts in suspended animation.

"How is it?" she called.

"Beautiful," he replied.

She giggled. "I meant the water."

"Oh. Cold."

Derrick was knee deep. He didn't dare go farther.

Jenny was at the shoreline now. She dipped one toe in, and quickly snatched it back with a hiss. "Geez, it *is* cold."

"No Kanye Wests, at least," he replied.

"You're funny."

Jenny forced herself into the water, wincing with every step. When she was close, she said, "I'm starting to reconsider my swim."

"Don't," Derrick said. "It's not *that* bad." With that, she cupped a handful of water and threw it at her. She screamed, threw up her arms, and turned, so that it splashed her side.

"That's *cold*, you jerk!"

She splashed him back, and in trying to move away, he tripped over

105

a rock and went down, the chilly water closing over him. When he burst back to the surface, Jenny was laughing. "Karma's a bitch!"

"Jenny!"

Mrs. Conner was standing on the shore, her one-piece bathing suit black and green.

"Sorry, Mom," Jenny said.

"You really should watch your language. It's unladylike."

"I said I'm sorry. What do you want me to do, rip my shirt and pour ashes over my head?"

Derrick laughed.

"Being smart won't get you anywhere, young lady."

Higher up, at camp, Tim Warner watched the proceedings with a half-smile. "She's a spitfire, alright."

"You can say *that* again," Dave Conner said.

They were sitting near the fire pit. Weak flames crackled in the stone confines of its belly.

"They seem to be getting along," Dave said.

Tim nodded. Derrick and Jenny were getting along just fine. Maybe *too* fine. He saw the way Derrick looked at her, and he also saw the way *she* looked at *him*. The last thing they needed on this trip was for someone to get someone else pregnant.

"I'll talk to him later," Tim promised.

Dave shook his head. "Don't bother. If they like each other they like each other. I'm not going to give myself a heart attack over it. At least Derrick's a good kid."

Tim shrugged one shoulder. "Yeah. I just..."

Dave shook his head. "Whatever. While they're down there goofing around, we oughta go hunting."

"I don't have a rifle," Tim said. "And most of the game is farther off in the hills; they don't come to the trail too often. Too much activity."

"We can at least *try*. You're not going soft, are you, Warner?"

Tim chuckled. "Alright. But *I* get the gun."

"We'll take turns."

"Let's go."

*

Night fell quickly in the woods. One moment it was purple twilight, the next it was pitch dark.

"How about a ghost story?" Mr. Conner said. "Something creepy."

He and Dad got back from their hunting trip just before dusk began settling in. "We got rabbit," Mr. Conner announced proudly.

"If you eat nothing but rabbit you'll starve to death because it doesn't have the proper nutrients," Jenny said.

"And if you keep talking back to me you'll overdose on Vitamin Fist."

Now they were sitting around the warm, orange glow of the fire. Mr. and Mrs. Conner on one side, and Derrick, Dad, and Jenny on the other. Dad was on his left, Jenny on his right. They held hands.

"No, David," Mrs. Conner said. "I don't want to hear anything like that."

"I do," Jenny said. "Tell one about zombies eating people's guts."

Dad laughed. "Okay. How about this. Twenty years ago, on a night like this, five people were camping in the woods."

"Is this a true story, Mr. Warner?" Jenny asked.

"It sure is," Dad said. "Anyway, they were sitting around the fire, telling scary stories, when one of them, a little girl, had to pee. So she got up and went into the woods. She was maybe fifty feet into the shadows when a zombie popped out and ate her guts."

Mr. Conner laughed. Mrs. Conner didn't look pleased. "Ghost stories," she said. "Not stories where people's guts get eaten."

"It was a good story, Meg," Mr. Conner said. "My turn. Okay. So, these two kids were out neckin at lover's lane, boy hand his hand up the girl's shirt..."

Mrs. Conner glared at him.

"I'm playing, I'm playing," Mr. Conner laughed.

"I think it'd be best if we all turned in," Dad said. "It's getting late and we have to be up early tomorrow."

"Yeah, you're probably right," Mr. Conner said, getting to his feet.

Derrick squeezed Jenny's hand, and she squeezed back. Leaning close, she whispered, "Later."

With that, she smiled and got up.

Later on, after the Conners had turned in and Derrick was getting ready to head into his tent and wait, *pray*, for Jenny to come to him, Dad clapped him on the shoulder and said, "So, you're not hating this trip as much as you thought you would."

Startled, Derrick turned. "No," he said, "it's okay."

Dad nodded. "That's good. Looks like you and Jenny are getting along pretty well."

Derrick nodded. "Yeah. She's okay."

"Funny girl."

"Yeah."

"Cute."

"Yeah. And?"

Dad leaned in close. "And precocious."

For a long moment neither one of them spoke. "Don't take things too far," Dad finally said.

*

Amu-Ne watched from the trail as, below him, the camp cleared out and the fire began to die. Next to him, Mau-Na-Noc, Ja-Ze-Da, and Ryleh-Ta waited for his orders. Each one of them carried a pack containing tape, knives, rope, and other assorted supplies. "Soon," Amu-Ne said, his voice a hushed whisper. "Soon."

*

Derrick was just beginning to drift into sleep when the tent flap opened and Jenny Conner slipped in. She was wearing a thin white nightgown and nothing else, her hair done up in pigtails.

When she entered, Derrick snapped awake and sat up. When he saw her, his penis stirred in his shorts, and his heart throbbed in his chest.

She zipped the flap behind her and turned to him, her eyes bright in the low, pale light of the moon.

"Hi," she said.

"Hi," he dumbly replied.

Then she was in his arms, her body lithe and firm against him. Her lips found his in the dark, and her tongue darted shyly into his mouth.

*

Amu-Ne stiffened as, in camp, someone moved. He had just given the order to go when someone left their tent. Amu-Ne held his hand up and watched; in the moonlight, he saw the girl, the prize, the child bride of the Great God of the Forest, stealing across the campsite, moving quickly and furtively.

When she unzipped the flap of the boy's tent and went in, Amu-Ne's heart sank. The little whore!

"Now!"

*

She was on top of him now, straddling his leg, the moist heat of her against his flesh too much to handle. She pulled the nightgown over her head and tossed it aside; her breasts were taunt, full, her areolas dark against her pale white flesh.

Derrick was lightheaded.

"Did you hear something?" she panted.

"No," he gasped.

Then he did. Footsteps.

Before he could act, the flap was ripped open and arms were reaching in. For a moment Derrick thought they had been caught, but then he caught a glimpse of one of the men reaching in. Bald, with steely blue eyes and ugly pink scars crisscrossing his leathery flesh.

Jenny screamed and tried to move back, but the man had her arm, and another person, this one an Asian woman, had her by the hair, dragging her out into the night.

As soon as she was out, Derrick followed, yelling. Before he could mount a defense, however, someone hit him over the head, and he collapsed back onto the tent, which collapsed under his weight.

"Fuck!" Derrick heard as he teetered on the edge of unconsciousness. "Come on!"

*

Tim Warner was just in time to see someone, a dark shape in the night, throw Jenny Conner onto their shoulder.

"Hey!" he cried.

The figure darted away, and Tim realized there were several of them.

Dave Conner was suddenly beside him, the rifle in his hands. "What's going on?"

"They have Jenny!" Tim replied.

Dave's face fell. "Jenny?"

Before Tim could stop him, Dave raised the gun and fired.

Someone grunted.

"Stop!" Tim yelled, shoving the barrel of the gun away. "You'll hit her!"

"They have my daughter!" Dave roared. He pushed Tim out of the way and started after them. In a shaft of moonlight ahead, Tim caught a fleeting glimpse of someone limping into the darkness.

At Derrick's side, Tim dropped to his knees and lifted the boy's head. He wasn't bleeding, thank God, but he wasn't entirely lucid, either.

"Derrick? Derrick, can you hear me?"

The boy's head rolled limply.

"Derrick!"

The mist seemed to clear from his eyes.

"What's happening?" Megan Conner asked sleepily. She was standing by the opening to her tent.

'Just stay where you are," Tim said, holding up one hand. Looking back at Derrick, he shook the boy. "What happened?"

"Jenny..." he finally managed. "They took her."

What was she doing in his tent in the first place? Jesus Christ!

Dave emerged from the night, the rifle in his hands. "Come on," he said.

"What?" Tim asked.

"I hit one of the bastard's and he's bleeding all over the place. We're gonna track him."

"What happened?" Megan asked again.

Dave told her, and she nearly sank to her knees in grief.

"Get hatchets, shovels, whatever you two can carry," he said to the

Warners. "We're going after them."

*

In the mouth of the cave, Amu-Ne collapsed to the ground, dropping Jenny Conner to the cold stone. Mau-Na-Noc grabbed the girl by her hair before she could flee and, with the help of Ja-Ze-Da, and Ryleh-Ta, tied her to the gallows along one of the walls. She fought, thrashed, screamed, and kicked.

"We must do it soon," Amu-Ne said, panting. "It's almost midnight. He Who Walks in the Woods will wake soon."

Mau-Na-Noc, once Heather Ming, glanced at the gaping darkness toward the back of the cave. She shuddered as she imagined Him coming forth and taking His bride.

"Your leg," Mau-Na-Noc said.

"I'm fine," Amu-Ne said.

"You might bleed to death."

In the days before this, before the hilltop and the strange, titanic god in the mountain, Heather had loved Ben Cramer, at first despite his strange religion, and then because of it.

They live below, he told her long ago, *but They will return. We, the faithful, will be spared. None others will.*

Now, she loved him only as much as she loved herself, which wasn't much. Human beings were weak, pitiful, and disgusting. Love or no love, however, he was their leader, and they needed him.

"I'll extract the bullet and sew the wound," she said. "While it happens."

Amu-Ne nodded.

*

Derrick shined the flashlight on the rocky hillside; splatters of blood marked the spot where they passed with Jenny.

"Alright," Mr. Conner said from beside him. Looking up, he saw the jagged summit of a hill. "Come on."

Dad was in the rear, carrying a hatchet.

At the summit of the hill, Mr. Conner stopped dead. Ahead and slightly to the left, a mountain climbed into the night. On one of its lower ridges, an opening shone with light.

"There," he said, crouching low; Derrick did likewise. Behind them, Dad said, "How are we going to do this?"

"Violently," Mr. Conner replied.

*

Midnight approached. Mau-Na-Noc watched the wall of shadows with a superstitious wariness. At any moment, He would come.

"It's a great honor," she told the girl who hung nude in the corner. She didn't believe her own words. "You have been chosen to bear His young."

"Fuck you, bitch," the ingrate sneered, and spat at her; the glob of saliva hit her chin.

Mau-Na-Noc smiled. "No. It's *you* who will get fucked."

In the darkness, something moved.

*

They were almost to the mouth of the cave before they were spotted; the bald man was sitting on the ground, nursing his wounded leg. When he saw them, he opened his mouth to scream, but Mr. Conner raised the rifle and fired. The round took him high in the head, exploding the top of his skull. He fell back.

Derrick could see Jenny now, hanging from a rail of wood, her arms tied above her head, her pretty little breasts thrust out. One of them stood before her, their hands behind their back. When they turned, Derrick saw it was the Asian woman.

Somehow, Derrick got ahead of Mr. Conner, and was in the cave before the woman could even register what was happening. He tackled her, driving her back and to the ground. She hit with a thud, her head striking the stone floor with such force Derrick was sure he heard her neck crack.

There were others around him, all dressed in robes, some of them wearing hoods. As they advanced, Mr. Conner appeared in the entrance and fired, taking one of them in the chest.

The others, wisely, backed off.

"Tim, get Jenny," Mr. Conner said. "Derrick...get up and come back here, son. Stay low."

Derrick, remaining low, scuttled back to Mr. Conner's side.

There were three of them, he saw then. They all had their hands raised.

"I'm okay," Derrick heard Jenny telling his father. When she saw him, she smiled.

"Who the fuck are you people?" Mr. Conner demanded.

No one spoke.

Jenny was at his side. He kissed her, sweeping her hair back from her face. "Are you okay?" he asked.

"I'm fine," she said.

"I said who the...?"

Mr. Conner's words died on his lips. The cave shuddered, the ground and walls shaking. Earthquake, Derrick thought.

111

Then the thing emerged from the shadows.

Long and lithe, scaly like a snake but thinner, much, much thinner, the thing resembled a tapeworm. The long, hairy legs upon which it moved, however, reminded Derrick of a spider.

Millipede, he thought hysterically. It looked like a millipede.

The cultists fell to their knees now; it struck Derrick as more ducking and covering than a display of reverence.

"Jesus Christ!" Mr. Conner screamed.

The thing shrieked as it came, a long, shrill, ear-piercing sound. Jenny screamed, and Derrick drew her close.

Mr. Conner fired.

Once.

Twice.

Three times.

The thing kept coming. Derrick could see its face now, gray and spikey, its many black eyes reflecting the cold light of the moon.

"Get out of here!" Mr. Conner screamed, shoving Derrick back.

"Come on!" Dad yelled, grabbing Derrick.

Unthinkingly, Derrick scooped Jenny up into his arms and started running down the long, rocky path toward the camp, toward civilization, toward sanity.

Once he glanced over his shoulder. Dad was ten feet behind him, looking up into the cave. "Dave!" he screamed. "Dave, come on!"

"Daddy!" Jenny wailed.

Against the light from the cave, Derrick saw Mr. Conner's silhouette, heard the gunshots, watched the monster overtake him.

*

Meg and Jenny Conner spent Christmas morning at the Warner house. Outside, the sky was a piercing blue and the sun shone hot upon Newport Beach.

"I still dream about it," Jenny said.

They were in the downstairs rumpus room, lying in each other's arms. On TV, the kid from *A Christmas Story* was trying to come up with a way to get his parents to buy him a BB gun for Christmas.

Derrick kissed Jenny's forehead. "I do too," he said, and he did. Every night that horrible *thing* appeared in his dreams, its face gray, sharp, and covered with eyes.

"I wonder what would have happened if...if it *did* fuck me."

Derrick shuddered.

"What happens if it *does* fuck somebody?"

Derrick didn't know.

He didn't *want* to know.

THE LAKE HOUSE

There was something about the house by the lake, something indefinite, something unnamable. Standing in the front yard that first day, cold wind washing over him, Jim Conner struggled to put a finger on it but couldn't. It was shabby, a two story Cape Cod wedged between a barren hillside and the craggy shore. The paint was peeling, the roof needed work, and the windows were dark and dirty.

Nevertheless, he wanted it.

"You don't wanna see the inside?" the old man asked. He was leaning against the front end of his pick-up truck, a red trucker hat with a white mesh back pulled low on his forehead.

"I don't think I have to," Jim said.

The old man shrugged. "Suit yourself."

Now, sitting in the Jeep and studying the gloomy façade through the rain sluiced windshield, Jim sighed and settled on *energy*. There was an energy here; it seemed to radiate from the house in waves. *It's the moon and I am the tide*, he thought, and snickered. Where did *that* come from?

Regardless, it was an accurate description. He felt *drawn* to the house, felt it in his bones and in his blood.

Shaking his head, Jim got out of the Jeep and hurried through the cold rain. Under the covered porch, the wind chimes tinkling from a hook in the ceiling, Jim took the keys from his jacket pocket and opened the front door. Ahead, a staircase led up to the second floor. To his right, a small, rustic living room opened up, its crowning centerpiece a stone hearth. The couch, he saw, was tan and threadbare; the rocking chair by the window was stationary and coated in dust. A record player sat near it, and beyond that was a bookshelf crammed with titles.

The air was damp and musky. The old man said no one had been out here for nearly ten years.

"I come by once in a while and clean and all that, but it's still pretty shut-up."

Past the living room, a tiny kitchen flanked the western wall. Light streamed in through the window over the sink, murky and dirty like day old dishwater.

Home, sweet home, Jim thought, shutting the door behind him.

Home...at least for the next six months, at least until the book was done and the memories of Connie weren't so strong. Out here, in the wilds of Vermont, he was safe; but back in Boston, where every restaurant and every street corner reminded him of her...

Jim cut the thought off and shrugged out of his jacket. The place had central heating, the old man said, but where was the thermostat?

Searching, Jim found it in the kitchen, just to the left of the threshold, by the cellar door. He set it to seventy-two, and it kicked on, groaning and shuddering like a dying dragon. A strange and unpleasant odor filled the house.

It hasn't been on in a while.

Through the window, a small patch of lumpy ground gave way to the forest. To the left, he could just see the muddy shoreline disappearing into the woods.

The kitchen, like the rest of the house, was terribly dated. Black and white checked tiles; seventies or eights model fridge; table with metal legs; floral wallpaper. The back door, its little window covered with a near translucent curtain, led out to the lake. There was a pier, but no boat. That was okay, though. It was mid-November; too late for watersports.

Jim looked right. Somewhere over the hill was a cemetery. A private, three-person affair. The old man's parents and his sister.

My daddy built this place with his bare hands in 1956, the old man said, *lived here until the day he died. Said he never wanted to leave.*

It was a nice place. Maybe he'd never want to leave, either.

The rain had let up a little bit, so Jim dashed back out to the Jeep and grabbed a couple of his bags. He sat them by the front door and went out for the others. By the time the rain had picked back up again, all of his luggage was inside and was ready to start nesting.

Upstairs, a short hall offered three different doors. One was the master bedroom, one was a bathroom, and the other was barren and washed in dusky light. The master bedroom was wood-floored, the walls mounted with prize deer heads and fish bodies, and the bed, a king, was made neatly, the top cover wool with a striped red and blue pattern. The old man said he washed all the sheets just before Jim came back up. Jim was glad for that. He already had too much crap as it is. When he first came up with the idea of getting away from the city for a while, he planned on taking one bag and one bag only; truly rough it, huh? But that didn't happen. Not that it ever did. Modern society reminded him of a Lay's commercial: Bet'cha can't eat just one. Well, bet'cha can't *pack* just one. You have your clothes, your laptop, your soaps, and sprays, and a thousand other things you don't need. Creature comforts, they called them. Creature comforts aren't a *bad* thing, but they sure are a pain in the ass.

Jim sat one of the bags on the bed and opened it. His clothes. A dresser sat in the corner between the bed and the window. He tossed his socks and underwear into the top drawer, his shirts into the second, and his pants into the third. Next came his toiletries. Body wash. Shampoo. Conditioner. Deodorant. Toothpaste. Toothbrush. Mouthwash. Geez. Might as well open a pharmacy. Come one, come all; get your potty items 10% off.

Back downstairs, Jim grabbed his laptop and took it into the kitchen. There was a power outlet by the table. He unzipped the bag, plugged his charger in, and then plugged the charger into the computer itself.

He checked his email (nothing) and logged onto Facebook. Sixteen friend requests, three messages, and five notifications. Jim moaned. Start a Facebook page, his publisher said, it'll help you connect with fans, they said. Jim didn't *want* to connect with his fans, God bless them.

Jim closed the laptop and sighed.

In a pantry closet, he found the cleaning supplies, just as the old man said he would, and started with the kitchen, because why not? By the time he finished in the upstairs bathroom, two hours had passed and it was starting to get dark. In the living room, he threw a couple of pre-cut logs into the fireplace and watched as the flames came to life. In a space under the record player, he found a cache of oldies. The Beatles. Tommy James. Frank Sinatra. One record stood out; the very last. HEADHUNTER it said over a picture of a metal skull with crossbones. KROKUS.

Hey, dad, I'm gonna put my cool metal album next to all your square shit. Is that okay?

Sure, son, just don't forget it's there. One bad apple...

Jim slid the record out of its sleeve and put it on the turntable. Hissing. Popping. Loud, riff heavy rock music. It wasn't half bad.

In the kitchen, Jim took a glass from one of the cabinets and a bottle of Canadian Mist whiskey from the fridge. As always, he failed to stop himself from looking over his shoulders, as if someone would appear from the ether and take his booze away. When they didn't come, he poured it into the glass and returned to the living room.

*

Jim started awake sometime in the night, his chest heaving and his breath coming in short, quick gasps.

Nightmare, just a nightmare.

Sitting on the couch, Jim caught his breath and steadied his racing heart. The fire had burned down to embers and the record player was off.

Unsteady, Jim got up and went into the kitchen. The Canadian Mist was on the kitchen table, half empty. He unscrewed the cap and tipped the bottle back. It was slimy and piss warm.

Grimacing, he put the cap back on and started into the living room, but a crash beyond the cellar door stopped him.

For a long moment, he stood where he was, his heart pounding inexplicably. It came again, a hard, metallic sound. The central heating system.

Damn it.

Jim went to the door and laid his hand on the knob.

It turned in his hand.

Screaming, Jim jumped back. The door swung open...

...and nothing came out.

Panting again, Jim went to the door and switched on the light. A rickety stairway led to a dirt floor. Everything else was out of sight.

"Hello?" Jim called.

No reply.

No one's down there.

To be sure, he checked.

The basement was empty. The guts of the heating system occupied one corner, its base a concrete slab. It looked clean and brand new. Jim checked it over and found nothing amiss. Then again, he had no idea what he was doing. Back upstairs, he killed the fire and went up to bed.

In the darkness sometime later, Jim laced his hands behind his head and stared up at the ceiling. The house grunted, groaned, and sighed under him. *Settling* he told himself. Sure it was. Still: It sounded *creepy*. Low, hollow, drawn out. He remembered a horror movie he'd seen years ago. A woman was lost in the shadowy corridors of an old house, turning left, right, trying to escape before coming finally to a door at the end of a hall. Inside, the door was dark, the hall light spilling over the bed. A hideous creature sat up and stared at her, moaning just like the house.

I'm going to twist your back like mine, the white-faced ghoul said with a horrible grin.

Maybe she's down there now, Jim thought, and forced a smile.

A low, empty moan filled the house.

Jim's heart sputtered. That wasn't a settling noise.

Jim clicked on the bedside lamp and sat up.

Something moved in the darkness below, a soft, furtive footfall.

Jim got out of bed.

The bottom stair creaked.

Heart throbbing, Jim went to the head of the stairs and switched on the light.

Nothing.

He chuckled. Nothing. It was nothing. Of course it was. Why would anything be standing at the bottom, looking up at him with cold, black eyes?

You're losing it, Jim told himself. Maybe he was. Maybe the grief had turned to madness. Oh well. Schizophrenia would be like a non-stop acid trip. Man, the things he could *write*.

Behind him, the second bedroom door creaked open.

Jim swung around.

Nothing.

Sighing, Jim closed the door and went back into the master bedroom. He laid down and closed his eyes, willing himself to sleep.

Oops, I 'forgot' to turn the lamp off.

Jim laughed.

The morning was clear and cool, the sky a piercing blue and the trees along the lake burning red and yellow. For a long time, Jim sat on the dock, gazing at the beauty of it all. Farther down the coast, another pier jutted out into the water. The McKenzie's. The old man said they were his closest neighbors.

When he'd had his fill of the lake, Jim decided to go and see the cemetery. Getting up, he sighed. From here, the hill behind the house looked rather steep, its bare ridge line rising and falling like frozen waves. A faded white path led up the hillside.

Jim picked the path up near the side door and followed it. At the summit, he stopped and looked out over the lake and the surrounding forest. In the distance, the Green Mountains rolled north and south. They didn't look so green now; they looked yellow and brown.

Nodding at the beauty, Jim turned. The hill sloped gently. At the bottom, three headstones occupied a flat space enclosed by a low stone wall. Jim went to it, climbed over, and stood before the graves.

Bill Carver 1928-1979
Margret Carver 1932-2001
Jim Conner 1978-2017
Jim blinked.
Sheila Propst, it said, *1950-2009*
Jim chuckled. Insane. He was going insane.

Back at the house, Jim made himself a sandwich and ate it at the table while he checked his email. A literary magazine in California had accepted a short story of his; *The New Yorker* wanted rewrites; and his publisher was asking when he planned to have the book done.

The book.

Jim didn't *know* when he was going to have it done. Sometime before spring. It never took him longer than three months. This one, though...this one was more personal. His main character, a schoolteacher/writer, loses his beloved wife to cancer and goes through a long period of grief.

Just like him.

Reliving those memories, purging them from his system...he had no idea how long it would take.

Might as well start, though, right?

Jim opened a Word document and went to work.

The air vents kicked on.

Only instead of blowing out, they were sucking *in*.

*

The sound of a slamming door woke Jim with a start. His mind was muddled and his heart was slamming.

Running feet. Clunk-clunk-clunk. On the stairs.

Jim jumped out of bed. The hall light turned on. Jesus Christ!

Standing there beside the bed, Jim waited for the intruder to appear in the bedroom, but he (or, oh God, *it*) never came.

Swallowing hard, Jim forced himself out into the hall, the back of his neck tingling and his stomach rolling.

Nothing.

He checked the bathroom, the other bedroom, *his* bedroom. Then he moved downstairs. Nothing. Nothing at all.

In the living room, with every light in the house blazing bright, Jim tried to get ahold of himself. It was a dream. That was all. As for the light, well...he must have left it on. In fact, he thought he *remembered* leaving it on.

Feeling silly, Jim went through the hall and turned off all the lights. At the last one, he lingered, listening. When he finally switched it off, his finger stung. Turning it back on, he looked at it.

The tip was red.

Looked like a...hickey?

Jim shook his head. Crazy. You're crazy.

When he woke up the next morning, however, he didn't feel crazy. The sheets *were* strangling him, *were* lashing his hands and his torso. He rolled out of bed and smacked his forehead on the nightstand. Fuck!

Sitting there nursing his poor, poor head, Jim struggled to grab hold of his bleary mind. The sheets weren't strangling him. He was half-asleep and freaked out. That was all.

Getting to his feet, Jim noticed a few drops of blood on the floor. He cut his forehead good. In the bathroom mirror, he determined that he wouldn't need stitches but *would* need a Band-Aid; the cut was an inch across and fairly deep over his right eye.

After attending to himself, Jim wetted a wash cloth and went back into the bedroom to clean up the blood.

It wasn't there.

For a long moment, Jim searched on his hands and knees. He *knew* he saw drops of blood on the floor.

But they were gone.

It was almost as if the house...absorbed them.

Jim looked around.

He needed to get out of here. Go into town and have breakfast or something, get around some people. If he stayed alone, he'd go *totally* crazy, and the thought of that *did* kind of bother him.

Fifteen minutes later, Jim was dressed and behind the wheel of the Jeep. Before he started her up, however, something caught his attention. It wasn't anything drastic, in fact, Jim had to think on it for a moment. The house looked...different. All the way down the bumpy dirt road to

State Route 10, Jim struggled to put his finger on it. Finally, as he turned onto the blacktop behind a logging truck, it hit him. It didn't look as dilapidated as it did that first day. The paint wasn't peeling quite as much, and the wood siding wasn't as dark.

Not surprising, considering it was dark and raining when he saw it that first (and second) time. Still, it didn't sit well with him.

Nutcase Jim. Voted most likely to take out the President two years running.

Smiling wanly at his own bad humor, Jim switched on the radio. Sugar Ray wanted to fly. How nice. Jim nodded his head politely until they were done.

The village of George River sat on a sloping hillside rising back from the titular river, its main drag lined with quaint shops and cafes. Beyond the trees lining the side streets, a white church steeple towered into the air, and several blocks south, Jim caught a glimpse of what he imagined to be the school: Low, two story red brick with a line of wide windows. Faye's Diner, which the old man mentioned that first time, sat across from the Union Bank. Jim parked at the curb and went inside.

It didn't look much like a diner (no counter, just tables and chairs), but the sound and presence of people cheered him. He wasn't much of a people person, true, but he wasn't a hermit either.

Jim sat in a booth along the far wall, and smiled as a pretty waitress took his drink order. When she returned with his Coke, he ordered a burger and fries.

Alone again, Jim realized for the first time just how *tired* he was. He hadn't slept well either of the two nights he'd been at the cabin. Now, the combined weariness of two bad days weighed heavy on him. His back hurt, his neck was sore, his nose was beginning to drip, and a slight headache flared up behind his grainy eyes. When the waitress returned with his food, his stomach growled.

He took the fries down first, with plenty of ketchup. Then it was burger time. By the time he was done, he was stuffed.

Ready for a nap.

He paid, left a tip, and went back to the Jeep. Golden sunshine filled the streets. People walked aimlessly to and fro along the sidewalk. Jim wondered if there was anything else to do. An arcade, maybe?

Arcade?

Shaking his head, Jim got behind the wheel and started the Jeep up. In the parking lot of a five and dime, he turned and set off toward the cabin. Out of town, he realized something. He kind of dreaded going back.

Crazy, crazy, crazy.

Jim turned the radio back on, found a political talk show, and let the droning voice of the host wash over him.

Ten minutes later, he pulled into the front yard of the cabin and parked under the drooping bows of a tree. Let's do this.

He got out, locked the Jeep (city habits die hard) and went to the front porch.

At the bottom step, he stopped.

There were muddy footprints on the stairs.

Jim didn't know why the sight of those prints sent a cold pang of terror through his body. The old man dropped by. So what?

When he stepped into the house and saw the same prints leading into the kitchen, however, he wasn't so sure. Would he just *walk* on in if no one answered the door? Jim didn't know. It was possible. Some landlords had no respect for their tenants. *It's my house,* they figure, *I can do what I want.*

Jim's heart was racing.

He closed the door behind him.

His hand stuck to the knob.

What the fuck?

Jim pulled, and his hand came free. Looking at it in the sunlight, it reminded him of his finger: A red circular mark, much like a hickey.

Shaking his head, Jim followed the trail of mud into the kitchen. Here and there, he noticed, clumps of earth had fallen away, along with leaves, beetles, and earth worms.

The kitchen was empty.

Back at the front door, he saw a second set leading up the stairs. He followed it up.

They terminated at the second bedroom.

The door was shut.

Jim's heart was pounding so hard it filled his head. His stomach rolled.

This is insane.

Yeah. It was. Jim started up the last two steps, but what he saw froze him.

Under the crack of the door, a shadow moved in front of the sunlight.

Jim's mouth went dry.

Someone was in there.

Or some*thing.*

Jim remembered the cemetery.

Dirt. Leaves.

"No," Jim muttered, shaking his head. No. That was crazy.

The shadow disappeared.

Breathing heavily, Jim took the last two steps and threw open the door.

Nothing.

The room was empty.

Save for dirt. And the smell of rotting meat.

The closet door stood open. Jim went over to it and swept it with his gaze. No one crouched in the shadows. When he looked up, however, terror overcame him.

An attic hatchway. The cover dropped into place just as he glanced up.

Slowly.

Deliberately.

Something was in the attic.

In fact, he heard it now, low, shuffling footsteps.

When he threw open the hatch and climbed into the space above the second floor, he saw only a dark swish of movement.

He stayed there for a long time.

*

Insanity. That's all.

Hehehe. Insane in the membrane.

Jim sat in the kitchen, gazing at the blank Word document, the black curser flashing mockingly. He deleted the five thousand words he'd written the other day. They were no good.

Later, as evening crested, Jim started writing something else, an account of what he'd seen and heard at the lake house. It was short, dry, without the usual adornments that marked his typical writing style. When he was done, he felt much better.

Upstairs, he undressed. In the bathroom mirror, he looked terrible. His face was pale and haggard, his eyes were dark and sunken, and his hair was wild. It had been two days since he came home and found the thing in the attic. His sleep was thin and fitful, and he woke even more exhausted than when he'd gone to bed. He spent most of yesterday on the couch, dozing, the thought of getting up and moving around so obscene he almost pissed on himself to avoid a trip to the bathroom.

Jim looked away and stepped into the shower, letting the hot water cascade over his aching body. When he was halfway done, he opened his eyes and saw the swirling blackness near the drain. Not blackness, really, but darkness, like the dirt and grime of a long, sweaty day.

He didn't have any dirt and grime on him.

It's washing my energy away, he thought madly, *sucking it down the drain!*

The thought was strange and wholly unbidden, but Jim cut the water anyway.

When he was dressed, he went back downstairs. He was thinking of calling the old man and telling him he'd had enough. Boston waited. Safe, warm Boston. The only thing stopping him was the fear...nay...the *certainty* that he'd experience the same thing back in the city. He could leave the house behind, but he couldn't leave his insanity.

What if it isn't insanity?

It better be.

A loud bang came at the back door, startling Jim.

The wind.

It came again.

The doorknob rattled.

All at once, Jim's terror turned to rage. He charged into the kitchen and went for the door. On the other side, he could see the vague suggestion of a face.

Jim reached for the knob.

Behind him, the cellar door slammed into the wall. Jim turned, and deargodinheaven, it was there, coming for him, its arms outstretched, moaning like the cold autumn wind in the barren treetops. A woman. Her long blue dress was rotted and falling off of her. Her face was nearly skeletal, the flesh clinging to the bone black and withered. Through the tatters of her dress, Jim could see her ribcage. Beetles and spiders scurried madly.

"Jiiiiiimmmm!"

The window smashed, and an arm reached through, wrapping around Jim's neck. It, too, was the arm of a thing, the covering fabric eaten away, revealing the bone underneath.

Jim screamed.

The woman came closer, her arms wide as if to embrace him.

"Give it your power, Jim. Give it your life!"

Screaming and thrashing, Jim kicked the thing when it was close enough. It fell back and came apart on the floor. The arm snaked away, releasing him, and he pitched forward, nearly falling. The door flew open, and the second ghoul entered. Tall and bent to one side, dressed in the tattered remains of a suit, it was in remarkably good shape for having been in the ground since 1979.

"Come here, Jim," it said.

Jim turned. The front door. He had to get to the front door.

The ghoul on the floor was reaching for him.

Jim kicked it away and ran into the living room. The old man was there, a shotgun in his hands.

"Help me!" Jim screamed.

"Now you just stay right there," the old man said, taking a step forward. "Put your hands up over your head where I can see 'em."

Jim looked over his shoulder. The man ghoul was helping the woman ghoul up.

"What's going on here?" Jim breathed.

The old man jerked the gun at him. "Put your hands up!"

Jim reluctantly did as he was told.

"Turn around and go into the basement."

Jim turned. The two ghouls were standing there, watching.

The old man shoved the barrel into the small of Jim's back, and forced him into the basement.

In the middle of the floor, a single grave had been dug. Jim swallowed.

"Get in the hole."

Jim spun so quickly he was knocking the gun away before he knew he was resisting. The old man grunted and pulled the trigger, sending a volley of buckshot into the stone wall. A low, rumbling groan rose from the house.

Jim punched the old man and pushed him back. He pulled his foot back for a kick, but something happened; something fell onto his head, knocking him down. A floorboard.

Blackness overcame him.

*

The old man threw the shovel into the bed of the pick-up and cast one last glance at the house. The paint was crisp, white, and the windows sparkled in the cold light of the moon.

Soon, he thought as he swung into the cab, soon it'll need another.

He just hoped it wasn't him next time.

CHOMO

The man woke in darkness, dazed and disoriented. He tried to move, but a lightning bolt of agony shot through his head, and he cried out in a high, reedy voice that wasn't his own. Where was he? The darkness was total, providing no clues. He lifted his arm, and heard an unmistakable rattle.

Panicking, he tugged at his tether, but it was no use. He was chained to the floor.

Suddenly, harsh white light flooded the room, stinging his eyes.

"Ready for round two?"

The man opened his eyes. There, standing in a doorway, was, unbelievably, he himself, clad in jeans and a t-shirt. There was a bulge in his pants.

The man's breath caught in his throat.

What was happening?

Then it started coming back. He was in the prison library, mopping the floor, when three young Hispanic guys with tattoos and wiry muscles surrounded him.

"What's good, Chomo?" the leader, a thin youth of about twenty with short black hair and ink on his neck, greeted. That's what they called guys like him in jail. Cho-Mo. Child Molester.

He opened his mouth to speak, his heart suddenly racing, but one of the guys slammed him in the head, and he fell without a sound.

Once he was down, the Mexicans went crazy, showering him with punches, kicks, and sticks from homemade shivs. All he could do was curl up and pray a guard came to protect him, but none came, and soon the world went gray, then black.

But where was he now? What the hell was going on?

The man looked at his hand, the one cuffed to the chain. His fingers were too small, slender, painted lime green. He knew those nails. Kaylee Anderson. Snatched from a Wal-Mart parking lot in Ormond Beach. Held captive in a basement for three days. Beaten. Tortured. Raped. She was only fourteen. The last one before they arrested him.

"I'm ready," the erect doppelgänger said, approaching, and he remembered uttering those exact words before taking her for the final time.

He screamed, and as the child molester mounted him, the man knew where he was.

THE TRAVELING SHOW OF 2016

Day Parker, sheriff of King George County, pulled into the dusty lot and parked parallel to US301, nose facing south, toward Dahlgren. It was a hot, dry afternoon, the sky unbroken blue and the sun raging directly overhead.

Nice day for a bust, Parker thought sarcastically as he got out into the sweltering heat. It was 98 degrees by the thermometer at the bank. Weatherman said it'd be 102 before all was said and done. At fifty-eight and heavyset, Day Parker was far past the stage of tolerating extreme heat...or cold, for that matter. He was up for reelection next year. Maybe he wouldn't run, move somewhere more temperate. Where...well, he didn't know. Georgia, maybe. His grandmother came from a little town south of Atlanta called Thomaston. He still had family there, cousins and nephews he'd never met. Maybe he'd go there.

Sighing, Parker hitched up his belt. Ahead, the white tent fluttered in the sandpaper breeze.

Every year, in late June, fireworks stands went up all over King George County. This one, at the junction of 301 and 205, next to the Family Dollar, was run by a guy named Packard from Fredericksburg. If what he was hearing was true, Packard was selling illegal product. In Virginia, heavy duty fireworks are against the law. Take your sparklers and your bottle rockets, but hold the big 'uns.

What you got there under that tent?

Parker went to find out.

As expected, folding tables laden with fireworks formed three makeshift aisles. Black Cat. Phantom. Roman Candles, Georgia Peach, big, fifty dollar packs containing everything you could think of.

On the opposite side of the tent, on another table, was a cash register, a small metal desk fan, and a radio from which low country music played.

No one in sight.

"Hello?" Parker called.

Almost at once, George Packard appeared at Day's arm.

"Hi there, Sheriff."

Day jumped.

"Jesus Christ, George! You 'bout gave me a heart attack!"

Packard laughed. A short, balding man with deep, faded blue eyes and a leathery face, Packard was eighty-one; he didn't look a day over seventy-five.

"Sorry, Sheriff. I thought you heard me."

"That's why I said 'hello?' right?"

"Guess so. What can I do you for? Lookin for fireworks?"

"No, George. I'm here on business."

Packard's eyes narrowed. "What *kind* of business?"

"The business of findin' out if you're sellin' people illegal fireworks or not."

Packard cackled. "Illegal? I don't sell anything here like that."

"Well, I heard tell from a couple people you sold their kids illegal fireworks, and you know I can't have that sorta thing here."

"Where'd they hear that? Straight from the kids?"

Parker nodded.

George Packard laughed. "You can't trust kids! They're probably tryin' to hide who they really got it from. Their daddies, most likely. Big brother. Teacher. Didn't come from me."

"You mind me takin' a look?"

"Look."

Parker did. He searched the wares on the tables, the wares in Packard's truck, and nowhere did he find any illegal fireworks. That didn't mean much, but it satisfied him. For now.

"I tell you this: If you were doin' it before, you stop *now*. Got that?"

Packard nodded. "Sure do."

"Good."

Parker turned to leave, but something caught his eye. A brightly colored piece of paper was taped to the front of the cash register. He hadn't seen it before.

"What's that for?"

Packard looked at it. "Aw, some damn circus down to the park this Friday."

"The fourth?"

"Guess so."

Parker went over to the register and looked it over. It said:

COME ONE, COME ALL! THE TRAVELLING SHOW OF 2016 WILL BE AT BARNSFIELD PARK ON FRIDAY THE 4TH. MAGIC! FUN! THRILLS! SHOW STARTS AT SUNDOWN. HAMBURGERS, HOTDOGS, AND SODA WILL BE PROVIDED FOC.

"Huh."

"What's that, Sheriff?"

"I didn't know someone was comin' to the park."

"Do now."

*

After visiting George Packard, Day Parker drove back to the county courthouse, where the police station was housed in a series of basement rooms.

Inside, where it was dim and cool, Parker paused, relished the change of pace, and then went to his office.

Just outside the door, he stopped. On the community corkboard was another flier for the 'Travelling Show of 2016'.

Hm. It wasn't there this morning. Maybe someone came around after he left.

Travelling Show of 2016, huh? Didn't sound very appealing to him. Magic? No, thank you. Fun and thrills? He could go for fun and thrills as much as the next guy, but what *kind* of fun and thrills? Were they like the carnivals that set up in the Wal-Mart parking lot every August? If so, what would a grown man want there? Cotton candy? Bumper cars?

Parker chuckled.

*

Later, as the sun sank in the west, its dying orange light lying heavy over the world, Parker went out on a round of the county, touching King George proper, Dahlgren, and Blyth. In Dahlgren, which sat between the Potomac to the east and a long, gentle hill to the west, Parker went by the Food-Lion to get a few things for later on.

The store was cold and nearly empty at this hour; a couple of old people, a couple of harried single mothers just off work. Parker got his things and checked out, the cashier, a young blonde girl with metal in her face, favoring him with thinly veiled disgust. Parker was used to it, and even gave her a smile; young people never like the police. Had something to do with the whole rebellion phase. Lately, with all the 'unarmed' black kids getting shot, even most adults didn't like the police.

As he was leaving the store, Parker caught sight of a familiar sight: A brightly colored piece of paper on the community board. This travelling show was really on the ball when it came to marketing.

*

The next morning, as he was getting dressed, Parker heard an ad on WGRQ, the oldies station out of Fredericksburg: "For fun, thrills, and magic, visit the Travelling Show of 2016 at Barnsfield Park in King George this Friday, July 4th. Hamburgers, hotdogs, and soda will be free to the public."

The voice was deep and monotonous.

At the station, the night receptionist and the desk sergeant were talking about the show. At the WaWa in Dahlgren, waiting in line to pay for his gas, Parker heard a couple of teens behind him talking about it.

The entire county was talking about, from the way it sounded. Not much happened in King George for the 4th. They shot fireworks off on the naval base in Dahlgren and that was about it. Most people went over to Colonial Beach, where they at least had vendors and music. With this kind of buzz, they'd be packed.

Parker decided to pay them a visit.

*

Barnsfield Park sits on the Potomac River just off 301; the last turn-off before the Nice Memorial Bridge crossed the river and went into Maryland. As far as parks go, it wasn't a particularly exciting place. There was a walking trail, a bike path, both of which wound out of sight through the woods, a playground for the kiddies in a corner, and a large, open area where impromptu games of baseball, football, and soccer were played by restless children with nothing else to do.

Today, the field was unobstructed save for a large red tent placed squarely in the middle. Next to the tent was an antique red Ford with TRAVELLING REVUE stenciled in white on the door. Slightly apart from that was a Winnebago.

Parker parked on the grass in front of the tent and got out. The day was still and hot, and the sound of kids frolicking in the river just beyond the trees was faint, almost as if from a dream of summertime youth.

Parker went into the tent.

Inside, several rows of metal folding chairs stood empty before a rough patch of dirt upon which sat an overturned metal washtub. Soapbox came to mind. Other than that, there was nothing.

"Hello?"

No reply.

Parker looked around, found nothing of interest, and went back outside.

"Anyone here?"

Nothing.

Strange.

*

Friday, July 4th dawned hot and clear. Burgers sizzled, firecrackers popped, and country music wafted from radios across the county. Day Parker spent most of the day on the Westmoreland County border, personally manning a drunk driving checkpoint.

When the sun began to go down, he got into his car and drove to Barnsfield Park. Hopefully he could talk to the proprietor before it opened.

By the time he got there, it was almost dark, and the once tranquil tract of grass was crammed with parked cars and holiday revelers, some tailgating, others walking toward the tent.

Parker got out and went straight for the Winnebago, which was still parked next to the truck.

The sun went down.

Parker knocked on the side door of the RV.

It opened.

"Yes?"

The man in the threshold was short, fat, and wore a thick mustache twirled at the ends. He wore a long red coat with cutaway tails and a tall black top hat.

"I'm Day Parker, sheriff of King George County. Can I talk to you?"

The man smiled, wide and toothy.

Day Parker started, and, impossibly, found himself sitting in one of the metal folding chairs facing the metal tub. The inside of the tent was crammed with people. People sitting. People standing. People milling. Children on their parents' laps. Parents sharing seats.

The lights went out.

Parker jerked again.

A spotlight came on, illuminating the soapbox. The man with the red coat was there, holding a megaphone. In the hot white lights, he looked *wrong*. His face was too pale, his eyes too black. He raised the megaphone to his lips, and Parker saw that his fingers were long and double-jointed, the nails yellow and sharpened to a point.

"Friends and neighbors!" he called, his voice booming hollowly. Parker recognized it: The ad on WGRQ.

The chattering, which had, hitherto, been a low roar, died gradually off, and silence hung heavily over the congregation.

"Welcome to the Travelling Show of 2016, Summer Revue. My name is Julius Lazlow, and I will be your humble host for this evening."

Lazlow took a deep and graceful bow, met with scattered claps. For the first time, Parker noticed there were others with him, standing blankly in the shadows. Men. Burly. Black T-shirts. One of them wore a long coat and pants.

It's too hot for that, Parker thought crazily. He didn't feel right. The world rocked back and forth like a ship at sea, and the edges of his vision blurred, cleared, and blurred again. He tried to stand, but his knees were rubber, and wouldn't support him. Something was wrong, dreadfully wrong. Already the encounter with Lazlow by the Winnebago was fading. How did he get here? What happened?

"Refreshments will be served after the show," Lazlow was saying. "Then, perhaps, fireworks!"

Clapping. Loud and dry. Stop it! Can't you people tell something's wrong?

"Now, let the magic commence!"

With a sound like ripping canvas, it happened. They came through the walls of the tent, their eyes glowing red and their mouths open, their teeth gleaming and razor sharp.

Someone screamed, and the lights went out, plunging the revue into darkness.

Parker tried to stand once more, but fell to the grass. Around him, screams of agony and terror rent the night.

Day Parker, sheriff and bachelor, kind-hearted but tough, fair but firm, died of a heart attack. His was the only natural death in King George County that night.

*

By midnight, they had pulled up the stakes and moved on, crossing into Maryland, a convoy of ten vehicles under the warm light of the summer moon. Their next engagement was in Mechanicsville, the day after tomorrow.

At Barnsfield Park, bathed in the same luminescent light, the bodies of the dead stared with open-eyed nothingness into the powdery black sky.

Then they began to move.

By morning, only one body remained.

EVILDOER

The Lord would be pleased!

Grinning with the delight of a demented child, Danny Hotchkiss tucked the chrome .9mm into his waistband and hurried down the tree lined road, great, glorious work ahead of him. Behind, the man moaned in the dust, his guts spilling through his fingers. Danny would have finished him off with a shot to the head, but the Lord had told him to let the bastard suffer.

Danny giggled as he remembered the way the man's eyes widened as he whipped out the gun. He went from jovial ("You're the first person I've seen in three weeks!") to terrified.

Terror was something that Danny was getting used to.

It had been nearly a month now since the plague came through Charleston, West Virginia, killing everyone in the city. A whole month. Danny marveled. It felt like a century.

It began at the end of June. People were coughing and sneezing all around him. Doctors, nurses, other patients. He was only allowed one hour of TV time in the dayroom, and while Danny preferred watching old movies in black and white, the orderlies and nurses strong-armed him into putting on the news each and every time. Riots. Looting. Hospitals closing. The government cracking down. Then, one morning, he woke and found the hospital empty. A dead nurse sprawled outside his door was the only sign of humankind anywhere. The halls were dark, quiet. His voice echoed.

He took the laminate pass card from the nurse's keychain (the keys to the kingdom!) and let himself off of the unit. It took him a while to find the stairs, but when he did, he crept quietly to the first floor lobby. Inside the little niche where guards checked people's IDs, Danny found another body, a beefy black man in a uniform. There was a revolver on his hip.

Danny took it and left the building, walking down the stone steps like a man emerging from a fifty-year stint in a cave. The sun was so bright, and warm, and the sky was so big.

There were a few cars in the parking lot (and one in the road, but it was flipped over), not that Danny could drive any of them. He'd been in the hospital a long time. Since before he could get his learner's permit.

So, on foot, Danny walked into Charleston. He was surprised at what he found. Fires raging. Smoke billowing into the sky. Storefronts shattered. Glass and garbage on the sidewalks. The main highway was crammed with abandoned cars. Well, not *all* of them were abandoned. Dead bodies manned some of them.

That first day, Danny met only one other person, a shirtless hillbilly coming across the Yeager Bridge. He was grizzled and scary, and Danny shot him.

After rummaging around in a 7-11 and gorging on junk (he wasn't allowed to have junk at the hospital), Danny made his way to a Holliday Inn, where he slept behind the check-in counter. That night, the Lord came unto him, eyes glowing red in the darkness.

"Daniel..." It said, "I have returned."

Danny smiled when he heard the dark, familiar voice. It had been so long since the Lord had come to him. The doctors at the hospital made him take pills, and the Lord didn't like those pills.

"Help me, Daniel. I've tried and I've failed. I didn't get them all. The plague wasn't enough. I need you. Only you can do it..."

The next day, the Lord led him out of town. His first target was a teenaged girl hiding in her house on the edge of the city limits. She was scared, like Danny, but she didn't have the Lord, so he shot her.

"Kill them all," Danny muttered as he struggled down the road from Charleston, loathe to forget the command, "kill then all, kill them all."

That had always been the Lord's plan. Kill them all. The last time, Danny only got as far as his grandparents. But this time, he wouldn't fail.

As a sign of their covenant, the Lord led him to a pick-up truck in Pocahontas County, and showed him what was in the glovebox. A beautiful chrome gun with EVILDOER etched onto the side.

Presently, Danny pressed on into the day summer heat, the sound of locusts in the trees like music to his ears. The Lord would be pleased with him.

And the Lord was...for a while. But then Danny stopped meeting other survivors. He walked across the mountains into Virginia, but Harrisonburg, the biggest city in the foothills, was deserted.

"Burn it, just in case..."

Danny spent an entire day wandering the streets, setting fires. By dusk, the entire city was alight.

But that wasn't enough. The Lord wanted men to die, not buildings. Danny pressed on toward Alexandria and Washington, where his chances of meeting other people were better. He walked by day (even with the Lord, night scared him), and, at night, slept in haylofts, fields, and abandoned houses. As time wore on, the Lord became angry, and Danny cringed at his wrath.

In the middle of August, panting and overheated, sunburned and nearly dehydrated, Danny made it to the outskirts of Alexandria. More death and destruction.

More nothing.

That night, Danny dragged himself behind the counter of a McDonald's, and listened to the Lord.

"You must have done it. You must have killed the last ones."

Danny smiled. He'd done well.

"But there's still one left..."

Danny nodded. He knew what he had to do.

A PERFECT LIFE

Bill Wexler woke at six, as he did every morning, and kissed his wife.

"I'm going for a run," he said.

She didn't reply.

Bill hurriedly and silently dressed in his sweat suit and left the house, being careful not to make too much noise; it was a Saturday, and Linda and the kids liked to sleep in.

Outside, the day was bright and warm, the scarlet light of the sun falling through the trees along Grover Street and casting shadows along the sidewalk. For a moment, Bill stood in the middle of his lawn, scanning the houses across the street; Fox Meade was a nice subdivision, but the neighbors were really letting the place go. Grass grew riot all around him, and the houses themselves looked strange, dirty. Gene Donovan's front door was even open, just *inviting* trouble.

Bill jogged across the street and followed the sidewalk south, toward US2, which bordered the subdivision to the north. He usually jogged all the way to the beach in the morning, past the shops and drive-ins, along the boardwalk, and then back home through the woods. It took him an hour and a half all told, but the time *flew* by.

Bill loved jogging. When he ran, all of his thoughts and cares melted away; lost in the rhythm of the run, he simply *was* and that was all.

At Fox Meade's richly appointed entrance, Bill stopped, caught his breath, and went on, running down US2's southern flank. No cars passed him as he went.

Fairview, a mile down, sat empty in the morning sun; approaching over the tall hill separating it from the rest of the county, it sparkled like a gem on the seashore.

In town, Bill passed the police station, the ice cream shop, the pharmacy, and the town hotel. There was a lot of broken glass on the sidewalk; at the intersection of Main and Beachside Drive, two cars sat tangled, metal twisted and burnt.

Bill didn't notice.

The roar of the sea and the cry of a gull whirling overhead kept Bill company on the boardwalk. He breathed deeply of the salty air, and sighed contentedly. For as long as he could remember, Bill had always wanted to live by the sea. When he moved Linda and the kids to California, it was like coming home.

Bill passed through town once more. A stand of forest stood between Fairview and Fox Meade, the initial leg of it up the hill. Bill walked this part, huffing and puffing; even from here he could hear the sea and the gulls. What a perfect life.

At the top, Bill paused and looked back over his shoulder. He thought of his life before Linda, back when he was nearly four hundred pounds and lonely, trapped in a basement in Iowa. It seemed so long ago, in a different life...a life he didn't think of often. He lost the weight, met Linda, had two beautiful kids, and moved to the sea. That was that.

Back in Fox Meade, Bill did a lap of the richly appointed clubhouse; the gated pool was empty.

Finally home, Bill stripped out of his sweats and hopped in the shower.

The water was off.

Huh.

He fiddled with the handles, but nothing happened.

Oh well.

He got back into his PJs and sat on the bed. "Linda? You up?"

*

They ate at the table, in the sun-washed kitchen. Linda and the girls weren't very hungry; none so much as *attempted* to touch their food.

"What's wrong with you guys?" Bill asked.

No one spoke.

"Are you...?"

Linda slid out of her chair and collapsed to the floor, her head thunking against the tiles. That sound, the wet, sickening crack, woke Bill briefly from his languor and for a moment he saw the world as it really was:

The girls, in their chairs, were dead, their faces blue-gray and their eyes closed, mouths slightly parted. Flies buzzed around their heads, looking for a landing point.

No.

On the floor, wearing the pink bathrobe she died in, Linda was rotting, her face nearly black.

No!

He was alone, his perfect life piled in rubble around him, taken cruelly by the plague.

No! God, please!

As sudden as it had come, the lucidity was gone; Bill was safely back in the delusion.

"Here, let me take you to bed," he said, standing. "You girls be good," he warned as he picked Linda up off the floor. "Mommy doesn't feel good."

Upstairs, he tucked Linda in and kissed her forehead.

"You sleep. I'll take care of the girls."

He didn't mind. He loved them so much.

"What a perfect life," he said as he closed the door and went back downstairs.

FURY

Why don't they like me?

Standing in front of the ancient brick middle school on the warm morning of May 8, watching as the other children streamed into the building, laughing, smiling, and chatting, Tommy Simmons asked himself the same question he'd been entertaining every day since the first day of school; today, he was no closer to an answer than he was back in August.

He took a step off the curb, but stopped himself, and drew back, like a frightened turtle into its shell. He knew what lay ahead of him. More taunts, more dirty looks, more cruel smiles and cutting words, and he dreaded it with every fiber of his being. Home. He should just go home.

The only thing stopping him was his father; Dad was probably still there, passed out in his Lazy-Boy, a smattering of empty beer cans drifted across the dirty living room carpet. Of all the bullies Tommy dealt with every day, his father was the worst...though Butch Hargrove was a close second. Butch was in eighth grade, so Tommy rarely saw him, which was good. Butch was worse than the other kids. He actually *hurt* Tommy. Just last week, he hit Tommy square in the nads. "What's the capital of Thailand?" he asked, and before Tommy could answer, he was on the ground, hot pain in his belly and tears in his eyes.

"You like that, you four-eyed queer?" Butch asked, standing over him.

Sighing, he steeled himself for what he knew would happen, and crossed Schoolhouse Road.

Cedar Point Middle/High School was a tall, two story building dating back to the 1920s. Its brick was dark and faded, and its windows watched with Jazz Age malice as Tommy approached; sometimes it seemed as though the school itself hated him, just like everyone else.

It's just a building, Tommy told himself. He was at the door now. The lobby beyond was flooded with students, most of them pushing their way toward the cafeteria. With a deep, shuddery breath, Tommy pushed open the door and went inside.

Instead of going to the cafeteria like everyone else, Tommy ducked right at the main office and headed for his homeroom. Whenever he went to breakfast, the feeling of the other kids watching him, and of knowing that they were whispering about him, pushed Tommy to the edge of tears. The last time he went, Butch stuck his foot out and tripped him as he made his way to the sole unoccupied table; he fell, getting eggs and yogurt all over his shirt, and how they laughed...

At first, Tommy thought it was because he was new. Of course the other kids were going to talk about him and look at him funny; in a town like Cedar Point, newcomers were few and far between. But instead of tapering off, it grew worse. They called him four-eyes, faggot, nerd, geek, dork. He overheard some of the girls saying he was 'weird' once. At home, he looked at himself in the mirror but couldn't find anything 'weird' at all. He *was* a little short for his age, and thin, wispy even, but not weird. His skin was fair and soft, and his hair was stark black against his cream-colored forehead. He thought his lips were too red, and his features too soft, but that didn't make him strange. Why would they say that? Because he didn't like the same things they did? Because he didn't play football? Maybe if they gave him a chance he would. The only time he ever gathered enough courage to ask in on a game in the park, last autumn, the boys only laughed and told him to piss off.

What did he ever do to them?

As he reached the door to his homeroom class, Tommy felt a familiar flush of anger spread over him. It wasn't fair.

In the classroom, Mrs. Barkey was sitting at her desk and grading papers, a steaming mug of coffee close at hand. She looked up, and smiled. "Good morning."

"Good morning," Tommy said, conscious of his reedy voice. Mrs. Barkey didn't make fun of him, at least. She genuinely liked him.

Tommy dropped his backpack next to a chair at the front of the class and sat down. Some of the other kids said he was a teacher's pet because he sat here, and others threw wads of paper at him. But when Mrs. Barkey caught them and yelled at them, Tommy couldn't help but think it was all worth it.

A few minutes later, other students began coming into the classroom. One of them, Donald Maddox, nodded in his direction. "'S'up, baby-dick?"

He said it so low that Mrs. Barkey didn't hear, and Tommy's face flushed. They called him that ever since Ben Cramer pantsed him in the gym. Tommy was so embarrassed when it happened, he pulled his pants up and ran out crying.

He hated them.

He hated them all.

*

James Parker, sheriff of Cedar Point, rose early on the morning of May 8, torn from sleep by a nightmare he couldn't remember. Something to do with Laura, he thought, but sitting in the spill of the bedside lamp, he couldn't be sure.

Wide awake at barely five in the morning, Parker heaved a sigh of resignation and trudged into the bathroom, where he turned the shower on as hot as he could stand and climbed in, letting the near-scalding water sluice over his achy body.

It was three years in July since he lost Laura, and still he hadn't gotten over it, not entirely. Once a month he dreamed of her, and while he couldn't remember every single one, he knew the gist: She was alive again, alive and *sick*, just like she was before she died. And the crazy thing? Parker *remembered* her dying, remembered holding her hand as the last breath rattled from her throat, remembered standing before her casket and looking dazedly down, but here she was. A zombie, Parker thought, but not really. She was back from the grave and sick, and all he could think was: *This isn't natural. You shouldn't be here.*

He supposed he was subconsciously dreaming of the days before her death, as the cancer slowly ate her alive. They were terrible days, and only now, looking back, did he realize the emotional toll they'd taken on him.

Parker didn't like thinking about them.

When he was done in the shower, Parker threw on a robe and went downstairs. Beyond the sliding glass door in the kitchen, feeble sunlight was beginning to spread over the hills surrounding Cedar Point. Switching on the harsh florescent lighting Laura had loathed, Parker set about brewing himself a pot of coffee. Five minutes later, he poured some into a mug and went out onto the back porch, the crisp morning air greeting him like a welcome respite.

Past a stand of trees marking the edge of the property, Cedar Point huddled against the waxing sun.

Parker never tired of the view, though he'd been living here nearly twenty years. From here, high above it all, Cedar Point resembled a postcard, with its blue water tower, red brick schoolhouse, and white church steeple. Looking at it in the wan early morning sun, Parker could almost forget the real, everyday problems that plagued it. The meth. The domestic violence. The teenaged hoodlums. The normal scourges of small town America.

When he was done with his coffee, Parker sighed, locked up, and drove into town, following Mercer Road, which wound casually through the hills. Past the town limits, he turned onto Schoolhouse Road, which passed the high school, and followed it to Main. A left and a block and a half brought him to the police station, an old stone building on the corner of Main and Sage. He parked around back in the shade of a drooping willow, and killed the engine. He thought of Laura, how much he missed kissing her before he left for the day, how he missed her mid-afternoon phone calls. Pain rose in his chest, and he forced himself out of the car. He hoped there'd be enough work to get his mind off of Laura today.

Most likely, there wouldn't be.

*

"You throw like a girl," Ben Cramer pronounced disgustedly. They were in the gym. Their exercises were done and dodgeball was on; naturally, Tommy was automatically assigned a team because no one picked him.

"I-I'm sorry," Tommy whispered.

"No one wants you here. Why don't you go sit on the sidelines?"

Mr. Marowitz, the gym teacher, was sitting in a metal folding chair watching, his muscular arms folded over his barrel chest. If Tommy tried to get out of dodgeball, Mr. Marowitz would be mad.

Tommy tried to ignore it. He picked up the red rubber ball and threw it again. Next to him, Marcus Warner snickered. "You *pathetic*."

The anger rose in Tommy, this time boiling over. He swung on Marcus, his fists clenched. "I'm not pathetic!" he cried, his tiny voice echoing through the gym. Marcus stood up taller, ready for a fight. Mr. Marowitz just went on looking.

"You best back up, baby-dick."

Tommy swung. Marcus saw it coming, ducked, and hit Tommy with a wicked right hook, his fist crashing into the soft flesh of Tommy's stomach. Pain exploded over Tommy. His knees gave out and he sank to the floor, a muffled *Ump!* escaping his lips.

"Hey!" Mr. Marowitz yelled disinterestedly. "No fighting!"

Hot tears welled in Tommy's eyes.

"Bitch," Marcus said, and walked away.

Tommy cried.

*

James Parker spent the morning going over paperwork and signing his name on arrest reports from the night before. Two good ole boys were picked up at Larry's Roadhouse on US2 for fighting. They were in the drunk tank when he came in, but by ten both of them were gone, neither one wanting to press charges on the other.

As the day wore on, the work ran out, and for a long stretch of time, Parker simply sat behind his desk, twiddling his thumbs and waiting for something to happen. At one, he went on lunch, walking the two blocks to Faye's Café, the sole restaurant in town. He sat in a little booth by the window and watched the lazy comings and goings of Main Street as he ate. When he was done, he left a tip and decided to head over to the park on Pine Street. Sometimes you could catch kids playing hooky there. Today it was empty save for a woman sitting on a bench while her toddler son played on the slide. He walked back over to the station then, and spent a few long minutes talking to Steve Graves, one of his deputies. Tall and thin, Graves had been with the force longer than anyone there, Parker included, and he was always good for an interesting story about local people.

Back in his office again, Parker inevitably thought of Laura.

I hope they all die!

Tommy Simmons looked both ways before crossing Schoolhouse Road; kids were streaming away in both directions, walking in groups of twos and threes and fives, and Tommy felt such hatred for them that he was shocked.

Screw them!

Instead of following Schoolhouse Road east toward Maple Street, where he lived, Tommy ducked west. A half a mile from Cedar Point middle, trees rise suddenly up on both sides of the road. It continues on for another couple miles of hilly forest before crossing the Steele River and turning into State Route 10. Eventually it went through Preston, and then onto the interstate, but not before passing Caruthers Manor, where Corwin Caruthers and his wife, Matilda lived. His dad said they were snobby rich people. Tommy didn't know either way, but he suspected his dad was just bitter because Corwin Caruthers had nice things and *he* didn't.

Several cars passed Tommy on his walk, but none of them slowed or stopped, as he was half-afraid they would; no one knew what he was doing.

A full mile from the school, Tommy stopped, looked both ways, and scrambled over the guardrail, dropping onto the crest of a slight ravine. Moving carefully, Tommy went down the hill and stopped. Ahead, a dry riverbed led up and over a humped hillock. He came here sometimes when his father was drunk and mean. It was so peaceful, so remote, that he could allow himself to believe that nothing outside existed at all, that Dad, Butch, and all the others were figments of his imagination, mythical creatures that weren't real, thank God, like the vampires and aliens he read about in the paperbacks he kept at the back of his closet, hidden away.

You always have your nose buried in a book, his father said once, disgustedly. *Why don't you man up and stop acting like a little queer?*

He hated his father, too. He hated all of them.

Tommy was so lost in thought that he suddenly came to and found himself in a section of forest he'd never seen before. The trees were higher here, their tops fuller, obscuring the sun, and the underbrush was denser, more snarled. Startled, Tommy came to a halt. Getting his bearings, he decided he'd gone straight and true, and that turning around and going the way he'd come would bring him back to the highway.

Tommy spun on his heels, his toe kicking something. Looking down, expecting a rock, he saw instead the smooth, rounded edge of what looked like a metal Frisbee jutting from the ground. It was perhaps two inches thick and six inches across.

Intrigued, Tommy dropped to one knee and inspected it closer. The edge was ribbed, like a quarter, and something was etched onto the face in raised letters, though the letters weren't familiar.

Reaching out, Tommy touched the ridged edge of the thing, but snatched his hand back. It vibrated.

"Whoa," Tommy breathed. He touched the obelisk again, and forced his hand to stay the course. Warm vibrations snaked up his arm, numbing it. He pulled away again, and waited until the tingle went away to touch it again.

Energy, he thought. It felt like energy. In moments, power coursed through his veins, and he no longer felt like the little helpless runt he was, but *strong.*

*

An hour later, just as he turned onto Maple Street, his body still buzzing from the encounter with the stone circle, Tommy heard a familiar voice behind him.

"Hey, dick-breath."

He froze but didn't turn. Butch Hargrove.

"Where you goin, cockbait?"

Ignore him.

But he couldn't. Butch Hargrove *hated* being ignored.

"H-Home," Tommy said, hating the way his voice quivered.

"You gonna go jerk off to *Playgirl*?"

Someone tittered, and Tommy realized Butch had his cronies with him, Johnny Vega and Curtis Yancy.

"No," Tommy said, still not turning. Anger welled within him once more.

"Don't lie to me, fag," Butch said. "I know you like it like that."

Tommy started walking, but Butch had him, spinning him around and wrenching his arm. Tommy cried out. Butch's face hovered inches from his own, long and narrow, dusted with angry pink pimples. Behind him, Johnny Vega and Curtis Yancy watched, the former small and swarthy, the other big and blonde.

"You like suckin dick," Butch said. "I got a dick you can suck."

Tommy tried to pull away, but Butch yanked him back.

"I got a *big* dick you can suck..."

Just then, a police car turned onto the street; Tommy saw it over Curtis's shoulder, white and green with a big yellow badge on the door. Thank God!

Like an animal, Butch sensed something was wrong, and turned. His body stiffened when he saw the squad car.

"You're dead meat," Butch said, letting Tommy go. The cop car pulled alongside them, and the driver window powered down. Sheriff Parker, grinning, stuck his head out.

"You boys okay?" he asked.

"We're fine," Butch said, motioning to his minions. They left, and Tommy was so grateful he could have kissed the cop.

*

Once Parker had made sure everything with alright with little Tommy Simmons, he moseyed down Maple Street, keeping an eye out for Butch Hargrove and his buddies, but they were nowhere in sight; probably went through someone's yard to get away.

Parker sighed. Butch Hargrove had been a pain in his ass for nearly two years now. Small stuff mostly, loitering, vandalism, drinking. Parker had heard from some of the storeowners in town that the kid had sticky fingers, but no one had ever been able to prove it.

I'll be seeing a lot of him in the future, Parker thought as he turned onto Oak Street and started back toward Main. Kids like Hargrove were the ones who grew into the barroom brawlers and ignorant thugs every small town suffered. Vega and Yancy were just along for the ride. On their own they were harmless. Following someone like Hargrove around, however...

*

Dad was drunk when Tommy got home, so he went straight to his room and tried to pretend he didn't exist. Maybe Dad would forget he was even there, though that was unlikely.

All evening as he laid in bed, watching the shadows elongate across the ceiling, Tommy thought of the obelisk in the woods, of how good it made him feel to touch it. He thought maybe he'd go to it tonight, but he didn't know if he should. Tomorrow, definitely.

Tomorrow.

*

Past the midnight hour, the thing watched.

Concealed in a stand of bushes, it waited, its eyes red and its fury total.

The house, a small ranch, was all dark save for the glow of a light in the living room. The thing, in a mindless way, knew that its prey was in there.

Moving with supernatural stealth, the thing slithered from the bushes and moved along the western wall of the house, past a hose spigot and a flowerbed. It was beginning to rain, and the cold drops of water elated the thing. When it reached the back door, it stopped and listened. A dog barked in the distance, and someone's baby cried.

142

With one long, boney hand, the thing reached for the door handle...

*

At 12:01 AM, Sheriff James Parker pulled into the Shell station at the end of Main Street and parked alongside one of the outer gas pumps. As expected, Sparky Johnson appeared at the window within seconds, as though he'd been expecting Parker. A tall, thin man with big Coke bottle glasses and curly black hair, Sparky had been running the Shell (and the adjoining mechanic's shop) since 2008, when old man Ramirez died.

"Hey, Park, how ya doin?" he asked, resting his arm on the roof of the car and leaning close. His gray overalls were stained with grease, and he smelled of motor oil.

"Hey, Sparky," Parker said, "just fill her up."

Sparky nodded, said, "Yessir," and took the nozzle from the pump and stuck it into the car's tank. While he pumped, Parker leaned his head back against the head rest and closed his eyes. He was tired, but was he tired enough to fall asleep as soon as he went to bed? He didn't know. If he wasn't, he'd lay awake thinking of Laura, and that was probably the last thing he wanted to do.

One more round, he thought. He'd circle through town and go out toward the Carruthers' place on Schoolhouse Road. By the time he was done, it'd be past one; surely he'd be tired by then.

"Anything else?" Sparky asked. Parker opened his eyes. The younger man was in his former position, as though he'd never moved.

Parker opened his mouth to speak, but the radio squawked into life.

"Unit One, this is HQ."

Parker took the handset from its cradle and lifted it to his mouth. "Unit One. Go ahead."

The dispatcher (sounded like Margret Evans, though her shift didn't start until one) replied almost instantly. "We got a code 15 at two-six-five Parnell Street."

Code 15 was copspeak for 'unknown disturbance'.

"You got any details?" Parker replied.

"Neighbors report screaming."

"Two-six-five Parnell?"

"Two-six-five Parnell Street."

"Roger."

Parker replaced the CB. Sparky had backed away from the car.

"Gotta run," Parker said. "You mind if I pay you later?"

Sparky flapped one dirty hand. "Go 'head. I know you're good for it."

Parker nodded, thanked him, and pulled out onto the street, unconsciously flipping the overhead lights on; streaks of blue and red shot through the night.

Parnell Street was six blocks west, a long, broad avenue lined with small ranch houses and trees dancing in the night breeze. Two-six-five was a small white bungalow with pink trim and neon green shutters. A light burned in the front window.

Parker pulled to a stop at the curb and got out. The night was airy and cool, the only sound the wind moving through the trees. For a moment Parker stood by the car, surveying the house. He hated Code 15s. You never knew what to expect. It could be anything from a stubbed toe to The Texas Chainsaw Massacre.

Hand hovering near his gun, Parker followed the flagstone walk up to the porch. At the door, he knocked and waited.

No answer.

"Sheriff's department," Parker said. "Open up."

Nothing.

Parker waited a few minutes more, then he left the porch and went around back. The side of the house was lined with bushes, garden hoses, and outdoor bric-a-brac Parker couldn't place. If he got no answer here, he'd call for back-up and force his way in.

In the backyard, Parker paused. The door, at the head of a brief set of concrete steps, hung askew, its center busted and splintered.

Uh-oh.

Forced entry if I've ever seen it.

Unholstering his gun, Parker went up the steps and poked his head in. A kitchen, small and dimly lit, the floor yellow linoleum and the cabinets old, faded. Through an open archway, the living room, a lamp burning brightly on an end table.

Books, knick-knacks, and other debris littered the floor.

Parker took the radio from his belt. "This is Unit One. I am at two-six-five Parnell Street. I need assistance."

When the dispatcher acknowledged, Parker clipped the radio back to his belt and went in.

In the middle of the living room, a person (or what was left of them) was lying on the floor. Blood splattered the walls, the floor, the sofa, the TV set.

"Jesus Christ."

*

Parker watched grimly as the paramedics loaded the stretcher into the back of the ambulance. Next to him, Steve Graves was breathing heavily.

"I've never seen anything like it," he said for the fiftieth time since arriving less than an hour ago. Parker couldn't blame him. He'd never seen anything like it either. The woman (Mary Smith, a retired schoolteacher) was *savaged*. Her throat was ripped out, her eyes were clawed, and her stomach was laid open for all to see, her long, ropy intestines piled beneath her. The CSI team from Mechanicsville said it looked like she was attacked by an animal. Parker couldn't say he disagreed. The scratches, hair, and teeth marks left little room for doubt, but what kind of animal crashes through a closed door? No kind of animal *he'd* ever seen. Sure, there were bobcats in the hills, but they rarely ever came into town, and when they did, they didn't break into peoples' houses and tear them apart.

Animal, they said, and the evidence supported that.

Still, something didn't feel right.

Parker had learned long ago to trust his gut, and his gut told him this wasn't as cut and dry as it seemed.

"Make sure no one says anything until the coroner's report comes out," Parker said, turning to Steve. Steve nodded. "As far as we're concerned, we don't know what happened."

Steve nodded.

As he rushed away, Parker turned back to the house.

What happened here?

*

Early the next morning, Parker got out of bed, showered, and slid into his uniform; the room was purple and dusky, but he didn't turn on a light.

He dreaded the day ahead; not only would he have an investigation to contend with, but he'd have to allay the fears of the town as well. That meant taking phone calls and meeting with visitors, two distractions he couldn't afford.

Steeling himself for the day, Parker got out of the car, shut the door, and slipped into the station.

"You have a visitor," the desk sergeant said when he saw him, and nodded toward Parker's office; behind the glass partition, Parker saw Corwin Caruthers sitting in a chair, waiting. Parker sighed. Caruthers had been a pain in his ass since day one; he was under the impression that coming from one of the wealthiest families in the area still meant something.

It didn't.

"Have fun," the desk sergeant said.

In his office, Parker closed the door and came around his desk. Corwin Caruthers watched with steely blue eyes.

After sitting down, Parker forced a smile and said, "Good morning, Mr. Caruthers. What can I do for you?"

Caruthers, a solid man with white hair and a thick white mustache that reminded Parker of Dick Van Dyke, shifted in his seat, his spine never losing the rigid, nearer-my-god-to-thee posture Caruthers and his ilk preferred.

"I am here, Sheriff, to inquire about the progress you've made in capturing the man who killed Mary Smith."

Is that what they're saying?

Parker knew that it was. Small town rumor mills are notorious things. Not only did they have a way of disseminating news faster than fiber optic internet cable doo-dads, they had a way of disseminating the *wrong* news.

At the moment, however, Parker couldn't say that it *wasn't* a murder. Who knew? It looked like an animal attack, yeah, but even now, in the light of day, he had his doubts.

Nevertheless, he'd keep his cards close to his chest.

"It's been less than twelve hours. The CSI techs need at least a day and a half to come back with anything. We've taken witness statements. No one saw anything. We're not even sure if it *is* a murder."

"Not sure?" Caruthers asked.

"There's no definitive evidence at this point..."

"She certainly didn't fall in the shower, Sheriff. Something, some*one*, killed her, and I intend to have it stopped before anyone else is killed."

Parker sighed. "The best way you can help me is by not bothering me. If I have to deal with a thousand people coming in here all day, I won't be able to do my job. Okay?"

Caruthers's face darkened slightly. "Very well, Sheriff," Caruthers said, and stood.

Good riddance.

*

All day, Tommy thought of the thing in the woods, his excitement growing with each passing hour; though each taunt made him feel small, he took consolation in the fact that later on, alone in the serenity of the forest, he would feel big.

At lunch, Butch Hargrove flicked peas and bits of chicken at him while his butt buddies laughed, and Tommy wondered if the thing could ever make him strong enough to beat Butch up.

Finally, the last bell rang, and Tommy stole down Schoolhouse Road. He climbed over the guardrail, eased down the embankment, and slipped into the bosom of the wilderness. He was just starting along the riverbed when a voice froze him.

"Hey, Simmons! What'cha doin?"

Oh no.

Tommy turned just as Butch Hargrove and co. climbed over the guardrail.

"Hey!" Butch yelled as Tommy ran, "where you goin? Pussy!"

Over the hillock, Tommy ducked right, leapt over a fallen tree, nearly lost his balance, kept it, and followed a ridgeline for another hundred feet before dropping into a little culvert hiding a cave mouth just big enough for him to slip into.

Panting, Tommy slithered into the cave and tried desperately to wrangle his breathing. Maybe they weren't even coming.

Then he heard them kicking through the leaves. "Tommy boy!" Butch yelled, his voice echoing in the afternoon stillness. "Come out and play!"

Oh no.

The closer they came, the more Tommy's heart thudded; when they were standing right over him, it was so loud he was sure they'd hear.

"Where'd he go?" Curtis asked.

"I dunno," Butch replied, "but he's gotta be around here somewhere."

Tommy held his breath.

"What about down there?" Johnny asked, and Tommy's heart sputtered.

Suddenly Butch was there, his lips spread back over his teeth in an evil grin. "Got'cha!"

Butch dragged him out and threw him to the ground. Curtis and Johnny were there, too, laughing.

Tommy tried to get to his feet, but Butch kicked him, the tip of his boot connecting with Tommy's soft stomach. Tommy gasped as red hot agony enfolded him.

"You're gonna like this, you little queer," Butch said. He was on top of Tommy now, his legs on either side of him. The world grayed out for a moment, and Tommy thought he was going to pass out. Then, when he felt his pants being pulled down, he came alive, tried to fight, but a hard punch to the ear ended his brief revival.

Butch was panting now. "You're gonna like it."

Curtis and Johnny were silent now.

Tears welled in Tommy's eyes, but he didn't let them fall. Only girls cried. That's what his dad said when he hit him, and that's what the other kids said when they made fun of him. Only girls cry.

His pants were around his ankles down. Butch grabbed his underwear and yanked them down.

"What are you doing?" Curtis asked.

"I'm gonna give the little queer what he wants," Butch said. His breath was ragged.

"What?" Johnny asked.

Tommy heard a zipper.

"Hey, come on," Curtis said, "that is too much."

"Fuck you, fat ass."

Tommy tried one last time to fight, but Butch slammed his head into the ground; dirt went into his nose, and several of his teeth went onto the ground.

"You're crazy," Curtis said. It sounded like he was leaving.

"You can go too, spic!" Butch spat, presumably to Johnny Vega.

Soon, they were alone.

"You're gonna like it," Butch said again.

When he thrust, Tommy shrieked.

*

Sheriff James Parker parked along the curb in front of Faye's Café and sat for a long moment behind the wheel. Since leaving the station around eight, he'd talked to everyone who was within earshot of Mary Smith's murder, and all he heard was 'I heard screaming, but I didn't see anything'.

No one had.

Heaving a sigh, Parker swung out of the car and went into the café. It was just past three, yet most of the tables were filled, as was the lunch counter. Though he could have been imagining things, the level of conversation seemed to drop a few bars when he walked in, and people stole quick, furtive glances at him.

"Hi, June," Parker said as he sat at the counter. June Marsten smiled and offered her own greeting. Fifty-three last winter, June had been working at Faye's since high school. And even today she was a knock-out, tall and blonde with soft blue eyes and delicate features.

"You want a burger?" she asked, not even bothering to hand him a menu.

"Yeah," Parker said, "give me a burger. Fries, too."

While June jotted down his order and slid it through the little window into the kitchen, Parker did a quick, subtle 180. Yep. People were looking at him. They were all probably bursting with the same questions. Who did it? Why? Do you have any evidence? Have you caught him?

He hoped none of them actually asked him those, because he'd have to say no, and that would worry them even more. 'There's a murderer on the loose and the cops have nothing,' he could hear them saying. News travels fast in small towns like Cedar Point, but it changes as it travels, going in one ear as one thing and out the mouth as something slightly different. By the time it got to the last gossip in town, it'd say a serial killer was walking through the streets with an ax and chopping people left and right, and old Sheriff Parker was too worried about stuffing his face to stop him. 'Wait 'til I'm done, then I might get him.'

A few minutes later, Parker's lunch came, and he ate it quickly. When he was done, he left a tip and walked out. Thankfully, no one tried to stop him.

His luck didn't hold, though. Outside, Corwin Caruthers was there.

"Have you found anything, Sheriff?"

"No, Corwin, I haven't. If you'll excuse me..."

Caruthers watched agape as Parker climbed into his car and drove off. No one *ever* called him by his first name.

When Tommy came to, it was twilight.

For a long moment, he lay still, hovering in and out of consciousness. His head ached, his stomach ached, and his butt ached. He remembered leaving school, but that was it; everything after was a blank. He was going to the disc...and blackness.

He tried to get to his feet, but a wave of agony washed over him. His pants were down, he realized then. God, his butt hurt so bad.

Then it came back to him.

Butch Hargrove.

Tommy's stomach clenched at the memory. Butch...did something to him. Hurt him. Bad.

Gritting his teeth against the pain, Tommy pushed himself up, tears streaming freely down his cheeks. When he stood, he realized his legs were covered in blood...and he was so *sore*. He bent to pull his pants up, and a cutting pain sliced through him, bringing a scream to his lips.

They'll pay for this, Tommy thought, *they'll all pay.*

*

Twenty-four hours.

Sheriff Parker was at his desk, a cup of coffee within easy reach, and trying for the life of him to understand what the hell the paper in front of him was trying to say. Inconclusive? So it *wasn't* dog hair? What did 'pesudohyperhibridial' mean? He'd have to let someone else read it in the morning.

The fingerprint analysis, however, was clear and easy to understand: The only fingerprints in the whole house belonged to Mary Smith.

Someone knocked on the door.

Parker looked up, and sagged a little when he saw Corwin Caruthers.

"What do you have?" Caruthers asked as he came in.

"I have a pain," Parker said tightly, anger suddenly rising within him. "A pain in my ass named Corwin Caruthers."

Caruthers's face hardened. "Sheriff, I..."

"If you don't leave me alone," Parker said, "and if you keep keeping me from doing my job, I'll arrest you for obstruction of justice. Do you understand me?"

"Quite," Caruthers said.

*

Tommy Simmons crawled most of the way to the obelisk. It was too dark to see where he was going, but he could *feel* it, throbbing in the night, calling him, inviting him, offering love and understanding.

Twenty feet away, Tommy saw it. It glowed softly in the night, its faint, eerie green aura beckoning him. *Here I am*, it said, *come here. Hurry!*

Breathless with wonder, Tommy ran his hands over the smooth surface; it was warm, and thrummed under his touch.

As he caressed it, Tommy watched his hands change. The backs became hairy, and his fingers elongated, his nails growing long and sharp.

"They'll pay," Tommy said again.

His mind went blank.

The obelisk was in control.

*

Who did that fool think he was?

Corwin Caruthers shuddered with rage as he navigated the Lincoln along Schoolhouse Road. Trees pressed closely against the guardrail, their leaves wavering in the warm breeze.

He'd make damn sure that son of a bitch lost reelection next year. He'd do whatever it took. That was the Caruthers way. By hook, crook, or bribery, his grandfather used to say. Why...

Something smashed into the front end of the Lincoln, knocking it to the left; Caruthers, panicking, spun the wheel, but it froze in his hands. He stomped the brakes, but it was too late. The car was rolling.

When it came to a rest, the door was wrenched open, and before the thing savaged him, the last thing Corwin Caruthers thought was: *My beautiful car!*

*

Butch Hargrove finished the last beer in the fridge, and tossed the empty onto the kitchen floor.

"You're outta beer," he called over his shoulder.

No answer.

Butch sighed. Dad was probably passed out in his chair again. That meant there'd be no more beer tonight. Whatever. He had a little baggie of pot in his room; he'd smoke it and go to sleep.

Closing the fridge, Butch rubbed his crotch; it was still tender from earlier.

Butch chuckled as he remembered Tommy Simmons screaming and fighting. The little fag wanted it, Butch knew he did.

Maybe he'd do it again tomorrow. At school.

The thought sent a shiver of pleasure up Butch's spine.

Someone knocked at the back door.

Cops, Butch thought. *The little fuck told!*

The door exploded open, and a tall, hunched *thing* with glowing red

150

eyes was suddenly on him.

Butch screamed.

When it pulled his pants down and did to him what he'd done to Tommy Simmons, he *wailed*.

*

Jeffery Simmons finished the last pint of whisky in the house, and settled into his chair for a long night of pay-per-view porn.

At 12:15, the first movie started. Anal Nurses 10. He slipped his hand down his pants and touched himself. This was gonna be *good*.

The front door burst open then with a sound like Armageddon. The thing standing in the doorway, hunched over, fixed its red gaze on him, and his heart froze. Sinewy and dog-like, its back covered in a rake of wicked quills, it reminded him of a wolf, but at the same time of a human skeleton.

When it pounced, he screamed.

*

Sheriff James Parker was just getting ready to leave for the night when Steve Graves popped his head in the door, his face a white mask of worry.

"James, something's happening."

Parker looked up from his paperwork. Not ten minutes before, two of his men left on a disturbance call. Worry suddenly filled him.

"What is it?" he asked, getting to his feet.

"Sloan and Mason..."

Before he could finish, a loud *whump!* filled the world; the floor shook and the windows rattled in their frames.

"The fuck?"

Rushing, Parker followed Steve out into the warm spring night. Flickering firelight bathed the buildings along Main Street. Looking south, Parker saw the Citgo on the corner of Spruce and Main; it was engulfed, the flames whirling high into the night.

"Jesus Christ," Graves muttered. Quickly, he told Parker what he'd been about to inside: Sloan, one of the officers dispatched to the disturbance, radioed in saying a 'thing' attacked him and Mason on Maple Street, ripping Mason from the car and throwing him against a streetlight. Sloan, behind the wheel, cut to the left, slammed into a fire hydrant, and scrambled out. In the spill of light from someone's front porch, he saw the thing *eating* Mason. "When it looked up he said it was a werewolf."

Other cops had come out now. Three had left just before the explosion to assist Sloan.

151

For a moment, Parker helplessly watched the flames. Thing? Werewolf? None of it made any sense.

Regardless, two of his men were in danger.

Now the Citgo.

Parker opened his mouth to speak, but closed it again as something moved in the fire.

"What the shit?" Graves asked.

Someone...*something*...emerged from the flames, its shoulders stooped, its profile human but somehow *not*, taller, leaner, more crooked. The thing lashed out, knocking a burning car aside the way a normal man would a beer can, and continued toward them.

"The hell is that?" Graves asked.

As if on cue, the thing jerked its arm; before Parker knew what was happening, a steel hubcap was slicing through the air. Parker screamed, ducked, and watched as it slammed Graves in the head. For a moment the deputy stood where he was, stunned, then, as the blood began to cascade over his face, he collapsed.

The other cops swarmed him. Someone took his pulse. He was dead.

The thing was still coming.

Parker fumbled his gun out and raised it.

The thing kept coming.

"Stop!" Parker cried.

It didn't stop.

Parker fired.

The thing didn't even flinch.

Panicking now, Parker ducked back into the station. The others, looking and babbling, followed. When they were inside, Parker slammed the door.

Outside, something else exploded.

"We gotta get outta here!" Parker yelled

Outside, crashing, scraping, twinkling.

Parker started toward the back.

The door crashed open behind him; a detached fire hydrant smashed through the wall next to him. Screams rose.

Stumbling, Parker caught himself and looked over his shoulder. The thing was standing in the doorway, seeming to huff and puff. Its face was wolf-like, long and angular, but its body was covered in spiky quills, and its claws were long, like kitchen knives.

Someone opened fire on it, and it absorbed the bullets like nothing. When it looked up, Parker saw its red eyes, its long, crooked fangs, its snout/muzzle, its scaly face.

He screamed and bolted. Behind him, the thing shrieked, a loud, piercing dinosaur-like sound. Gunshots rose.

Outside, jabbering with hysteria, Parker climbed into the car, and squealed out of the parking lot, turning west. Main Street was in ruins from the station to the Citgo. Storefronts were smashed, sidewalks were torn up, trees and newspaper dispensers littered the street.

He didn't realize he was turning onto Schoolhouse Road until his headlights flashed across the ancient brick façade.

He'd go to Preston, he decided. Call the state police. The National Guard. Somebody, *anybody*.

When he came to the wreck two minutes later, his stomach clutched. Corwin Caruthers was scattered across the highway, a leg here, an arm there.

His battered Lincoln blocked the road.

Parker executed a U-turn and started back toward town. At Schoolhouse Road, he went to turn, but stopped. In the wan light of the moon, he saw the thing pawing at the door of the middle school. When it couldn't open it, it smashed through in epic fury. Parker was so transfixed by the sight that he almost got out and followed.

The sound of breaking glass brought him out of it. The thing was savaging the school.

At his house five minutes later, Parker picked up the phone in the living room, but it was dead. The thing must have taken the phone lines out.

Half the electrical lines too, by the looks of it. A large section of Cedar Point was dark, and the rest was on fire. Parker's eyes were inexorably drawn to the school.

As if on cue, it exploded.

*

When they searched the rubble of Cedar Point Middle School six hours later, they found only one body. A child. Roughly twelve or thirteen.

"Keep looking," Parker said. The National Guardsmen obeyed.

"It's gotta be out there somewhere," Parker said nervously, scanning the dark hills surrounding Cedar Point.

But it was over.

Tommy Simmons's fury had been spent.

They paid.

They *all* paid.

In the woods, the thing from outer space glowed.

PAINT

Beep-beep-beep.

Sean Barnes opened his eyes. The bedside clock's digital readout was a red smear. He blinked, and the picture swam into focus: 5:57.

Sean moaned, hit the snooze button, and rolled over, bumping into Jen, who snorted, stirred, and fell silent.

Beep-beep-beep.

Sean was catapulted from the murky depths of sleep once more. He turned, saw that it was 6:02, and slammed the snooze button again, sudden anger rising in his stomach. It was too early for this shit.

"You getting up?" Jen asked sleepily.

Sean settled onto his back. Cold, dreary light had begun to seep into the room. He could make out indistinct shapes in the gloom. The dresser. The TV. The half-open door to the master bath.

"Sean?"

"Yes," he snapped, "I'm getting up."

Jen shifted position. "Grumpy," she said.

Sighing, Sean sat up, swinging his legs from beneath the blanket. For a moment he sat there, his head swimming. When he trusted himself to move without falling over, he slid a cigarette from his pack and plopped it into his mouth. He lit it, drawing the heavy smoke into his lungs, and closed his eyes. When he felt himself beginning to drift, he opened them again.

It was going to be a *long* day.

When he was done with his cigarette, he stamped it out in the glass ashtray next to the clock, turned the alarm off completely, and got up. He pissed, washed his face, and looked at himself in the mirror over the sink. His eyes were bloodshot. Dark bags drooped halfway down his face. He thought he looked like a raccoon. A sleep-deprived raccoon.

Back in the bedroom, he dressed in a pair of camouflage shorts and a dark brown t-shirt. He pulled his socks and shoes on, lit another cigarette, and went into the kitchen. As he waited for the coffee to brew, he gazed out the window at the courtyard between his building and the next one over; a light mist clung to the ground. Over the terra cotta roof of the complex across the way, the sky was a cold mixture of orange and purple. The weatherman said it would be in the high fifties in the morning, but by noon it would be in the low eighties. He shivered.

When the coffee was done, he drained a cup and then poured some into a thermos. He went back into the bedroom, dropped onto the bed, and patted Jen's hip. She turned over.

"I should tell 'em I'm sick."

"No," Jen said.

To be honest, Sean didn't even want to go; the idea of spending two whole days traipsing around the woods with a paintball gun appealed to him far less than the prospect of spending two days on the couch, recuperating from the long week just passed. The only reason he was going was the fishing. Bob said there was a river near the cabin and that you could throw out a bare line and catch massive trout till Judgment Day. Sean was an avid fisherman, and couldn't resist the promise of a righteous fishing spot.

Sean patted Jen again. On the nightstand, his phone buzzed, the screen going from black to white.

Great. They were already busting his balls.

He grabbed the phone and read the text. It was from Bob. "You coming?"

Sean shoved the phone into his pocket and leaned over, kissing Jen on the cheek. "I love you," he said.

"I love you too," she muttered. "Have fun."

"I'll try," he said, standing. At the front door, he grabbed his bag, which he had packed the night before, and slung it over his shoulder. It was heavy; the strap dug into his flesh. Oh well. It was all the shit he needed.

Outside, the morning was crisp, and Sean shuddered, wishing he'd dressed better. His Tahoe was parked in a spot next to a Honda. He unlocked it, climbed in, and started the engine. Iggy Azala filled the cab. Wincing, Sean found a station playing Biggie Smalls.

The streets of El Morro were empty at that hour. On his way to Bob's place, he saw only a cop and a few assorted vehicles most likely belonging to the poor bastards who worked the night shift at the power plant on US6. In town, the storefronts were dark and shuttered. A homeless man lay on a bench, a thin blanket pulled over his emaciated frame. Knowing how cold it was, Sean felt for the guy.

At the intersection of Main and Oak, guarded by a blinking caution light, Sean hung a right and then a left. The street ahead was narrow and lined with small ranch houses. He pulled to the curb in front of the bungalow Bob and Joe shared, and whipped out his phone, firing Bob a simple, "Here."

While he waited, Sean studied the grimy façade of the house, its white siding smudged with dirt and dust. The yard was bare and brown, and the detached garage was falling apart. He'd offered to help Bob fix it, but he kept refusing.

Five minutes passed, then someone came out the side door. Squinting, Sean saw who it was. Joe, dressed in a long-sleeve shirt with a yellow 1 on the back. He was lugging a heavy bag. Bob followed right behind, setting his bag on the porch so he could close and lock the door.

Joe and Bob were a study in contrasts. The former was short and chunky, while the latter was tall and thin. While they looked nothing alike, their personalities matched like puzzle pieces. They both enjoyed dark humor, pop culture, and general misanthropy. At the restaurant, they routinely bad-mouthed the customers, lavishing particular hatred on the regulars.

"How pitiful," Joe had said on Thursday. He was leaning against the sink, his gray T-shirt soaked with water from the sink. *"You come in here every day and always eat the same thing. I'd hate to be that predictable."*

"It's sad," Bob agreed.

Their crap got old after a while, and Sean told them to knock it off. *"You don't like it, bro, you can go work somewhere else."*

That comment was directed at Joe; ninety percent of the time he was the one who started it.

Fucking whiners.

Presently, Joe tossed his bag into the back of the Tahoe and climbed into the passenger seat.

"What's up?" Sean asked.

"Nothing," Joe replied. He sounded like Sean felt: Tired.

Bob threw his own bag into the back and climbed in behind Sean.

"Bobby! How's it going?"

"Alright," Bob said, pulling the door closed. "Tired."

"Yeah, me too," Sean said as he pulled away from the curb.

At the end of the street, Sean turned right, drove back to Main, followed it, and then took a left.

"You're going the wrong way," Joe said.

"Yeah," Bob said, "the freeway's back there."

"We're picking up Kristen."

Joe's head whipped around. In the back, Bob made a small noise of disgust. "I thought she was riding with Derrick," Joe said.

"She was," Sean said, spinning the wheel, "until he decided to leave at five in the morning."

Kristen Hocksetter was a server, front of the house whereas the rest of them (with the exception of Derrick) were back of the house. No one in the kitchen particularly liked her. She was sloppy, forgetful, and pushy. On days Joe washed dishes, she badgered him every five minutes for silverware. By the end of the day, he was shaking and muttering under his breath. Bob, stationed at the grill, was driven into fits of barely suppressed rage by her sloppy handwriting.

"Great," Bob said now. "Just what my morning needed."

Joe chuckled. "And you get to sit next to her. Lucky dog."

"Yeah. Yeah. Real nice."

They turned onto Kristen's street, and parked next to the driveway, a brief concrete slab sloping up to the house.

Kristen must have been waiting, for as soon as they pulled up she emerged from the side door, a backpack over her shoulder. She was tall, thin, and pushing forty-five, her long brown hair already showing signs

156

of going gray. Her face was long, narrow, and her nose was too big. Joe said she looked like a horse, and Sean couldn't say that she didn't. Her rack was nice, though.

Unconsciously following the pattern established by Joe, she threw her bag into the back and climbed in behind the passenger seat.

"Hey, girl," Sean said, glancing back.

"Morning," she said as she slipped her seatbelt on. "How's everyone feeling?"

"Just peachy," Bob said.

"Just peachy?" She let loose a braying laugh, and in the passenger seat, Joe winced.

I fucking hate her, he mouthed.

Sean shook his head and drove to the end of the street, turned around in someone's driveway, and started toward the freeway. Six minutes later exactly, they pulled onto the onramp and joined the already busy flow of traffic heading north.

By now, the sun had fully risen, bathing the world in golden light, and Sean slipped on a pair of sunglasses. The light stung his eyes.

For the first twenty miles, houses and shopping centers sloped away from the road, protected by metal fences and concrete retaining walls. North of Malcasa, the farmland started. Vast, rolling hills receding from the roadside, dotted with barns, grain silos, and grazing pastures.

"Anyone hungry?" Sean asked. His stomach had been growling since before they got on the freeway.

"Yeah," Joe said. "I haven't eaten since yesterday afternoon."

"I made dinner," Bob said. "You could have eaten."

Joe snorted. Turning to Sean, he said, "Get this. Dickhole back there makes a lasagna. When it came out of the oven, it looked like a fucking soup."

"What?" Sean asked, glancing in the rearview mirror. "How'd you manage *that*?"

"I cooked it in the dishwasher," Bob said sullenly.

"You can actually do that, you know," Joe said.

"Yeah, I heard that," Bob said. "I think they tried it on *Mythbusters*."

"I saw it on *Hack my Life*," Joe replied.

"The dishwasher?" Kristen asked.

"Yeah," Bob said. "You have to cover it really tight with foil."

"That's when you wanna slow cook something," Joe said.

"Yeah," Bob chuckled. "Cook and do dishes at the same time."

"Leave your ribs in there all day."

"Watch your electric bill rise."

Joe turned in his seat. "You ever see that episode of *Seinfeld* where Kramer has a garbage disposal installed in his bathtub, and he makes salad and shit while he's taking a shower?"

"Gross," Kristen said.

"No, I didn't see that one," Bob replied. "Wonder how many pubes wound up on the plate?"

Joe laughed.

"You guys are sick," Sean said. He tried to change lanes, but a little red sports car zoomed up from behind them and blocked him. Come *on*.

The car inched ahead and put on its signal; then it came into his lane, sped up, and changed lanes again.

Dick.

Throwing on his own turn signal, Sean pulled into the westernmost lane. Signs flashed by. Food. Lodging. Gas. Up ahead, the freeway rose over a tiny smattering of buildings that might have been a town. He could see a McDonald's sign.

His stomach roared.

Sean took the off-ramp and followed it to a surface street. Next to the on-ramp was a Dunkin Donuts. When the traffic light changed to green, he crossed the street and pulled into the parking lot, falling in line behind a brown Toyota.

"Who wants what?"

They wound up getting two dozen donuts and one iced coffee apiece.

Back on the highway, Sean shoved a Boston Cream into his mouth and got back in the center lane. The highway continued into the rugged foothills surrounding Inca. Bob said the place was about three hundred miles out. When Sean checked Google Maps the night before, it said it was more like 350.

While Sean drove, Joe and Bob talked about a thousand different things, all of them sailing clear over Sean's head. *Angry Video Game Nerd* this, *Rocko's Modern Life* that. Sometimes he wondered if they just made shit up to fuck with everyone around them.

After a while their voices started getting on his nerves, so he turned up the radio. Some Drake song he'd never like was on but he didn't care.

"This shit, really?" he heard Joe ask.

Sean liked Joe and Bob, he did, they were funny and they worked hard, but sometimes he wanted to strangle them.

Kristen was oddly silent. When he looked in the rearview mirror, he saw her leaning against the window, her eyes closed and her lips twitching.

He knew how she felt.

Sixty miles past Victoria, Bob leaned between the seats. "Get off at the next exit," he said.

Sean took the off-ramp.

"Take a right."

Sean turned the truck onto a narrow two-lane highway. Up ahead, it curved steeply to the left, disappearing into the mountains.

From there, the road became a series of twists, turns, and switchbacks. For most of the length, a rocky hillface flanked the right side, while a sheer drop dogged the left. Gazing out over it, Sean had a sweeping view of the valley below, crisscrossed with highways and rivers, dotted with houses and towns. It reminded him of home, the steep foothills of eastern Oregon.

A half hour after leaving the interstate, the road leveled out and bent to the right. Dense forests pushed against the highway on both sides like the vanguards of sentient armies.

"The trailhead's up there," Bob said, pointing.

One final bend, and they were there: Derrick's black Ford F-250 was parked in the tall grass between the road and the treeline, the ass end facing them. Derrick was sitting on the tailgate, his legs lazily kicking the wind. Robert was next to him, a blue can in his hand. When he looked up and saw them, he nodded his head. Derrick looked up, smiled, and shoved himself off the tailgate.

Slowing, Sean rolled down the passenger window. Poking his head in, Derrick's smile widened. "Howdy, howdy! You boys ready for some paintball?"

Kristen cleared her throat; Sean didn't know she was awake.

"Boys and girl," Derrick amended with mock embarrassment.

"I'm ready for some fishin'," Sean said, and that was the truth. Screw paintball.

"Well, let's go. Me and Robert been waiting for you for almost two hours."

Derrick stepped back, and Sean drove off, passing the Ford. He did a U-turn and pulled onto the grass, bringing his bumper to within inches of Derrick's.

"Alright," he said. He cut the engine, put the keys in his pocket, and hopped out. While Kirsten, Bob, and Joe grabbed their gear from the back, he smoked a cigarette. Robert came over, bummed one, and nodded as he lit it. At six feet even, Robert was tall. He wore his blonde hair long and his beard nappy. He was wearing a tie-dye shirt and a pair of ripped jeans.

"You're gonna stick out like a sore thumb," Sean said, taking a drag.

"Whatever," Robert said, shrugging. "I'm quick."

When he was done with his cigarette, Robert went back to the Ford's tailgate and stood next to Derrick. Beefy and broad, Derrick stood six inches taller than Robert. He was a linebacker in high school, and was on the team during their perfect season back in 2000. Sean was the goal kicker that year, but messed up his leg in the second game and had to sit the rest of the season out. Though he never let on, he kind of envied Derrick for playing the full season; from what he heard they were *still* talking about it.

Joe, Bob, and Kristen were done getting their things. Leaning over the side of the bed, Sean grabbed his own bag. Zipping it open, he pulled out his gun (a Spyder with a top-loading drum...it cost him a fortune, but it was one of the best) and a pair of goggles, which he slipped on. The world took on a yellow tint.

When he joined the others, they were laughing, gathered around the tailgate and drinking beer as though they were waiting for the Superbowl to start. "What's so funny?" he asked, bending down and grabbing a Bud from the Styrofoam cooler on the ground.

Brushing away a mock tear, Derrick asked, "When do you know it's bedtime at Michael Jackson's house?"

Sean chuckled, already knowing where it was heading. "When?"

"When the big hand touches the little hand."

Sean laughed. It wasn't really funny, but none of Derrick's jokes ever were. It was the corniness that made them palatable.

Shaking his head, Derrick went over to the tailgate, zipped open his bag, and brought out a flimsy plastic gun. Sean didn't know what brand it was, but at a glance he guessed Derrick picked it up at Wal-Mart or somewhere.

"Alright, Bobby," he said. "It's your show."

Bob, already wearing a pair of goggles, shrugged. "The path goes about a mile in before forking. Both lead to the cabin. I guess one team can go one way and the other team can go the other."

"Speaking of teams," Derrick said, "how we doin this?"

Joe, cradling his gun in his hand (Sean noted it was a Tiburius...good brand), shrugged. "I just wanna be on the team opposite Bob so I can cream his ass."

"Okay," Bob mocked.

"Show you what it feels like to be a Nazi on D-Day."

"Show *you* what it feels like to be a Jew in Dachau."

"Girls," Derrick said, holding up a hand. "Focus."

Shrugging, Bob said, "I dunno. Me, Sean, and Robert against you, Joe, and Kristen?"

Derrick nodded. "Yeah, that works."

When they were ready, they went into the woods.

*

Richard Granger, fifty-three and balding, pulled the white sedan off the main highway and started down a long dirt road lined with dense underbrush. He checked the rearview mirror, inexplicably certain that he would see a cop car in his dust, and breathed a sigh of relief when the dirt cloud was empty.

The road dipped and bent to the right; Richard navigated it with the care of a man walking through an unfamiliar room in the dark. He'd been out here plenty in his life, but not in fifteen years; fallen trees were a real hazard on the roads crisscrossing the mountains.

Several miles farther on, the tees fell away from the roadside, and to the left he could see the Rock River meandering past. Its further bank was crowded with pines.

Going off road, he followed a narrow dirt tract through the clearing and to the tree line. He swung the car around, and backed carefully to the trees.

He killed the engine, got out, and went around to the trunk. Pressing the button on his key fob, the trunk popped open.

Curled into a tight ball, Missy Granger looked asleep.

But she was dead.

For a moment, Richard lingered over her body, his hands braced on either side. He remembered their wedding day, how they exchanged sentimental vows on Fisherman's Warf, how she looked in her wedding dress. Young and bright and happy. His heart ached.

Then he remembered finding her in bed with that Jefferson asshole, the one from her work. He remembered the devastation, the horror, the tears. And how she laughed.

"You can't even get it up," she snorted. *"How am I supposed to get off on a limp dick?"*

She was so cruel, so uncaring, it shocked him, though in hindsight, she had slowly become that way over years, not overnight. She browbeat him. She criticized him. She emasculated him in front of his friends and his family. Though no one ever said anything to his face, he knew they all thought he was a henpecked wimp. The flash of anger he felt right before he strangled her surprised him, but, he supposed, it shouldn't have. It had been simmering for years, so low and slow that not even he himself was aware of it.

Shaking his head, he grabbed the shovel from the trunk and closed the lid. He scanned the road, hoping no one happened along and saw him, and ducked into the woods. The forest floor was thick with fallen leaves from autumns past. They crunched as he waded through them. Back from the treeline, the woods opened up a little, becoming less densely packed. He found a nice flat spot and began digging.

As he worked, he thought of his alibi. What would he tell the police? He knew they always suspected the husband first, so he had to come up with one quick. Maybe he could get Dave, his brother, to lie and say they spent the weekend at Lake Tahoe, or in Vegas. He didn't know for sure, but he suspected Dave would back him up. It might take a couple kilos of free coke, but that was no big deal. Richard knew people who dealt.

He was so lost in thought that he didn't hear the crunching leaves behind him, didn't feel the nearness of someone else. He didn't know he was being watched until he turned, his forehead and armpits damp with sweat.

Then he saw.

The hole was roughly four feet deep at that point, the surrounding forest flush with his chest. At first he saw only the rounded tips of sturdy hiking shoes. His heart catching in his chest *(Discovered! They'll eat me alive in prison!)*, he looked up. Jeans. A leather jacket, tight on a small frame. A motorcycle style helmet with a face shield.

The last thing Richard Granger saw was the gun. It looked like an Uzi, he thought wildly as the stranger raised it.

Gunshots echoed in the forest, scaring birds from the treetops.

That's how Richard Granger wound up buried in the forest instead of his wife.

*

Sean stumbled through a screen of branches and came to the bank of the river, the grass reaching up to his waist.

"Man, it's hot," Robert said. He dropped down next to a tree and pulled out a metal flask, from which he drank.

"That's water, right?"

Robert shook his head. "Jack," he said with a sheepish grin.

Sean sighed. "That'll dehydrate you even more."

As Robert shrugged, Sean sat next to him, resting his back against the gnarled trunk of a twisted redwood. Before them, the river, at this point roughly fifty feet across, moved sluggishly. To the north, it bent around a rocky peninsula jutting from the forest, and continued west. Past the bend, the land rose, the trees covering it like shag carpeting. Somewhere over the smaller rise but before the larger one, Sean thought, was the cabin. Bob said it was small but nice; last week he and Joe drove up and stocked it with everything they'd need for the weekend.

"My dad hasn't been up here in years," he told them as they walked along the path before splitting at the fork. "Basically, it's mine."

Derrick, Joe, and Kristen went off on their trail, and for a while, Sean, Robert, and Bob stuck to theirs. A mile past the fork, however, Bob suggested they split up, saying it would be easier for the other team to take them out if they were grouped together. It made sense, Sean thought, agreeing; Bob instantly took off into the woods, and as he stalked through the brush, Sean caught flashes of him along the path. He finally lost sight of him ten minutes before coming to the river.

"I can't wait to fish," Robert said, lighting a cigarette. His gun sat forgotten in his lap.

"Yeah," Sean said. He liked Robert, but whenever they fished together, he, Sean, would have to bait Robert's hook and, sometimes, cast it out for him too. He wasn't much of an outdoorsman, that is...the only nature he cared about was weed.

For a moment longer they watched the river. The damp, earthy smell of the water was overlaid by the acrid tang of Robert's smoke.

Sean sighed. "I think you should follow the river," Sean said. "I'll go back to the path. That way we'll have one guy on the left, one on the

162

right, and one in the center."

Robert nodded, flicking his cigarette away; it landed in the soft mud flanking the river.

Grunting, Robert got to his feet. "See ya," he said, starting off along the river, the grass concealing everything below his thighs.

"Keep your head low!" Sean called after him.

Robert lifted one arm in acknowledgement.

When he was gone, Sean leaned back against the tree trunk and gazed absently at the trees crowding the far shore. A sense of tranquility settled over him, and for the first time in years he realized just how much he loved the outdoors. Growing up in rural Oregon, Sean had been a great lover of Mother Nature. On weekends, he would rise early, before everyone else in the house, make a lunch, and then go off into the woods, sometimes hiking as many as ten miles. He remembered lazy afternoons on high peaks overlooking the forested hills, with the fresh blue sky above, and a dull ache clutched his chest. It was like nostalgia, but stronger. Loss?

Shaking his head, he pulled out his smart phone and checked it.

No service.

He put the phone back into his pocket with a sigh. For some reason he wanted to text Jen, to tell her just how much he loved her. Though he knew he took her for granted, he missed her, and the thought of not seeing her until Sunday evening pained him.

He looked at the gun in his lap. He imagined raising it, opening fire, plugging Derrick or Kristen with a stream of red balls. When Bob first brought up the trip, it sounded like fun, even if only vaguely. Now it seemed stupid. Childish, even.

He sighed.

Maybe he *should* have begged off. Right now he and Jen could be having lunch at a restaurant on the beach, or snuggling on the couch and watching TV. Even the thought of lying on the couch bored sounded nice. It was hot, sticky, the clear blue sky having turned flat gray, and already his feet and back were sore. Given the circumstances, even the promise of good fishing later on didn't appeal to him. He wondered briefly if he could pawn Kristen, Joe, and Bob off on Derrick and then go home alone. There would be space enough in the Ford for all of them to fit.

He decided against it, however. He would stay, he thought, and he would have fun. Getting up, he pulled his goggles on and grabbed his gun.

*

Derrick Johnson crept along the winding path like a cop from *Law and Order*, the gun before him, but held close to his body. He read somewhere that cops on TV always held their guns wrong: their arms reaching out. The writer of the article (or was it in a book?) said that a perp could easily knock the gun aside and jump the cop. He doubted anyone would try that here, but he wasn't taking any chances. Robert wasn't a concern; he was probably off somewhere smoking a blunt. Sean and Bob, however, worried him. Both were crafty.

Stopping, Derrick scanned the trees on both sides of the path. Through their twisted bows, he could see only fifteen, maybe twenty feet; *anyone* could be hiding just beyond his line of sight. He listened, but heard nothing.

Leaving the path, Derrick crouched behind a tree and removed the mossy oak walkie talkie from his pocket. Before they split up at the fork, Bob handed one to each of them. "To keep in touch."

Now, he twisted the knob on top, turning it on, and depressed the TALK button.

"Joey, you there?"

Joe's voice cut through the static. "I'm here."

"Where are you?"

For a minute Joe didn't reply, then: "I don't know. In the woods. I'm pretty sure the path's off to my left."

"How far to the cabin?"

"Two-and-a-half miles from the fork."

Derrick nodded. The rules of the game were simple. At the cabin, perched on a ridge overlooking the mountains, two flags were hung carefully from the porch, one red, one blue. The object of the game was to grab the opposing team's flag and bring it back to the trailhead, through the forest, without being hit. If you were hit in the chest or back, you were out. You could take a hit to the arm or leg and stay in the game, but if you snatched the flag and got back to the trailhead covered in paint, you were disqualified, and the other team automatically won. Derrick liked the premise of the game, but thought it would work better with more people. As it stood, each time had only three chances at the flag. He didn't think Kristen would make it; she'd probably be the first one shot. Joe *might* do it, but Derrick doubted.

The responsibility, then, fell to him.

"Keep going," Derrick said into the radio.

"Alright."

Derrick turned it off and slipped it into his pants.

He stood, crept back onto the path, and started toward the cabin. The path bent ahead, and the land suddenly became steeper; hills buffered both sides.

Derrick glanced over his shoulder.

No one.

When he turned back around, someone was standing in the path.

Derrick froze.

The man wore jeans, a tight leather jacket, and a motorcycle helmet with the wind visor down, covering his face. A gun was cradled in his hands.

Derrick way maybe fifteen feet from the guy; just far enough away that he couldn't see whether the gun was real or not.

He was pretty sure that it wasn't Bob or Sean. Definitely not Joe.

Derrick opened his mouth to say something, to ask the guy who he was, but the guy swung the gun up and fired.

A hot fist slammed into Derrick's stomach, fire enveloping him. For a wild moment he couldn't believe what was happening, couldn't believe that he had been shot. Then a second bullet hit him, tearing into his right shoulder and driving him back.

I'm being shot! he thought.

The gunman was coming forward then, raising the gun.

This can't be happening! This...

The final shot hit Derrick in the forehead, passing through his brain and mushrooming out the back of his skull, sailing through the air in a mist of blood and gray matter.

Derrick was dead before he hit the ground.

*

Sean crouched behind a fallen tree covered in moss and watched as Joe moved past the pines thirty feet distant. He aimed, but there were so many trees in the way that he couldn't get a good shot.

When Joe emerged from cover, he quickly ducked behind a large rock.

Damn.

Holding his breath, Sean climbed over the fallen oak and quietly dropped into the leaves. Joe's head appeared from behind the boulder. Shit.

Before he could act, Joe brought his gun up and fired. A blue ball splattered on the ground in front of him.

Leaping back over the tree, Sean crouched down.

"I see your bitch ass!" Joe called, his voice echoing in the forest.

Sean, gritting his teeth, popped up and returned fire. Three of his balls crashed into the boulder next to Joe, who ducked down.

Before he knew what was happening, Bob stepped from the brush behind Joe and fired twice. Yelping as the paintballs stung his skin, Joe sank to the ground.

Sean laughed. "Bobby!" he yelled triumphally, raising his gun into the air.

"Motherfucker!" Joe screamed, getting to his feet and throwing the gun into the leaves. "You snuck up on me!"

Bob was laughing. "You shouldn't have been out in the open."

Joe was about to reply when a gunshot rang out, followed by three more in rapid succession. Birds flew from the treetops, startled, cawing to one another as if in warning.

Sean, Joe, and Bob looked at each other.

"The fuck was that?" Joe asked, looking around.

"Someone's shooting," Bob said.

Sean scanned the forest. He couldn't see anything.

"Is it hunting season?" Joe asked.

"No. Hunting season doesn't start 'til November."

Sean came over the tree and joined them by the path. "Maybe someone's target practicing."

"I don't know," Bob said, "maybe, but..."

Kristen screamed.

Sean's heart leapt into his throat.

Joe and Bob were already running, already crashing through the underbrush. Sean followed, leaping over rocks and twisted tree roots. Gruesome images danced through his mind: Kristen lying across the path, blood seeping from wounds to her chest and back; Derrick or Robert curled up as the life drained from their shattered bodies, a half-wit yokel standing nearby, shocked that shooting randomly in the woods could *possibly* hurt someone.

Sean came back to reality as he crashed through the trees lining the second path.

What he saw stopped him in his tracks.

Derrick was lying on his back, his feet spread and his arms thrown out, reminding Sean hysterically of Christ on the cross. Blood splattered the path around him.

Kristen was nowhere to be seen.

Bob and Joe were both kneeling by Derrick. As he got closer, Sean could see that one of the bullets took Derrick in the forehead. Brains and bits of skull lay in ugly clumps around his head.

"Oh, my God," Sean muttered.

From the woods, Kristen screamed.

Like a shot, Bob was up, plunging into the woods with his paintball gun. For a moment, Sean froze, didn't know what to do, where to go. Another shot rang out, and he dropped to the ground.

Joe was sprawled beside Derrick, his hands on his head. He was facing Sean. His eyes were wide and frightened.

A few minutes later, Bob emerged from the woods. His face was drawn and pale. "He shot her," he mumbled. He stared ahead like a man who's just watched his hometown struck by a tornado.

Sean got to his feet just as Bob sank to his knees.

"What happened?" he asked.

Joe was sitting up now, looking worriedly into the woods.

Bob acted as though he didn't hear.

"Bobby, what happened?"

Sean was kneeling beside him now, shaking him.

Bob shook his head and looked up. "He was dragging her away. When he saw me, he shot her in the head and took off."

A hammerhead of horror struck Sean's heart. He glanced up into the forest, which seemed darker now, more malevolent.

"Who was it?" he asked.

Bob shook his head. "I don't know. He was wearing a helmet."

"You're sure she's dead?"

Bob nodded. "I felt for her pulse. It died under my hand."

He shivered as he remembered.

"We gotta get the fuck outta here," Joe said, getting to his feet. "He's gonna come back and waste us all."

Bob looked at Sean.

"We scared him off," Sean said, but didn't believe. He squinted into the woods but couldn't see anything past the tree trunks.

He was out there, watching. Sean knew it like he knew his own name. Even if Bob *did* momentarily scare him off, he would be back, realizing he couldn't leave any witnesses.

The cars. They had to get to the cars. Sean said as much, but Bob shook his head.

"We'd be better off going to the cabin," he said. "It's closer."

"How far?" Sean asked.

"A mile. It's three to the road."

Sean and Joe looked at each other. The same thought passed through their minds. Going back to the cars would leave them exposed too long. If the guy was going to come back, they had a better chance of reaching the cabin than the cars.

Sean sighed. At the cabin, they'd be stuck.

Joe, seeming to read his thoughts, said: "There's a CB at the cabin. We can call someone."

"There are guns, too," Bob added, getting to his feet.

Sean looked down at Derrick. Flies were already landing on his gaping head.

"Alright," he said, pulling out the walkie talkie Bob had given him. He depressed the TALK button. "Robert? You there?"

Nothing but static.

"Robert?"

No reply.

They looked at each other.

"He probably doesn't have his radio on," Sean said, but wondered, his stomach twisting.

"I hope so," Bob said.

So did Sean.

Robert Hellsmen followed the river until it curved, and then picked up a deer path which led up a gentle, grassy rise. Trees lined either side, their branches dancing in the warm wind. At the top of the rise, Robert saw the cabin, a rustic one story house with a wraparound porch sitting on a ridge. To get there, Robert would have to cross a wide, open field, go through a cluster of trees, and then climb a fairly steep hill. Bushes and the occasional tree dotted the hillside. He figured he would be able to use them to pull himself to the summit.

Going over to one of the trees guarding the forest, Robert sank down and rested, the damp heat of the day sapping steadily at his energy. He wasn't much of a strategizer, but he knew damn well crossing an open field with virtually no cover was a risky move. If one of the other team members was in the forest, they'd have a clear shot at him. Once he reached the grove of trees he would be okay for the moment, but then he would be exposed again. The hillside really worried him. It was so steep that he would probably have to crawl. To do that he would have to sling his gun over his shoulder, rendering him helpless: At least crossing the field he would be able to shoot back.

Setting his gun and pack aside, he reached into the right front pocket of his tattered jeans and removed a small cellophane baggie. He held it up in the light and examined the contents. Subtracting the few stems and seeds, he would have enough for three bowls. One now, one tomorrow, and one on Sunday morning.

He should have brought more.

Robert had been smoking weed since he was thirteen. From the time he was eighteen, he smoked at least twice a day, often three. He wasn't addicted (he could stop anytime and had in the past), but he didn't feel right when he wasn't high. He felt...dull, drab, tired and without energy. When he was high, rolling and laughing, he felt good, felt...normal.

The other guys made fun of him, but he didn't care. They called him a stoner, they called him a junkie, Joe and Bob said he couldn't handle being a sober adult so lost himself in drugs. Well, fuck them. Haters gonna hate. He liked having fun, and when he was high, he had lots of fun. When Derrick picked him up that morning, they smoked a bowl in Robert's driveway, and the long trip into the mountains was a blast. They sang along to Cindi Lauper and The Eagles on the radio, told jokes, and stopped at a McDonald's in McLaren to have an Egg McMuffin eating contest. Derrick won, naturally, but only by one.

Speaking of Egg McMuffins, Robert's stomach didn't feel too hot. He figured that by the time he reached the house, after running and climbing, he would have to shit. He wondered briefly if the front door was open. If not, he'd just squat in the backyard and wipe his ass with a leaf. He'd done it before.

Getting his bowl from his bag, Robert packed it and put it to his mouth. He held the first hit for nearly a full minute before letting it out in a long plume of smoke. Almost instantly, his weary body reacted to the drug, his aches and pains diminishing. He took another hit, and laid back against the tree. Ten minutes later, when the bowl was empty, his mind swam. He was happy and at peace with the world.

Later, he tapped the bowl against his shoe and stuck it back into his bag. Before putting the baggie back into his pocket, he extracted a stem and popped it into his mouth.

Ready, he grabbed his pack, slung it over his shoulder, and picked up his gun. At the summit again, he looked down at the stand of trees.

He was ready.

With a sigh, he started running, the dry grass whipping his knees and shins. As he ran, he surveyed the forest on either side of him. He saw no one waiting in the shadows.

By the time he reached the stand of trees, he was sweaty and winded. Resting against the trunk of an elm, he caught his breath and looked around once more.

Again, he saw no one.

Pleased, he ducked out of the grove and headed for the bottom of the hill. He glanced up at the forest rising above him on his right. If someone was there, he couldn't see them.

At the hill, he slung his gun over his shoulder, glanced once more at the woods, and started up on his hands and knees; at several points he had to grab onto a jutting root. One near the top gave way, and he tumbled head over heels down the hillside, crashing into a bush. Insulated, he felt no pain, and, thinking only of reaching cover, started back up again.

At the top, a dirt road curved past the cabin. Climbing a wooden split-rail fence, Robert dropped into the yard and stayed low. The only sounds were the cries of birds in the sky and the rustle of wind in the trees.

Confident that he was alone, he stood up and started toward the house. He saw the flags nailed to the porch railing, and grabbed the blue one with a "Ha!"

They probably didn't think he could do it. Stupid stoner. He'll fall down and pass out before he wins the game. Yeah, right. Look at me now, bitches!

Chuckling, he climbed the stairs to the front door. A canned rocker sat to his right near a table. Wind chimes twinkled.

Robert tried the knob, found it locked, and sighed. Backyard it is.

Coming down the stairs, Robert started around the side of the house.

Someone hit him in the back of the head then.

The world went gray, then black.

Robert passed out after all.

From the spot where Derrick lay, dead, the path became first wide, the trees on its flanks evenly spaced. Then, it became dark, narrow. Bob led the way, with Joe in the middle and Sean in the rear. As they walked, Sean kept glancing around, dreadfully sure that he would see the killer standing in the woods, a gun in his hands. He kept his Spyder at the ready. It wasn't much, but at least it was something. If he saw the guy he'd start firing, and unless he was wearing armor, the sting of the paintballs striking him would *hopefully* drive him off.

Several times as they trekked, Joe tried to get in touch with Robert over the radio, but couldn't. Sean knew Robert must not have it on, but pictures of Robert dead, floating face down in the river, flashed through his head, and he had to fight to dispel them.

Presently, the path curved, and the trees screening its eastern edge fell away. Across an open valley, the cabin stood proudly on its ridge.

They stopped.

"There's another path up here," Bob said, speaking quietly. "It goes down the hillside and lets out on the road."

Sean nodded, glancing nervously behind them.

The path was in actuality a narrow strip of dirt winding through the brush. They walked carefully lest they lose their balance.

At the bottom, Bob stopped, held up his hand, and looked around. "I don't see anyone," he said over his shoulder.

He left the cover of the trees and started up the sloping road. Joe was next. He looked around. "I don't see the fucker," he said, and motioned for Sean to follow.

They were on the road now, walking one behind the other. Sean looked back. The road slid down into the forest before rising and bending out of sight. To his left, jagged peaks thrust up against the iron sky.

Bob jumped over the fence. Joe followed. Sean slipped underneath.

At the foot of the steps, Bob stopped. "The blue flag's gone," he said.

Sean looked. A red flag was nailed to the railing.

"Robert must have been here," he said.

Bob took a deep breath.

"Here," Sean said, pushing past Bob. "Let me go first."

He held the paintball gun, his finger on the trigger. If someone was there when he opened the door, he was going to light them up.

"Hand me the keys."

Bob passed him the keys.

Keeping one hand on the gun, Sean inserted the key into the lock and turned it.

Behind him, Joe grunted breathlessly.

Sean turned. The killer was there, Joe crumpled at his feet. He was wearing a motorcycle helmet with a shiny visor covering his face.

Sean raised the paintball gun.

Bob shot him in the leg.

And not with a paintball gun.

*

Sean came blearily awake, his head swimming and his body throbbing. For a terrible second he didn't know where he was, and the blackness around him was total, silent, tomblike. He tried to move, but a rocket of agony shot up from his leg, and he cried out, rolling to his side.

Then he remembered:

The killer standing behind Joe, the gun held straight up in the air (must have cocked him with the handle); Bob raising the revolver, firing; the hot sear of pain as the bullet smashed into his leg.

Bob was on top of him then, grinning as he smashed his fist into Sean's face over and over.

Then darkness.

Sean was on the verge of passing out again when harsh white light filled the chamber. He opened his eyes.

What he saw shocked him.

They were in a hole. Him, Robert, and Joe. Joe was slumped against the wall, his eyes closed and his teeth clenched. His hand was clapped to his head. Robert was sitting up, his legs straight out in front of him. Dried blood was caked to his forehead.

Someone laughed.

And Sean looked up.

Backlit against the light, two figures looked down at them. For a moment Sean couldn't see who they were, then recognized Bob and Kristen.

"Alright, guys," Bob was saying, "now we're gonna play *Silence of the Lambs*."

"Would you fuck me?" Kristen asked, giddy.

"I'd fuck me," Bob said without looking away. He was looking right at Sean.

"I'd fuck me *hard*," they finished in unison, Kristen giggling.

Sean opened his mouth to speak, but the words wouldn't come. He was suddenly very weary, and wanted only to curl back up and go to sleep.

"In the movie, Buffalo Bill makes his victims put lotion on their skin," Bob said with evident delight. "That way it's easier for him to peel it off."

For a moment Bob disappeared. When he returned, he was holding something in his hands. A pot. Sean noted he was wearing oven mittens.

"We don't have any moisturizer," Bob said, "but we do have grits."

With that, Bob tipped the pot, and a shower of white splattered them, the bulk of it landing on Sean's right side. Instantly he was on fire.

Screaming, he jerked up and tried to brush the grits off, but succeeded only in getting them stuck to his hands, where they burned even worse.

Robert drew his legs to his chest and flicked off a glob that had landed on his knee. He made no noise as he did this. Joe, on the other hand, who had escaped the napalm-like dump, screamed. "You pieces of shit! You better fucking kill me or I swear to fuck I'll come up there and kill your asses."

Kristen giggled.

"Have fun climbing up, fat boy," Bob said, and tossed the pot. Joe ducked, and it clanged off his skull. With a shriek, he toppled over and lay still.

Sean passed out again.

*

He didn't know how long they were down there. A day. A month. It was hard to say. Every once in a while Bob would throw down a Gatorade or a baggie of chips, and he and Robert would share them evenly. Joe didn't need any. The pot-to-the-head killed him. He lay face down, motionless.

The last meal Sean ate down there was a cold hamburger. He was ravenous. Only when the world began to spin around him did he realize it was drugged.

When he woke up, he was lying face-down in the dirt. Robert was beside him. It was dusk, warm and breezy, and both of them were handcuffed.

"It's like this," Bob said, uncuffing them. "We'll give you a five-minute head start. If you make it to the road, we'll let you go."

Sean, his mind still muddled, tried to process what Bob was saying.

"Now get up. Clock's ticking."

Sean pushed himself up, hot pain snaking up his leg.

Robert glanced at him, and then he was gone, running up the road.

Sean looked over his shoulder. Bob and Kristen were standing there, watching him. "Four minutes," Bob said.

That spurred Sean to action. He turned and started for the hill, each step sending bolts of pain up his leg. He carefully picked his way down the hill, and rested at the bottom.

The clock was ticking.

Gritting his teeth and ignoring the pain, he pushed to his feet and started running. At some point he must have blacked out, because he found himself by the river and had no recollection of getting there.

Dropping to his knees by the water, he splashed some in his face, wincing at the cold, and shook his head.

The sky above was a smear of orange and purple. A wind sprang up in the west. It was cold. Needling.

They were coming.

He had to get away.

Getting to his feet, he looked around. He didn't see Bob *or* Kristen, but he knew they must surely be after him by now.

The woods weren't safe.

He had nowhere to go.

But the river.

With a final glance over his shoulder, Sean waded into the river; he made a hell of a racket splashing. There was no way they wouldn't be able to hear him.

The rocky river bed eventually gave out under him, and he swam. When he reached the other side, he flopped onto the ground, his leg burning, and fought to catch his breath. It was almost full dark now, and he was cold, sodden.

He pushed himself up to a sitting position.

Bob was standing on the other side, watching him.

"Oh, Warriors!" he called. "Come out and play!"

Scrambling to his feet, Sean ducked into the woods. Behind him, Bob's gun roared.

Lost in a frenzy of fright, Sean bounded through the rapidly darkening forest. The land was hilly, like frozen waves, and several times he tripped, sprawling in the leaves. He moved so slow. Like a man in a dream. Faster, goddamn it! His leg hurt so bad. He shivered against the touch of his wet clothing.

In the distance, barely audible over the sound of his own ragged breathing, a gunshot rang out.

Too far to be Bob, he thought, lightheaded. Kristen.

She must have gotten Robert.

The thought disturbed him.

"Hey, Sean!" Bob called. He sounded far away, but Sean's heart jumped nonetheless. "Look, I'm sorry about all this. I just got carried away. Come on out and let's have a beer, okay?"

More gunshots in the distance, pushing Sean faster. His mind was a blur. *Escape. Escape. Escapeescapeescape.*

His foot hit something then, and he fell.

Get up. Get up. GET UP!

Pushing himself to his feet, he brushed something hard and jagged.

A rock.

His breath caught. A rock. Yes. He clawed at it, but it was stuck deeply in the ground.

Behind him, a hundred feet or less, the sound of leaves crunching.

Come on. Come on. Come on.

"Oh, Sean!" Bob called in falsetto. "It's me, Spongebob! I'm here to help you get away!"

Shit! Shit! Shit!

Sean ripped at the rock, bending one of his fingernails.

It was loose.

He grabbed it with both hands and staggered to his feet.

In the darkness, Bob appeared.

He had a flashlight.

"Got'cha!"

The gun roared. Bullets whizzed past Sean's head. He ducked, almost fell, and threw himself behind a tree, kept running, pumping his legs faster, the pain entirely forgotten now. He looked back. Bob was waving the flashlight like a sword, its beam cutting left, right, behind.

"Sean!"

Up ahead, a boulder rose from the night.

Sean ducked behind it. He was breathing heavy, his throat hot and burning. He clutched the rock. He was gonna do it. When the son of a bitch showed his ugly face, he was gonna smash it to bits.

Pushing away from the boulder, he slipped behind a tree. Bob was coming, leaves crunching underfoot. He closed his mouth in an attempt to hide his breathing, and winced when the light fell on the boulder.

Silently, he moved around the side of the tree trunk, coming out behind Bob.

"I got you now, you little balloon," Bob said. He leapt at the boulder and shone the light behind it.

Sean raised the rock.

Sensing him, Bob turned.

The rock left Sean's hand and disappeared in the night.

Umf!

The flashlight beam went wild.

Energized, Sean jumped at him then. He was stumbling back, on the verge of losing his balance, when Sean slammed into him, knocking him to the ground. The gun clattered out of reach.

Sean punched him. Once. Twice. His nose shattered under the assault. He thrashed and fought, but even in his weakened state, Sean was the stronger of the two.

Punch. Punch. Punch.

Sean felt Bob's lips split and his teeth crack, but he didn't stop, *couldn't* stop. His mind had become detached from his body, and it was as though he were standing beside himself, watching, powerless to intervene.

He was crying now.

The only thing that stopped him was the radio. Lying on the ground, near the gun, it crackled into life. "Bob? Bob, I got him. Where are you?"

The sound of Kristen's voice woke him from his trance.

"Bob?"

Panting, Sean crawled off Bob and grabbed the radio. He held it for a minute, thinking of what to do. "Bob! You're scaring me! Are you okay?"

The plaintive sound of her voice, the perverse concern, enraged him. Derrick was dead. Robert was dead. Joe was dead. She laughed. But now that it was Bob she was on the verge of crying.

Sean pushed the TALK button. "I got your boyfriend." He was panting still.

"Don't hurt him!" she came back almost at once, a cold, hard edge in her voice. "I swear to God, Sean, if you hurt him..."

"I already did," Sean replied, finding sudden, savage pleasure in it. "I broke his nose and his mouth. He'll probably die."

She wailed into the radio. "I'll kill you!"

"I'm already on the highway, bitch. You're going to jail."

With that, he sat the radio on Bob's chest. He had begun to stir, his eyelids fluttering. Sean grabbed the gun, clicked off the flashlight attached below the barrel, and checked the magazine. Half full.

"Nice gun," Sean said. "M4. Scope. It's mine now."

With that he walked away.

*

Mumbling through shattered teeth, Bob directed Kristen as best he could. Lying on the ground, his face aching, he drifted in and out of consciousness, sometimes coming awake to Kristen screaming at him through the radio, hysterical and close to tears.

"Don't die," she wept. "I love you."

"I love you too," he'd whisper.

And he meant it.

In the six months that they'd been together, Bob had fallen so deeply in love with Kristen that he could no longer see the light of day, and he didn't care. She was twenty years older than he was, but that didn't matter. She was the only one to ever truly understand him. He thought Joe understood him. His hatred for humanity. His love of self. But Joe was a poser. They made plans to shoot up shopping malls and daycare centers, but Joe wasn't serious. He thought it was all fun and games. But Kristen...she was the first one to get him, and, he suspected, he was the first one to get her, too. Psychopaths, some called them. Soulmates, Bob said. She had that spark of rage in her heart just like he did, and she knew how good it felt to stroke that spark. Even before they met Kristen was feeding her fire. Two babies. Smothered. Unwanted.

"He had this stupid look on his face," she told him once, referring to her first son, Dean, whom she bore when she was twenty-two, the product of a drunken one night stand. "Just staring into space and drooling down his shirt. I put the pillow over his head and held it there. Little fucker."

Bob had laughed then. He told her about the dogs and cats he took off the street and killed.

You need bigger prey.

They devised the game right then and there.

There's a short story, Bob said. The Most Dangerous Game. About a guy *who hunts humans.*

Kristen liked it.

She liked it a lot.

And Bob loved her for it.

"Bob!" she called, her voice clear and ringing. For a moment he thought it was through the radio, but then he saw the jostling beam of her flashlight.

"Here!' Bob croaked.

She found him then, and when she saw him, the breath went out of her. "Oh, my God," she whispered and sank to her knees. "What did that faggot do to you?"

Her face was above him then, her smell in his nose. Beyond her, stars twinkled in the night sky, cold flecks of ice on black velvet.

"He hurt me," Bob whispered.

Something moved in the brush.

"Got'cha," Sean said.

Kristen turned; the bullet took her in the forehead and flung her back. Bob saw (or imagined) the spraying mist of blood as the bullet exited the back of her skull.

Bob screamed.

Gone.

Wailed

She was gone.

His life.

His love.

When the tears came, they were hot and heavy.

"Kill me," he whispered. "Please, just kill me."

"Fuck you," Sean said, and left.

Bob didn't know how long he was lying in the leaves, drifting on the verge on consciousness, looking into the sky, before the bear came, but it felt like eternity. When the animal ambled from the bush and pushed its nuzzle against his head, sniffing, his blood ran cold. And, as the bear found his soft, squishy middle, Bob realized there *were* worse things than losing the love of his life.

There were teeth.

NIGHT OF THE DOG

A full moon hung heavy over the city of Fredericksburg, its face sporadically obscured by passing clouds. Seen through the lattice of barren treetops, it resembled a grinning skull, seeming to look down upon the killer's work with gruesome approval.

Shuddering against the chill, the killer stuffed his hands into the pockets of his oversized pea coat and turned onto College Avenue, which flanks the southern edge of the University of Mary Washington campus. Opposite the college, residential homes slumbered among dead trees, their windows black and their doors shut tightly against the cold. The killer followed the sidewalk for several blocks, listening to the silence of the night, his ears attuned to catch the slightest sound.

Save for the wind, there was nothing.

Deflated, he crossed to the residential side and walked back to Highway 1. On his way, he met only a cat streaking from one bush to another.

Back where he began, the killer checked the time on his cellphone. 2:30am.

It was getting late.

Highway 1, which cleaves through the heart of Fredericksburg, is lined with restaurants, shopping centers, and gas stations. Here, south of the college, the only businesses still open were a Pizza Hut (which closed at three), and a McDonald's which stayed open 24/7, mainly for the benefit of the students. He briefly considered walking into the McDonald's and opening fire, but while the orgy would temporarily satisfy the Dog's bloodlust, it wouldn't be enough to truly sate him.

Standing now by an El Camino parked next to a utility pole, the killer scrambled for an idea. He had to kill *someone;* if he came home empty-handed...

An idea struck him then. He took his cellphone back out and went to Google. Five minutes later, he was talking to a woman.

"Where are you?" she asked.

He gave her the address of the McDonald's.

"It'll be ten minutes," she said.

"That's okay," he replied and hung up.

Revitalized, he walked up the sloping street to the restaurant, its ubiquitous golden arches glowing soft yellow in the night. Being careful to avoid the security cameras he knew must be watching him, he sat down at the curb and faced the street. Across the way, a strip mall hunkered against the light of the moon, waiting impatiently for day.

Several cars passed in the street, one of them a city squad car, all white and blue and gold trim. Through the darkened window, he caught a glimpse of blue computer light bathing a tired and haggard face.

Fifteen minutes after sitting down, the taxi arrived, its headlights washing over him. He got up, went to the back door, and got in.

"How you doing?" the cabbie asked.

The interior was dark. The killer couldn't see the cabbie's face, which, he figured, was just as well. "I'm good."

"Where you going?"

The killer gave him the address of someone he knew long ago.

"Alright."

From the McDonald's, the cabbie followed Route 1 to Alvey Drive, which cuts through a wooded corner of the UMW campus. At the end, he turned onto Sunken Road, which passes between a comfy residential neighborhood and a massive hill, its summit dotted with the ancient brick tombs of academia.

When they reached the corner of Sunken Road and Hanover Street, the killer, his stomach rolling, said, "Here's fine."

"You sure?" the cabbie asked.

"Yes."

The killer took the revolver from his pocket, wincing at the heavy, slimy feel of it, and put it against the cabbie's head.

When the killer jerked the trigger, the sound of Judgement Day filled the car, deafening him. The cabbie flew forward in a spray of blood and brain matter, slumping over the steering wheel. The car began to roll forward, and the killer scrambled out.

The car angled across the street, over the sidewalk, and down a short embankment, coming to rest against the gnarled trunk of an oak tree.

Shaking (and not from the cold), the killer shoved the gun into his pocket and disappeared into the night.

*

Detective Dean Whitehead parked the Crown Vic behind a squad car and got out, wincing at the damp chill of the day. Deke Morgan, his partner, did likewise. "Too cold for this shit," he said, slipping on a pair of sunglasses even though it was overcast and rainy.

"Yeah," Dean said.

Ahead, an intersection was closed, uniforms diverting traffic like high school crossing guards. To the left, the ass end of a yellow cab poked from a gully, its front half hidden by the barren branches of dead trees.

"Some people go to Yelp and complain," Deke said as they crossed the street. "Our guy goes to Smith and Wesson."

"Hilarious," Dean said.

Uniforms buzzed busily around the scene, looking for evidence. An officer talked to a few rubberneckers over fluttering yellow police tape.

When Dean spotted Sergeant Dan Avis, he raised his hand. Avis, a plump little man with a mustache and thinning hair, nodded, said something to the uniform he was talking to, slapped him on the shoulder, and came forward, meeting Dean and Deke in the street.

"What do we got?" Dean asked.

"Male, thirty-five or forty. Single gunshot wound to the back of the head."

"Nice," Deke said.

"Messy," Avis corrected.

"You ID the vic?" Dean asked.

"The ID card taped to the seat says his name's Paul Horgan. But since the bullet entered the back of the head and came out the front, you wouldn't know him from Adam."

Dean shook his head. This was *not* what he wanted to deal with right now.

"Who spotted him?"

"Guy out walking his dog."

"What time?" Deke asked.

Avis shrugged. "Hour and a half ago."

"It must have just happened then," Deke said to Dean.

They were in the gully now, alongside the driver door. Through the blood-splattered window, Dean could see the vic slumped over the steering wheel. The bullet entered the back of the head, leaving a neat little pinprick, and exited the forehead, mushrooming out and reducing the poor cabbie's face to bloody diarrhea.

"We're thinking it's a robbery gone wrong," Avis said.

"Maybe," Dean said. He looked at Deke.

"Maybe."

"Where's the guy who found him?"

"Over here."

The dogwalker was a chubby middle-aged man with glasses and wearing a gray UMW sweatshirt. His dog was a dark blonde golden retriever who panted and smiled as Dean and Deke walked up. Unthinkingly, Dean reached down and petted his head.

"I'm Detective Whitehead, this is Detective Morgan," Dean said.

"Gene Donovan," the man said.

Dean shook his hand.

"Tell us what happened."

The man sighed. "I was coming down Hanover" – here he pointed up the canted avenue – "when I noticed the taxi. I went over to see if anyone needed help, and that's when I saw him."

"What time was that?" Deke asked, producing a notepad.

Donovan shook his head. "Six-thirty, six-forty-five."

"Did you call?"

"Yeah."

"From a cell?"

"Yeah."

"Check what time you placed the call."

Donovan took out a smart phone. "Six-forty-one."

"Did you see anyone hanging around?" Dean asked. "Maybe running away?"

Donovan shook his head. "No. Nothing like that."

"We might want to talk to you later. Can we have your number?"

"Sure," Donovan said, and gave them the number.

Done, they wandered over the police tape, where the officer was still conversing with the crowd.

"Do any of you live nearby?" Dean asked.

A couple nods and 'yes's'.

"Does anybody remember hearing anything strange last night?"

"I do."

The speaker was a thin middle-aged woman in a red coat.

"Let her through," Dean told the cop.

The cop nodded, and the woman ducked under the police tape.

"What'd you hear?" Dean asked her.

"Well, I was in my kitchen when I heard this muffled...noise," Charlotte Wiles said.

"What time?"

"Three-ish."

"What were you doing in your kitchen at three in the morning?" Deke asked.

The woman favored him with a withering glance. "I have insomnia."

"Alright," Dean said.

"So, I heard this noise, and when I looked out the front window, I saw someone running away."

Dean and Deke looked at each other.

"Did you get a good look?"

The woman shook her head. "He passed through a streetlight, but all I saw was he's white. Youngish."

"Tall? Short? Fat? Skinny?"

"Tall and skinny."

Deke jotted that down, as well as her number for future reference.

As they were finishing up with the woman, Sergeant Avis came over. "The press is here," he said.

"Great," Deke said. "Where?"

Avis nodded.

An NBC news van was parked along the curb. People hurried to set up camera equipment.

"The Free-Lance Star, too."

A man in a tweed jacket and holding a pad much like Dean's talked to a uniform. He looked up, saw Dean and Deke, and tried to come forward; the cop placed a hand on his chest and motioned him back.

"They're gonna have a field day with this," Avis said.

Murder was rare in Fredericksburg. Spread out between the Rappahannock River in the east and Interstate 95 to the west, Fredericksburg boasted a population of nearly thirty-thousand people, making it a fairly small city, but large (ish) by Virginia standards. Gangs such as the Bloods, the Crips, and MS-13 had a presence, but violent crimes were surprisingly few and far between. Every time someone got killed, the media turned it into an event. IS OUR CITY BECOMING TOO VIOLENT??? the newspapers asked.

The last violent crime Dean investigated was the arson of a local Islamic community center. The fire broke out late at night, when no one was there; when he arrested the neo-Nazi who did it, he said he didn't want to 'hurt anybody.' Despite the lack of causalities, the media turned it into Fredericksburg's 9/11.

"Don't talk to him," Dean said.

An hour later, after the body had been removed and the car towed from the gully, Dean and Deke went back to the Crown Vic. The TV reporter tried to ask them questions, but they ignored her.

In the car, Dean started the engine and put it into reverse.

Someone knocked on the window, startling him.

The newspaper man. He held up a press badge. "I'm William Holloway, Free-Lance Star..."

"Get outta here!" Dean said, slapping the window.

Holloway jumped back. "I have a few questions..."

"Not right now," Dean said.

He backed the car up and pulled a U-turn. In the rearview mirror, Holloway stood in the middle of the street, watching.

"Jackals," Deke said, leaning back in his seat.

"Yeah," Dean replied. "You hungry?"

It was pushing ten-thirty now, and neither one of them had had a chance to eat breakfast.

"Sure."

They stopped at Faye's Diner on Princess Ann Street in the heart of Old Town. As they waited for their food, they went over the crime.

"Robbery's the most likely motive," Deke said, sipping a cup of coffee.

"Maybe," Dean said. "What about time? There's a three-hour discrepancy. Charlotte Wiles heard the gunfire at three, which means the taxi was there for a good three hours."

Deke shrugged. "Maybe no one happened by. Hanover isn't a main drag. I can see it being dead at that hour."

"Yeah, but we're talking *three* hours."

Deke shrugged again.

At eleven, the vic was positively ID'ed as Paul Horgan. He lived across the Stafford County line with his wife.

"Call her in," Dean said.

An hour later, she appeared, a thin woman with long brown hair. Her eyes were red and puffy as though she'd been crying. Sitting at their joint desk in the bull-pen, Dean questioned her as gently as he could. No, she said, Paul didn't have any enemies. No, he never mentioned any weird fares or stalkers or anything.

After she left, Sergeant Avis came by to tell them that Paul Horgan's wallet was found in his back pocket, where it should have been, and that there was a crisp fifty-dollar bill inside.

"So no robbery?" Deke asked.

Avis shrugged. "We don't know. Looks unlikely, though."

"If it wasn't a robbery," Deke said when Avis was gone, "then what is it?"

"Someone getting their rocks off?"

"Man, don't say that," Deke said, shaking his head. "The last thing we need is some sicko running around and shooting people for fun."

Dean shrugged. "That's how it goes sometimes."

*

Kill. Kill. Kill.

The killer crossed Route 1 and turned onto College Ave. There was no moon tonight, thus the only lights came from the streetlamps lining the sidewalks.

Kill.

"I'm killing," he muttered.

It began nearly a year ago. The Dog, tied to its post, spoke to him from the night, its eyes glowing red. "Kill," it said. "Kill."

He resisted. He fought. He tried to rise up and kill the Dog instead, but demons spoiled his aim. When it came to him, a bandage wrapped around its chest, he fell before it and worshipped it as a god.

I'll kill! I'll kill!

Coming from a fugue, the killer found himself on the campus proper, following a flagstone walk past sleeping buildings. The land rose and fell on either side of him, frozen and dark like winter waves on the sea. The occasional light shone from a window, but for the most part, the college was dark.

The killer thought back to his own days at UMW. So long ago it seemed. He remembered walking the campus at night, going into buildings and stalking the vaulted marble halls. Some of them stayed open all night, patrolled by security guards and late-night studiers. In fact, one of those buildings, Amos Hall, was up ahead, to the left of the path.

Stroking the gun in his pocket, the killer paused, checked the path and, finding it empty, slipped in.

The chamber was warm and well lit. The roof was a dome and an open walkway overlooked the tile floor.

Several halls branched off from the antechamber. The killer took the one closest to the door, and took it all the way to the end, passing closed doors and shuttered windows. Meeting no one, he walked back to the lobby and listened.

Nothing.

He started toward another hall, but stopped when a security guard appeared, a large black woman in a blue shirt.

She smiled. "Hello."

The killer pulled out the gun and fired without aiming.

The first shot took her low in the stomach. The second in the shoulder. Forming a perfect O of surprise with her mouth, she half-turned and went down, making noises of pain.

The killer came forward, aimed at the back of her head, and fired again.

The shots echoed through the building for a long time afterward.

*

Dean Whitehead parked in a spot marked FACULTY and cut the engine.

Across the commons, a group of students clustered around the police tape. They were visibly shaken, scared.

Sergeant Avis was standing on the steps of the building. Two ambulance men wheeled a gurney from the double doors. A plump figure covered in white rested on top.

"Black female. Five gunshot wounds."

Dean looked at Deke.

"How much you wanna bet it's related to yesterday?" Dean asked.

The official line around the office (so far) was that the cabbie was murdered for his money, even though fifty dollars was found crisp and safe in his wallet. Ballistics had been taken from the gun, and the CSI team did a full work up of the car. If this was related, that theory went right out the window and *stayed* out the window.

"Looks like it might be," Avis said.

Inside, Avis went over the story. A professor coming in for work about six-thirty found the guard lying in a pool of blood. She was dead.

The professor, a tall man in his late sixties, told Dean virtually the same story.

"There are similarities alright," Dean said later. They were sitting in the car and watching the uniforms guarding the police tape. The Dean of the school canceled all classes for the day, but a group of students remained; some in shock, some shouting angrily at the police, as if it was *their* fault someone got shot.

The medical examiner said Horgan was killed about three in the morning (how his car sat in that gully unseen for three hours still puzzled Dean), and chances were the security guard was killed around the same time. Patterns were good, but they were also bad. At this point, it looked like they were dealing with a serial killer.

Dean didn't like that.

He didn't like that at all.

Back at the station, the bull-pen was a flurry of activity. After meeting with Captain Mayfield, they retired to their desk.

The ballistics on the most recent murder would be back in several hours, the lab said; then they would know if the gun used on the security guard (ID'ed as Shana White) was the same one used on Horgan. Dean suspected it was.

"We won't..." Deke started, but was cut off by someone clearing his throat.

The newspaper man, Holloway, was standing meekly behind Deke, his head hung. "Detectives," he said.

Dean sighed. "Not you again."

Holloway nodded. "Me again."

"Look," Deke said, "we're in the middle of an investigation, can you...?"

"I need to know whether these murders are linked," Holloway said. "If there's a serial killer on the loose..."

"No one said anything about a serial killer," Dean said. "We don't even know what's going on."

"It stands to reason that two similar murders, occurring in close proximity over two days, would be related," Holloway said. "I need confirmation. If the people don't have hard facts to go on, they're going to get scared. And when people get scared, bad things happen."

"I know what happens," Dean said, and he did. Gun sales went up. And when jumpy people were carrying guns, innocent lives wound up lost, impacted, or at least threatened. "All we can tell you is that two people are dead and we're working hard to get to the bottom of it. Okay?"

After Holloway left, Dean sagged back in his chair.

"He doesn't care if people are scared or not," Deke said.

"No, he doesn't," Dean agreed. "He wants a good story. Typical journalist."

Journalists, in Dean's experience, were all fearmongers whose only interests were selling papers and making a name for themselves.

Holloway served one purpose, at least. He occupied them long enough for the ballistics to come back.

It was official.

The same gun killed Horgan *and* White.

The killer walked the streets of the city, his hand in his pocket. He started in Old Town and moved west, following narrow streets lined with quaint shops and massive colonial-style churches.

Inevitably, he found himself back near the college. Cruisers were out in force, passing at a rate of three every ten minutes.

He had to be careful.

Just before dawn, he found himself in front of the city bus station. People milled about the platform, waiting for the fleet of buses to open their doors. One bus idled close to the street, its doors open and its driver on his knees, checking the tires.

Taking the gun from his pocket, the killer walked up to him, put the barrel against the back of his head, and pulled the trigger.

The report was covered by the roar of the buses' engines.

When he was sure no one heard the shot, he slipped the gun into his pocket and started toward the river. In Old Town, he got into his car and drove home; in the rising sun, he drifted to sleep, pleased with himself.

The Dog was silent.

*

Captain Mayfield, dressed in a black uniform complete with cap, stood before the podium like a general going to war. The reporters assembled in the lobby of the police station snapped photos in dead silence.

"There is a serial killer loose in Fredericksburg," he said. "So far he has killed three people."

Dean and Deke watched from the sidelines, their arms crossed. Spotting Holloway in the crowd, Dean shook his head.

"They're slurping it up."

Deke nodded. "Yep."

It was late in the evening; the sun was down and a cold wind swept over the city. That day's edition of the *Free-Lance Star* speculated that a serial killer was loose in town. The byline: William Holloway.

The department hadn't confirmed yet that the same gun was used in both murders. But the slaying that morning of Jim Weathers, a city bus driver, left little doubt. A serial killer *was* working the streets of Fredericksburg. To prevent panic, Captain Mayfield called the press conference currently in its opening salvo. As far as Dean was concerned, it was too late. There was a palatable sense of dread in the air. People were scared. Captain Mayfield mentioned that he was considering talking to the mayor and imposing a dusk to dawn curfew, but Dean suspected that the good citizens of Fredericksburg wouldn't *have* to be told to stay indoors after sundown.

Sighing, Dean thought back to the events of the day. The dreaded

185

early morning call, the rush to the scene; the all too familiar sight of a body lying in a pool of blood while uniforms buzzed restlessly around. A few witnesses standing on the platform and waiting to board their buses said they saw someone running away. The description was the same as Charlotte Wiles's: tall, skinny, white. That precluded Gene Donovan, the dogwalker from the first murder: A routine background check revealed that Donovan spent some time in jail after shooting a guy in a bar fight back in 1993. Digging deeper, the department uncovered that he was arrested after beating his then-girlfriend to a bloody pulp in 1989; the woman refused to press charges, however, so Donovan was turned loose. Sitting in Donovan's living room that morning, Dean couldn't help but notice the man's eyes. They were cold, reptilian.

Donovan worked for the Salvation Army as a district manager. He served three years in the army back in the late eighties/early nineties, saw action in Desert Storm, and once went to jail for beating his girlfriend in the head with a frying pan. His alibi for the first murder checked out, however. Horgan was killed about three 'o'clock; at three 'o'clock, Donovan was at the Salvation Army center on Plank Road, accepting a shipment of office supplies.

Even without a solid alibi, Donovan didn't match the description they kept getting. He was white, sure, but none but Fredericksburg's blindest could mistake the short, fat Donovan as 'Tall and skinny.'

In effect, they were back at square one. Hell, they hadn't even *left* square one.

Presently, Holloway was grilling Captain Mayfield. "What is the police department doing to catch this guy?" Holloway was asking. "He's already killed three people. What *else* can he get away with?"

"We're increasing our presence on the streets," Mayfield said. "Especially in the college district, including having plain-clothes officers patrol on foot."

"Is that enough?" Holloway worried.

"We have other avenues of investigation at this point." Mayfield took a question from someone else; Holloway jotted in his pad and looked thoughtful.

When the press conference was over, Dean was perturbed to see the journalist coming their way.

"Great," Deke said. "Clark Kent cometh."

Holloway nodded.

"We don't have anything for you," Dean forestalled.

Holloway held up his left hand. "I'm not here as a journalist. I'm here as a citizen."

"Okay."

Holloway sighed. "This is scary. Okay? There's some asshole running around shooting people. It would be one thing if he was going after a specific type of person, but no one's safe. A bus driver. A black woman.

A white guy. He's killing everyone. It's crazy."

He paused, seemingly in an effort to compose himself. For the first time since meeting him, Dean felt something other than annoyance toward him. Pity? Sympathy?

"I just want to know you guys have a lead...or *something*."

"Look," Deke said. Dean noticed his tone was more tender than it had been previously. "We're doing everything we can. I promise you."

Holloway nodded. He didn't look any more reassured. "Alright. I'm sorry if I came on strong earlier."

"You're just doing your job," Dean said.

"If there's anything I can do to help..."

Deke chuckled. "Just don't try any Nancy Drew shit."

Holloway laughed. "I'm not brave enough for that."

After wishing them well, Holloway left, stopping to check his pad. After a moment, he came back. "What kind of gun is this guy using?"

Charter Arms Off Duty .38. A small, compact 'snub-nose.' Dean knew why he wanted to know, so he didn't tell him.

"We're already talking to gun dealers in the city, so don't even try."

Holloway sighed. "Alright. Hey, you guys have a good night."

When he was gone, Dean shook his head.

"You think he's gonna pull some Nancy Drew shit, huh?"

"Yeah."

"Gonna have to wind up rescuing him."

Dean sighed. "If he finds the killer before we do, I'll be happy to rescue him."

*

Kill! Kill! Kill!

The killer's eyes flew open. The room was dark, the only sound coming from a radio he tuned to a vacant station each night so that he could fall asleep to the static.

Kill! Kill! Kill!

An hour later, he pulled into a 7-11 near the college and parked near the air pump abutting the street. For a long time, he sat in the car, listening to the radio. The Dog interrupted every song with a demand for blood. Walk the Moon. Shut Up and Kill With Me. Adele. Hello...I Want Blood.

Finally, he got out and went inside. The bright light stung his tired eyes.

He selected a candy bar from the snack aisle and brought it to the counter, where a sleepy-eyed fat woman with dull red hair scanned it.

"1.50."

He took the gun out and shot her. She fell back.

He shot her again.

Back home, the Dog was waiting in the kitchen, its face long and sleek.

"Did you kill?"

"I killed."

"Good."

In bed, struggling to fall back asleep, the killer listened to the Dog barking in the next yard over.

He was already thirsty again.

*

Dean Whitehead waited impatiently as the store manager pulled up the video from the night before.

It was six in the morning and raining. The ambulance bearing the cashier had left fifteen minutes before. Her wounds were serious, but it looked like she had good chance of surviving; luckily, someone came in right after the perp, found her, and called 911.

"It was a white guy," the Good Samaritan said. His name was Devon Parker. He was young, black, and worked as a nurse's assistant at Mary Washington Hospital. He was on his way home when he realized he was running low on cigarettes. "Tall, skinny. Blue eyes. He ran out of here and almost knocked me over."

"Could you describe him to a sketch artist?"

"I could *draw* him if you want me to."

Working quickly and with the skill of a surgeon, Parker drew up a likeness of the killer. It was well-done, displaying artistic talent; the killer's face was narrow, his hair shaggy.

"I got the impression his hair was shaggy," Parker said. "I don't know why. I didn't see it."

Dean looked at the picture for a long time before handing it to Deke. The man was obviously not Gene Donovan, but his eyes were similar. Flat. Cold. The eyes of a fish.

Presently, the manager, an Indian man with blue eyes, sat in the office swivel chair, a computer screen before him. Deke stood in the doorway, observing the uniforms as they did their thing.

"Got it," the manager said.

Dean leaned over his shoulder. Deke, in turn, leaned over his.

On the screen, the store was empty. A man in a hat came in, grabbed a case of soda from the back wall, paid, and left. Through the window, Dean noticed a pair of headlights.

"That him?" he asked.

"I don't know," the manager replied.

Onscreen, a man entered the store and turned down an aisle so quickly that Dean didn't see his face. He was white, skinny, and tall.

His heart began to pound.

Come on, you piece of shit.

About a minute later, the man came to the counter.

"Jesus Christ," Deke breathed.

*

Fifteen minutes later, after calling the Free-Lance Star's main office and getting his address, Dean Whitehead kicked down William Holloway's front door and ran in low and fast.

"Police!"

Deke came in behind him.

Holloway lived in an apartment complex on Plank Road, near an I-95 overpass. The apartment was neat and tidy.

"Holloway!" Dean yelled.

The reporter appeared in a darkened doorway, dressed only in a pair of boxers.

He was holding a gun.

"Drop it!" Dean screamed.

Holloway raised it instead.

Dean fired three times: The first bullet smashed into Holloway's chest, knocking him back. The second tore out his throat in a spray of gore. The third caught him in the lower jaw as he fell.

In the distance, a dog barked loudly.

Also available:

THE CHAMELEON MAN by David Williamson
ISBN: 978-0-9935742-9-3

A PLACE OF SKULLS by David Ludford
ISBN: 978-0-9935742-6-9

HAUNTED GRAVE by Ezeiyoke Chukwunonso
ISBN: 978-0-9935742-3-8

INTO THE DARK by Andrew Jennings
ISBN: 978-0-9935742-5-2

TOUGH GUYS by Adrian Cole
ISBN: 978-0-9935742-2-1

CLASSIC WEIRD 2 selected by David A. Riley
ISBN: 978-0-9932888-4-5

OTHER VISIONS OF HEAVEN AND HELL by Jessica Palmer
ISBN: 978-0-9935742-1-4

A SAUCERFUL OF SECRETS by Andrew Darlington
ISBN: 978-0-9935742-0-7

THE WINTER HUNT AND OTHER STORIES
by Steve Lockley & Paul Lewis
ISBN: 978-0-9932888-9-0

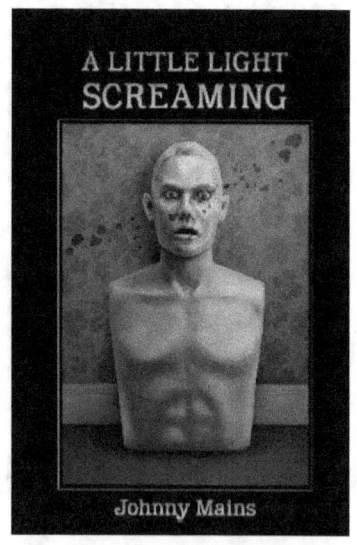

A LITTLE LIGHT SCREAMING by Johnny Mains
ISBN: 978-0-9932888-5-2

ENGLAND 'B': 90 MINUTES OF HELL by Richard Staines
ISBN: 978-0-9932888-7-6

AND NOBODY LIVED HAPPILY EVER AFTER by Kate Farrell
ISBN: 978-0-9932888-8-3

FISHHEAD: THE DARKER TALES OF IRVIN S. COBB
ISBN: 978-0-9935742-4-5

KITCHEN SINK GOTHIC: Selected by David and Linden Riley
ISBN: 978-0-9932888-3-8

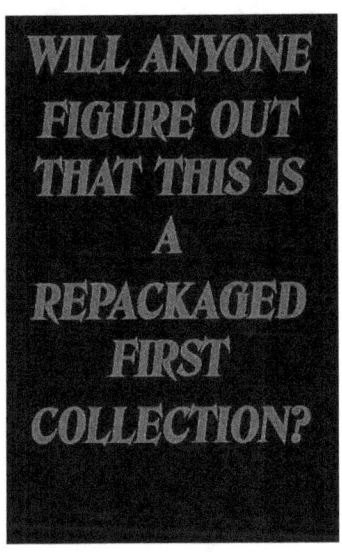

WILL ANYONE FIGURE OUT THAT THIS IS A REPACKAGED FIRST
COLLECTION? by Johnny Mains
ISBN: 978-0-9574535-7-9

BLACK CEREMONIES by Charles Black
ISBN: 978-0-9574535-5-5

HIS OWN MAD DEMONS:
DARK TALES FROM DAVID A. RILEY
ISBN: 978-0-9574535-8-6

THEIR CRAMPED DARK WORLD by David A. Riley
ISBN: 978-0-9574535-9-3

THE HEAVEN MAKER AND OTHER GRUESOME TALES
by Craig Herbertson
ISBN: 978-0-9932888-2-1

GOBLIN MIRE by David A. Riley
ISBN: 978-0-9574535-4-8

THINGS THAT GO BUMP IN THE NIGHT
selected by Douglas Draa and David A. Riley
ISBN: 978-0-9574535-6-2

CLASSIC WEIRD selected David A. Riley
ISBN: 978-0-9574535-3-1

MOLOCH'S CHILDREN by David A. Riley
ISBN: 978-0-9932888-1-4

Check our website:

http://paralleluniversepublications.blogspot.co.uk/